Manor

Gillian,
For the last dance!

[signature]

THE AUTHOR

I. K. Watson was born into a military family in 1947 and grew up in a succession of military quarters, being educated at St George's in Hong Kong, and St John's in Singapore. Prior to becoming a full-time writer, he worked as Head of Quality Administration for British Aerospace. In the early 1980s, he was editor of the infamous *Pin Green Chess Magazine*. He lives in Hertfordshire with his wife, Alexandra, and their two children. His second crime novel, *Wolves Aren't White*, will be published by Allison & Busby in spring 1995.

Manor

I. K. Watson

ALLISON & BUSBY

First published in Great Britain in 1994 by
Allison & Busby
an imprint of Wilson & Day Ltd
5 The Lodge
Richmond Way
London W12 8LW

Copyright © 1994 by I. K. Watson

The moral right of the author is asserted

This book is sold subject to the condition that it shall not, by way of trade or otherwise, be lent, resold, hired out or otherwise circulated without the publisher's prior written consent in any form of binding or cover other than that in which it is published and without a similar condition including this condition being imposed upon the subsequent purchaser.

A catalogue record for this book is available from the British Library

ISBN 0 74900 280 8

Typeset by TW Typesetting, Plymouth, Devon
Printed and bound in Great Britain by
Biddles Limited, Guildford, Surrey

Manor is dedicated to
Thomas Alexander Baldwin

Manor is fiction. All the characters and events involving the Smith family are fictitious. Any resemblance to real persons, living or dead, is purely coincidental.

MANOR – an estate held by a lord under the feudal system and worked by serfs or tenant farmers as a largely self-sufficient economic unit. The tenants rendered dues in kind, money or services in return for their land, and the lord enjoyed certain rights over both land and tenants.

Chapter 1

1976

The telephone rang out across the air-conditioned room. It seemed louder, like an alarm, and it had the same urgency about it.

In the bathroom Dave Smith heard the call but continued to gaze into the mirror. He placed his razor on the basin ledge and picked up a freshly laundered towel. Slowly, while the ringing persisted, he rubbed away the excess shaving cream that clung to his ear lobes. For a moment longer he studied his expression and saw the first sign of annoyance as it drew a veil across his eyes, then he threw the towel aside and opened the bathroom door with such force that it bounced back from the doorstop.

Enjoying his nakedness, he moved across the tufted Axminster into the lounge. It was a huge room dominated by glass; floor to ceiling windows comprising an entire wall looked out across the city skyline.

He stood at the window and as he lifted the receiver he gazed out at the familiar landmarks.

'Yes?'

'David?' A woman's voice, wrapped in an American accent, triggered a vague memory. 'Hello?'

'I'm here.'

'Do you recognize me?'

'Yes. It's been a long time.'

'Twelve years.'

'That long?'

'You made a lasting impression,' she said and laughed, a clotted laugh that focused his memory so that her image came flooding back.

The hairs on his arms prickled. He saw his narrowed eyes in the glass. For a second his reflection surprised him. Without his clothes he seemed taller and younger.

'Where's Tony?' he asked. 'Are you still with him?'

'Unfortunately.' Her voice lowered. 'We're over here for some shoppin'. At least, that's what he says. But you can guarantee it's business.' She paused before adding quietly: 'Nothin' happens around Tony that ain't business.'

Dave nodded into the handset.

'I've gotta see you, Dave,' she went on, breathlessly now. An edginess had crept in. 'Can you make it?'

'When?'

'Now. You know how it is? You gotta make the most of it. I can't be sure of gettin' another chance. He's out for the whole day. I'm supposed to be shoppin'.' Another pause, longer this time. 'I've thought about you. It ain't ever happened with anyone else.'

'Where?'

'Same place. For old times' sake ... He's taken everyone with him. I'm here on my own.'

'It's bloody dangerous, Sharon. Can't you get out?'

'He might have someone tailin' me, Dave. You know what he's like. They could be waitin' in the lobby. But you could get in. Nobody would know you're comin' up here.'

'OK. Give me half an hour.'

Dave dropped the handset on to its cradle. He remained motionless at the window.

The late morning August sun broke through the cloud and bounced off the distant Thames. Suddenly it was a different place. Concrete wavered and glass exploded with light.

Twelve years earlier Sharon Zinn had appeared naked in *Playboy*. She was seventeen. The touch-up artist had not been necessary. Later that year she married an American gangster, Tony Valenti. He was a part of the New York mafioso and she married him for his power and for his money. He was a small wiry man of forty. She was a beautiful blonde, six inches taller than him. Love had not been involved but he was happy and he liked to show her off. He would not allow the resumption of her modelling career.

In April of 1965 Tony Valenti accompanied Angelo Bruno on a trip to London. He brought Sharon along so that he could keep an eye on her. They stayed at the London Hilton. Bruno had come over to meet the Krays to discuss some hot Canadian securities he wanted to offload in Europe. He was also keen to expand his involvement in the Mayfair clubs and, at the time, he thought that the Krays might be ideally situated to handle his interests. That was not important. What was relevant was that Sharon noticed the eighteen-year-old Dave Smith in one of the Hilton bars and she could not take her eyes off him.

Dave was on reasonable terms with the Krays and was introduced to Bruno and his entourage and, when the others retired to a quiet corner to discuss business, Valenti had no hesitation in asking Dave to keep his wife company and to escort her, when she had had enough, to their room. 'She was a *Playboy* centrefold,' he boasted. 'And a movie star. If you ask her real nicely, kid, she'll give you her autograph.'

She was perched on a bar stool toying with the stem of her drink. She watched his approach through the mirror behind the bar.

'Did my clothes just disappear, or did you take 'em off one at a time?'

Her eyes flashed in the mirror.

Dave laughed out loud.

'That obvious, eh?'

'I hope no one else noticed. Tony's kind of funny about things like that.'

'He doesn't strike me as funny at all.'

She lifted her drink.

'You're bored?'

'Kind of.'

'How can anyone be bored in London?'

'It's like a strait-jacket,' she said. 'Bein' married to these guys is worse than marryin' into your Royal Family. You can't make a move without them knowin'!'

'That bad, eh?'

'You can believe it.'

'Tony told me about the films.'

'He tells everybody about them. They were the beach movies. Remember them? Surfin' and bikinis. I was the one playing volleyball. I was the one in the blue bikini. It matched my eyes.'

Dave smiled and glanced in the bar mirror. The far table was animated. Knowing Ronnie, the meeting would last well into the small hours.

'Drink up,' he said. 'I'll take you home.'

'Your place or mine?'

With scant regard for their own safety it began in the lift, continued in the corridor and climaxed on the floor of Valenti's suite. He left her there, on the carpet, with the hem of her evening gown around her waist and her pants hooked around one ankle. She smiled at him and said, 'You English are kinda friendly.'

Twelve years later Dave remembered it all. As he motored across to see her again he was stirred by the memory of their first meeting.

He parked the car at the Ballroom entrance and made his way through the plush foyer. It was checking out time and the reception area was busy. It suited Dave. The more faces on the ground the less likely he was of being recognized. He took the lift to the twelfth then used the stairs to Valenti's suite. The corridor with its deep spotless carpet was empty.

The years had done nothing to change her. Even now she could have stepped right out of the centrefold. She stood framed by the doorway. Her blonde hair cascaded over her shoulders and flared in the light that piled into the room behind her.

'What kept you?' she said. 'You're thirty seconds late.' Her eyes flashed as her mouth widened into a smile.

'I forgot how many stairs there were.'

She waved him inside. Her silk slip rippled.

'You're looking good.'

'So are you,' he said.

'Come on, let's not waste time. We've only got about eight hours. They won't be back until eight.'

'Don't you want to be courted? Has foreplay gone out of fashion?'

'Just come here and make love to me. I've been waiting twelve years for this.'

He closed the door and pinned her against it. Her lips were hot. Her tongue fluttered against his.

'Jesus!' she said when he pulled away and she gulped in air.

He picked her up and carried her toward a leather sofa. Half way across the deep pile he paused to kick off his shoes. He laid her down as though she weighed nothing and sank beside her. His hands worked beneath the ivory-coloured silk. He drew her pants down and raised her slip, for a moment savouring her thighs. She rubbed her legs together, moving her blonde hair. It was a novelty. It hid nothing. He put gentle pressure on her knees so that her legs parted.

He used his mouth and felt her stiffen and heard her tiny catch of breath. He increased the pressure, pushing his tongue inside her.

Suddenly she was pulling his hair, digging her fingernails into his shoulders. Her body coiled, her grip became almost unbearable until, slowly, she relaxed and he heard her sigh as she released a long breath. He looked up and smiled. His lips were wet and sparkling. A thread of something, spittle or her, wavered between his mouth and her crotch and glistened in the light that streamed in over Hyde Park.

'Take your clothes off,' she said. 'I want you to abuse me. Be rough!'

'I think I can manage that,' he said as he struggled out of his pants. While he unbuttoned his shirt she caught hold of him. She needed the best part of both hands.

'Jesus, I remember you,' she said. 'It's like meetin' an old friend.'

'How long are you over here?'

'We fly back tomorrow. We live in Miami now.'

'We'll have to make the most of today, then.'

'That's what I was counting on.'

He nestled between her legs. He brought her slip up to bare her breasts and the years were stripped away. It was all so familiar. The tiny nipples, the soft curves rising to them. He kissed her, burying his tongue deep into her mouth. At the same time he thrust into her. She arched, grimaced in pain and caught her breath. That shadowy idea, perhaps the thought of domination, thrilled him. He felt the end of her and every time he slammed in he heard her gasp and every time she gasped his smile of satisfaction widened a little more.

In those quickening moments before he let go she squealed and clamped her legs tightly around him.

She laughed. 'God, this is bliss. I've waited years.'

He cradled her head against his shoulder. She felt damp against him.

'You know,' she said, 'apart from when I've been on my own that's the first time I've come since . . .'

He turned to her. 'You're joking?'

She shook her head. 'No. It's been twelve years.'

'Fuck me! That's diabolical. Why don't you buy him a book?'

'It's not the technique, Dave. It's how I feel.'

'You tellin' me there's been no one else? In all this time?'

'Does that surprise you?'

'Yeah, you could say.'

'You don't know how it is. Over here he feels safe. I get some freedom. In Miami when I go downtown I get to be escorted by two gorillas. Sometimes I think I'm suffocating, you know what I mean?'

'Why don't you leave him?'

She snorted. 'You marry these guys for life, you know that. Where would I go? Where could I hide?'

Dave nodded, understanding even more than she knew.

'So this is it, eh?'

''Till the next time,' she said. She reached up and stroked his cheek. 'I love you, Dave. I know it's crazy. I know we barely know each other. But thinking of you has kept me sane all these years. Now you've filled my tank again I can go on a while longer.' She sighed and pressed closer. Her left breast flattened against his chest. Her right nipple brushed against him and tickled.

'Did you think of me in all that time?'

'Course I did,' he said honestly. 'I study that *Playboy* spread every night.'

'I've got older since then.'

'Not so I notice. I just wish the snaps had been taken now instead of then.'

'Why?'

'They'd be more explicit now. Split fig, pictures on horseback.'

She nudged him. 'I think I know what you mean. Is that Cockney?'

'No, sweetheart. It's Anglo Saxon. It's what God promised the circumcised: the Promised Land.'

Her laugh was smoky, as he remembered.

'If ever he dies,' she said, 'and if wishin' has anythin' to do with it, he will. I mean, he smokes three packs a day. But if he did die could I look you up?' She turned to face him. 'I mean, would you want me to?'

It was a serious question.

He nodded meekly. ''Course I would. Blimey, I can't think of anything I'd like better.'

She settled down again.

'That's what I thought,' she said.

It was late afternoon when he finally made a move. She watched him dress then threw her slip on and followed him to the door.

'Let's not leave it so long next time,' he said.

'I'll dream about you, David Smith.'

His smile was hesitant. He nodded and opened the door. She held him back and draped herself against him. Dave half turned as he heard a shuffle behind him.

Tony Valenti stood in the doorway, his wiry Italian features darkening by the moment.

'What the fuck is this?' His voice was high pitched. It filled the room like a siren.

As if dazed by what he saw Valenti took two steps backward.

Sharon dropped her hands from Dave's neck and followed Valenti into the corridor.

'It's not what you think, Tony,' she said feebly.

'What the fuck am I thinkin'? Eh?' He pulled the strap of her slip. It snapped. She held the front up to cover her breasts. He hit her hard, in the mouth. A fine spray of red dotted the wall. Dave saw her go down and heard the thud as she hit the carpet.

Valenti shook, his wild eyes fixed on Dave.

'I know you. Don't I know you?' He pointed at Sharon.

'That's my fuckin' wife!' he yelled. 'That whore's my fuckin' wife!'

Dave shrugged and moved past him.

'Where the fuck are you going you motherfucking son of a bitch?'

Valenti was a tiny man; his threats toward Dave were absurd. He kicked out. His chiselled toecap landed heavily into Sharon's stomach. She rolled over and slammed into the wall.

Dave turned back to face him. 'Leave her alone,' he said.

Valenti let out a strangled cry and head lowered he charged at Dave. Dave hit him once. His fist caught the little man squarely in the face. His heavy signet ring caught the flesh and ripped away the side of Valenti's big nose. Valenti staggered backward. He clutched at his face. Blood streamed from between his fingers. He began to scream. Doors along the corridor opened and people peered out.

Valenti rushed again. The pain had dulled his brain. His hands still covered his face as he tried to butt Dave with the top of his head.

Dave caught him again, hard, in the middle of the chest, and Valenti collapsed in a heap over Sharon's feet.

At the end of the corridor two men fought their way through the crowd. Dave looked up as he heard their approach. They were both black, built like Japanese wrestlers. They charged towards him. There were twenty yards between them as Dave made the corner to the stairs. He went down four at a time, crashing against the corners. He covered three flights before pausing to listen. Nothing. He decided they had stayed to help Valenti. Taking his time now, dusting himself and straightening his clothes as he went, Dave made his way to the lifts and five minutes later he was in the car park.

He was awoken just after one-thirty by a loud knock on his door. Jimmy Jones stood in the corridor. He was one of his father's key men. He looked drawn and tired.

'I've been ringing,' he said irritably.

'Pulled the phone out.'

'And banging on the door for the last ten minutes.'

'I killed off a bottle,' Dave offered. 'I was out for the count.'

Jimmy nodded. His dark features mellowed. 'Your old man's been goin' spare trying to get you.'

Dave shrugged and glanced at his watch. 'What's happened?'

'I thought you'd tell me.'

Dave knew, or he thought he did.

'There was a bit of bother earlier, at the Hilton,' he explained.

'What sort of bother?'

'You know what these Wops are. Can't control their women.'

Jimmy Jones grinned. 'Women! I might have known you'd be sniffin' around if there was a tart involved.' His face dropped again. 'Anyway, your old man's phone's been red hot for the last two hours. It's gotta be something pretty important to keep him out of bed at this hour. By the time he spoke to me he was pretty pissed off.'

Dave nodded gloomily. He didn't relish the prospect of facing his father, especially since his head was still reeling from the assault of half a litre of vodka.

'I'll throw some clothes on. You better drive me over there.'

Jimmy smiled quickly and sat down to wait.

His father was a big man. His white hair was ruffled, the collar of his worn dressing-gown rucked. He sat in his favourite armchair, his legs crossed, his foot tapping angrily so that his slipper slapped against his heel. The expanse of plain blue pyjama bottoms that Dave could see seemed somehow old-fashioned. His father looked tired, and older.

'You've caused me a lot of grief, boy. When are you going to learn? How old are you? Twenty-nine? Thirty? Then why is it you still act like an adolescent?'

'Are you going to tell me what I've done, Pop? It's too early in the morning to guess.'

'You've messed with the Mafia, boy, that's what. And half their fuckin' armed forces are on the way over here!'

Dave pulled a face as if he had tasted something nasty. Explanations were unnecessary. What worried him more than Valenti was that he did not know how to handle his father who was known to be strait-laced over such matters. He shrugged and filled a glass with vodka.

'It's my fault, Pop. He started slappin' her about and I went ape.'

'What did you expect him to do? He brings his wife over here for a little shopping to buy presents for their celebrations and some local piss-artist gets his leg over. For God's sake, aren't there enough local girls? His wife!'

'Blimey, Pop, if you'd have seen her. *Playboy* centrespread.'

His father scowled.

'They've flown him home. An ambulance job for Christ sake! Two broken ribs, eh? And half his nose is still in Park Lane!'

Dave swallowed half his drink.

'But worse than that, boy, you know what the worse thing is?'

Dave remained impassive.

'You left her to face the music. You ran out on the woman. How could a son of mine do that? Tell me?'

'He had two gorillas with him, Pop. There wasn't any return in me stayin'.'

His father nodded sadly. 'Well, for your information, he's half killed her. She'll be in hospital longer than the Wop. I hope you're proud of yourself.'

'I'm not. If I could do it over things would be different.'

His father's eyes narrowed reflectively.

'Meanwhile,' Dave said. 'I better get some muscle together.'

'You'll do nothing!' his father snapped. 'You'll make yourself scarce, and I mean scarce, like invisible, until I tell you otherwise. Your transport's outside. Get your shaving gear together then get in the back of the car.'

'Where?'

'You'll find out. It won't be a holiday. When I've sorted things out I'll let you know.'

'Pop! How long?'

'As long as it takes, boy. I don't know what I'm going to tell your mother. Pour me a whisky.' Dave filled another glass and carried it to his father. 'Treat it as a lesson, boy. Learn. Now remember, you're going to a good friend of mine. Do exactly what he tells you. Keep your mouth shut and your head down. I'll see you when it's all over.'

Chapter 2

Dave Smith was driven north and arrived at his destination with a late, overcast dawn that dribbled its grey watery colours from a bank of low cloud. His mood was darkened by the prospect of enforced idleness and when he saw what was to be his home for an indefinite period it turned uglier and he silently cursed every American he could think of. Dave knew the city; the lights, the smells, the incessant sounds, and already he felt uncomfortable.

During the journey he had considered his various options and he felt certain that his father was making a mistake. His best bet was to fight on ground that he knew with people that he trusted. It was not his way to run. He would have handled the Yanks with his own men and given them a permanent piece of dockland. That is what they always wanted anyway. His father's decision, which was bound to lose him some credibility, came as a surprise and, to his knowledge, it was the first time the Smiths had backed away. Perhaps his father was losing touch. Perhaps the last few years of relative peace had blunted his cutting edge. Respect was the key word for survival and respect came from strength and fear, not from running and hiding.

Through the tinted rear windows he saw a small village, little more than a single road lined with old cottages and one or two newer bungalows. The road forked in one place into a tiny cobblestone market triangle and beyond that, before the roads joined again, grass footpaths widened to a village green. Everything dripped.

A strange mix of sensations churned his stomach; tiredness was there, burning into his eyes, but he felt as a refugee might, or a displaced person, as though the roots of nourishment had been cut.

Throughout the journey the driver, his father's personal driver, had remained curiously uncommunicative, as though it had been an instruction. He had been polite but his answers to Dave's prodding had been to the point and conversation was non-existent. Dave was left in no doubt that for the time being his links with the family were well and truly broken.

From the village the road swung to the coast and ran parallel with the beach. The north-eastern air was damp and pungent; a watery sun glared through the grey and gave the froth at the water's edge a silver tint. The narrow B road curled away inland and now the light shafted through the trees. A small cottage with a poorly maintained thatched roof and weathered timbers stood only twenty paces from the road and with a thick hedgerow concealing its path until the last moment the driver overshot and had to reverse. To the left of the drive, beyond a group of derelict sheds, a carpet of windfalls lay beneath the trees and a couple of fat, long-haired pigs grunted around them.

Dave remained seated, motionless, while the driver climbed out and took a suitcase from the boot. He carried it to the front door then returned and opened the rear door of the car.

'This is it Dave. I suppose you'll get used to the smell.'

Dave studied the man for a moment searching for a hint of emotion. There was none. Eventually he nodded, resigned to his fate, and climbed out.

'See you later. Take care.' For the first time there was a kindness in the man's voice.

'Fuck you, son!' Dave said.

The driver shrugged as if to say it was not his doing, climbed quickly back into the car and turned the ignition. Dave watched the car back out until it disappeared from view behind the thick hedgerow.

The rusty hinges of the paint blistered front-door squealed into the silence as he pushed it open.

'Shit!' Dave said and dropped his case at the door. A small square parlour, musty and damp, was all but inaccessible because of a huge wooden table that left just a couple of feet of space around its sides.

He found some narrow, dangerously worn stairs that led from the one small room to a small bedroom with its ceiling slanting with the roof. A three-quarter size bed was made up and a dresser had been polished. A tiny bathroom adjoined the bedroom. He caught sight of his haggard looks in a mirror and scowled before making his way back down the creaking stairs.

In the parlour there was barely room to move around the table and no room at all if the four upright chairs tucked beneath the table were drawn back to use. The kitchen equipment was meagre: a porcelain sink with an unfinished work surface, a grease-filled crack along the wall, an antiquated gas cooker with a loose door and rings that were submerged in years of spillage, a small refrigerator with just enough room inside for milk, bacon and butter, an old cast-iron stove with a store of logs beside it and an enamelled kettle on top. From the stove's open door wood ash had spilt from the grating on to a raised concrete bed before it. A larder was filled with groceries and cleaning utensils. Dave smiled cynically. He was going to lose weight. He couldn't remember the last time he had prepared a meal.

The murky light in the room filtered in through casement windows and was just sufficient for him to find his way around. He found a tea caddy and teaspoons and some stained and chipped mugs hanging on hooks in the larder. He made some tea but could drink only a mouthful before creeping back up to the bedroom. He fell asleep thinking that his exploration of the warm, secretive areas of the American's wife had not been worth it.

Dave was awakened by noises from below. He negotiated the stairs and found a big white-haired man holding a boiling kettle above the teapot. The red face, wide muddy eyes, a nose criss-crossed with map-like formations of purple lines turned toward him. Broad shoulders were thrust forward as if to meet some challenge. Thick eyebrows raised and the face broke into a rugged smile.

'I'm Joe Daley. You look like shit!' His shoulders relaxed. His eyes remained curious under the shock of white hair. 'Dave?'

Dave nodded and accepted a mug of rich tea. He noticed a .410 leaning against the wall.

'Well, remember the name, Daley. You're my nephew, visitin'. My place is two hundred yards up the road. I've been told to keep an eye on you, so I'll do that. I'll be down from time to time to see to the pigs anyway. Just remember, a London accent is a dead giveaway up here so keep away from the locals.'

Dave gulped at his tea. It tasted better than his earlier effort.

'You need to run the water before you use it. It tends to lie in the pipes,' Daley said as if reading his mind. 'Someone will come in from time to time to clean up and change the towels. If you need anything special that's the time to ask. You won't see much of me but I'll be around, watching. If you keep your head down we don't expect any trouble. We like the peace and quiet.'

'This is Coddy Hughes' manor. Do you work for him?'

'That isn't your business. There's books and there's the telly. If you want to walk out, get some air, that's OK. But you walk away from company, right?'

'It's your show, my son.' Dave shrugged.

'I ain't your son,' Daley said sternly. He finished his tea, picked up his shotgun and moved heavily to the door. 'I'll leave you to do the dishes. See you around.' He had to bend slightly in order to get through.

For two days Dave barely ventured from the four white-washed cottage walls. He worked his way through two tattered thrillers and watched television until close down. By lunchtime on the third day he had had enough and was ready to take on Daley or anyone else who tried to stop him. It took him the best part of ninety minutes to walk to the tiny village and find the Royal Oak, a red-bricked building he had noticed on his way through.

The bar itself was typical of the country pub; panelled walls covered in watery prints of the hunt, treated ceiling joists and a spitting log fire that threatened the clothes of anyone standing within two yards of it. The fire was absurd. It was August and the temperature even outside was in the mid-seventies.

A balding English publican wearing a RAF moustache and tie stood behind his bar with a heavily made-up woman in her fifties who might have been his wife. There were a few others in the room, a cross section of rural life; some elderly couples sitting around the edge, some men playing dominoes, and a group of youngsters standing at the bar. Quite naturally most of them glanced his way; it was the sort of place seldom visited by strangers. Dave ordered a bitter and carried the drink to the far end of the bar, away from the youngsters.

A screech of brakes and the slamming of car doors heralded the arrival of a tall youth who led in a woman wearing spectacles. Before the other youngsters gathered around the couple her glance skated across the room and fell momentarily on Dave. In that instant he felt that he knew her. She was in her mid-thirties, straw blonde, attractive. Her mood was fickle as though she was unsure of herself; smiling to share a joke perhaps, smiling out of politeness, composed for an introduction then deliberate to cover a stifled yawn. She was older than the others and uncomfortable. There was something puzzling about her apprehension. Her movements were uncomplicated and confident, but her expression, more particularly in her brown eyes, gave a clue to her restlessness: she was bored.

With every opening of the street door more people arrived in groups of twos and threes until the small room was crowded and noisy. Smoke, curling in layers about the yellowing lampshades was whipped into spirals by the draught. Most of the youngsters were of similar stock to those found in any country public house but there were exceptions: the pedigreed, the bloodstock, parading.

Dave decided it was time to leave. He had been warned away from gatherings. In any case he was sick of the spoon-fed crap he was hearing. He finished his drink and noticed that the bright eyes slightly enlarged by the spectacles had fastened on to him again. Her face, framed by her curling blonde hair, held a trace of humour. Her wide mouth curled into a careless smile. Dave felt momentarily flustered. He was amazed at the feeling. He wondered whether he had been staring, for it was that knowing sort of look she gave him. Her escort, one of those exceptions, diverted her attention.

Dave made his way from the bar and began the long walk home. He had gone about one hundred yards when he caught sight of his minder. He chuckled to himself. It was going to be a long holiday.

He dreamt of the smoke, the picture-post-card city, Tower Bridge, the river, Oxford Street, Covent Garden, the stations, the complex road systems cutting through the grand buildings and the superstores with their vast windows of glistening goods. Then he crawled down to the lower levels, to the Underground and subways, to the hoardings and the graffiti, down with the degenerates and the filth where needles plunged into scabby arms in places decorated with smears of blood and excrement, a place where prostitutes hawked their bodies and children their souls, a place of dark shadows where pathetic creatures craned forward to glimpse the flash of pubic hair, where even more furtive creatures sat in tiny cubicles to masturbate while they gazed through slots at cunts beyond, where wailing pensioners hid behind their barricaded doors listening to the sounds of smashing glass and West Indian and Irish slang, then up again to the packed pavements and jammed roads, to the piles of litter and market trays spilling with rotten fruit, from the sleek opulence of Knightsbridge to the East End traps, from the King's Road to Berwick Street, from

Piccadilly decorated in superficial neon to St James's, from the abortion clinics around Oxford Circus marked for the overnight stayers who carried their unwanted lumps, by the Post Office Tower, to St Paul's Cathedral, where perhaps those overnighters could stop to pray for the souls they left behind.

Thunder crashed and Dave sat up sweating. The strong North Sea wind gusted, trees swayed and creaked, the rain beat the cottage walls and above the clatter of nature, he heard the sounds of a slamming door.

Armed with a torch he had discovered earlier and wearing a huge canvas raincoat that had hung on the kitchen door, he went out to the sheds. The loose door was swinging on the last of the four sheds used as storage space for gardening equipment and an assortment of rusty tools. He was not surprised to find a series of wet footprints on the dusty surface of the shed floor. His minder, Joe Daley, had been doing his rounds and no doubt stopped for shelter. He heard the pigs grunting in the next shed. The wind strengthened and rushed through the trees. Dave secured the door, pulled up the wide lapel and splashed back to the cottage.

It was late morning when Joe Daley pulled up in a battered green Austin. Dave was leaning on the orchard fence watching the pigs wallow in the spongy ground. The sun glared from a clear sky into air purified by the night rain. The subtle gradations of light and shade were lost. Daley's huge shoulders bunched over the wheel as he pulled on the hand brake. Driving had taken all his concentration. His eyes were curiously threatening.

'Getting around a bit?' He spoke slowly and Dave got the impression that Daley was unsettled.

'Just a stroll.'

The eyes narrowed.

'You been strollin' a lot these last few days.'

'Just seeing the sights.'

Suspicion mixed with hostility marked Daley's leathered features. He grunted his resignation.

'The boss wants to see you. Dinner. I'll pick you up at eight. Be ready.'

Dave smiled. So that was it. The invitation had rankled the big man. Special treatment for the man from the smoke was playing on Daley's nerves. Wet-nursing him was probably irritating enough, checking the grounds in the middle of the night in the middle of a thunderstorm was damned uncomfortable, but actually picking him up and acting as chauffeur was an absolute shit.

Dave grinned.

'Is there anywhere local I can get my suit pressed?'

The car roared off and on the corner took a thousand miles from the life of the tyres.

That evening Dave was entertained by Coddy Hughes in a manor house beyond a series of low-slung, red-brick buildings that housed stables and a pool room.

His father had once told him about Coddy and a friendship that had developed over the years. He had described Coddy as a lunatic and the most dangerous person he had ever come across, a thick-bodied man almost bald even at that young age, with a round scar right between his eyes. Coddy said it was a bullet that had bounced off his thick skull but his father had discovered later that it had been a wooden arrow fired from a bow by Coddy himself. The arrow had snapped and whipped back at Coddy's face. He had been nine years old at the time and lucky not to have been blinded. Not many people knew the truth. The bullet sounded better.

Dave met a sixty-two-year-old bald man in a neck collar who needed a walking-frame to get about. He was thin and weak and the only hint of his past came from his fired eyes, a fierce, stabbing gaze that missed nothing. But time had been unkind, a car accident in his fifties, a whiplash, had left him crippled and all but housebound.

It was an intimate yet cheerless party with Coddy heading the table, eating one handed while his other rested permanently on a silver-tipped walking stick, his wife, Mavis, to his left and Dave opposite her. Three others, girls aged six, ten and twelve, sat at the bottom end of the gleaming table. They were involved in other things, whispers and chatter and girlish giggles. They were the daughters of Coddy's daughter who was out for the evening, Coddy told him and added, 'Such a handful they need a minder a piece!'

Dave felt uncomfortable, conscious that they were all watching him.

Once dinner was over Mavis took the girls through to an adjoining room to play Scrabble and left Dave and Coddy together. It was time for business.

'The girls have taken to you,' he said in quiet clipped tones, his cruel mouth remaining expressionless. He waved his free hand. 'You went to the Oak. It's not a good idea. Your father has asked me to look after you until he can sort out the trouble. How can I look after you if you don't take advice?'

Coddy leaned forward in his chair and filled two glasses with whisky. He pushed one towards Dave then settled back again.

'The village is a small place with few secrets; the stranger stands out like a nigger in the Royal Family. If you need for something you let Joe know and he'll get it for you.' He raised his head slightly from the pink neck brace and emphasized coldly, 'This is not a request. You understand?'

Dave nodded. A mix of embarrassment and admiration ran through him. He understood clearly what made Coddy Hughes great in the eyes of some men. He was royalty, immediately dominant.

'All I want to do is get back to civilization. No one is going to look for me up here,' he said defensively.

'Dave, it's where I've chosen to live. It's my HQ. That makes it important.' He lifted his glass and emptied it in one before continuing. 'You can guarantee that the Yanks have at least one contact up here because of me. Sure, it's off the beaten track and it's a lot safer than most places, but don't drop your guard. These people have a network bigger than the CIA. I don't expect trouble, especially if you keep your head down, but you've got to understand, in this game there's no such thing as a certainty.' He grunted. 'It's not so bad. Your father tells me he hopes to have it sorted in two or three weeks.'

Dave's heart sank. Three more weeks in the country would drive him crazy. Coddy grunted again as he recognized Dave's despair.

'I'll send the girls around to keep you company. That will get them away from me for a while. The summer holidays are too long. All I'm hearing all day is noise. Pop. Men dressed as fairies leaping about the stage.' He indicated the bottle of malt on the table and Dave poured out more drinks. 'I prefer this to brandy,' Coddy said and swallowed two measures. 'I shouldn't drink at all with all the pills.' He chuckled. 'I've gone through life doing things I shouldn't, so what the hell!'

'I know you met my old man during the war but he's never discussed it. As far as he's concerned the war never happened.'

Coddy nodded thoughtfully.

'That's not a bad thing. Some men never stop talking about it.'

'It was only recently that we discovered he'd caught one in the shoulder. He didn't tell us about it. A geezer who boxed out of Peter Woodhead told my brother Tommy. When he asked Dad about it all he got was a shake of the head and something about a scratch on the shoulder.'

A wry smile ended Coddy's look of amazement.

'That's a bloody gem. A scratch on the shoulder!' He laughed out loud. It was the first time Dave had seen any humour in the man. Coddy swallowed half his drink before glancing up. Dave toyed with the crystal, turning the glass, waiting for Coddy's explanation.

'You heard of Scratch Fox?' The old eyes narrowed to examine the answer.

Dave shook his head.

'Scratch Fox was a sergeant in your old man's outfit. It was just before the war started. They were on exercises on Salisbury Plain when one of the squaddies got himself hurt and needed stitching up. Fox had your father drive him and the squaddie back to the hospital but it meant kippin' overnight at Fox's married quarters. During that night your father crept out of the house and drove into town to take care of a couple of goons who had put your grandfather out of action.'

'Took care of them?'

Coddy nodded.

'Years earlier they had cut up your grandaddy for not coughin' up protection. Paralysed him. It led to him topping himself.'

Dave knew that his grandad had drowned in the Thames; he hadn't known that it had been suicide.

'What happened?'

'Your dad took care of it. He waited ten years for the right moment.'

'He topped them?'

'Wouldn't you?' Coddy paused then went on. 'Unfortunately, in the early morning the sergeant heard him get back. But when the filth eventually arrived Fox gave your dad an alibi. He never did understand why the sergeant lied to the police but, as it turned out, Fox was the lucky one. Back home everyone knew what had happened. They treated your father differently. The thing unspoken remained between them; not respect, exactly, unless it was the respect you have for dangerous things. When war broke out they ended up in France. Sergeant Fox got half his head blown away in Dunkirk, the town. The same volley caught your dad in the shoulder. They were left behind. That's the way it was. The stretcher bearers would pick 'em up later. Trouble was, the stretchers had enough to do on the beaches. Your dad carried the sergeant down to the beach on his good shoulder and found what was left of the platoon. He was pretty busted up himself by then. Between the two of them they looked like something out of a butcher's window.'

He paused to fill his glass then went to top up Dave's and saw that it was still full.

'You want a beer?' The question was clipped.

Dave lifted his glass.

'This is fine.'

'Listen, son, a conversation that stops you drinking isn't worth holding.'

Dave finished his drink in one and allowed Coddy to fill the glass.

'You're telling me things I've never heard.'

Coddy smiled briefly in acceptance.

'It's a funny business, Dave, that as you get older and the war gets further away, you dwell on it more and more. In the end your memory turns it from being some kind of fucking horror story into something you enjoyed. I suppose that's why so many of the old guys go back to the battlefields. They're gettin' off on what their memories made of it. They've started to believe their own stories.' Coddy grunted. 'The glory! The few! All the heroic stuff. We were running backwards like no one ever ran. And as for all those little boats! The navy must get really pissed off hearing about them. It was chaos. There were bodies all over the shop. The stink was unbelievable. The planes never stopped. Getting on a boat during those first few days was impossible. At one stage they stopped taking stretcher cases. Your dad and the sergeant got a change of clothes from a couple of bodies. Not that Fox could do much. He was unconscious for most of the time. No one thought he'd make it. The rest of the squad had to hide both of them to get them on board. They were only taking able-bodied by then. Anyway, they made it.

'Outside Dover all the old people's homes, schools and the like had been converted into military hospitals. It was in a place called

Cheriton that I first met your old man. I caught one in the neck so I must have looked a bit like Fox.' Coddy touched the red scar that ran below his left ear. 'I'd been shipped back before the evacuation but I was still too ill to move. These places were only holding units until you were well enough for transfer to a pukka hospital and that could have been anywhere in the country. Everyone in the ward was pretty poorly. This guy who ended up in the next bed to mine had a bullet through his shoulder and was down with pneumonia and God knows what else. He was unconscious for two days. They didn't think he'd make it. That was your dad. We spent a week together in that shit-house.'

The time approached eleven; the war was spent and so was Dave's description of the family and London in general. They had opened a second bottle of malt when the sounds of a car halting on gravel marked the arrival of the tall youth from the pub, and close on his heels, in tight trousers and open-necked shirt, the woman.

'Hello Daddy, are we interrupting?' she asked Coddy.

'No, we've just about finished it. Come in and have a drink. This is Dave Smith. You've heard me mention his father. This is Pat, my daughter, and her boyfriend, James Osbourne.'

'Hello,' Dave said but the word got caught in his throat.

Coddy Hughes splashed whisky as he poured more drinks. The couple carried them to the bar stools at the far end of the room. Dave forced himself from the sneaked glance; he found her incredibly attractive; had it not been for similar feelings during their previous encounter he would have put it down to the malt. He heard them talking while he talked to Coddy, her low voice polished of its accent, hints of Lincolnshire. They discussed everything and nothing in particular. She was there, on the periphery of everything, even when he faced the other way, easing off her seat to reach over the bar, stretching material across her wide hips, scratching her knee, raising her glass, beating a silent rhythm with her loose foot; a continuous movement to attract the eye.

Coddy leaned forward.

'James is a bit of a wanker,' he said quietly. Whether the statement was rhetorical or an indication of Coddy's real feelings toward his daughter's boyfriend was hard to tell.

Chapter 3

The following morning Dave decided to call London. He left his breakfast dishes on the table and began the walk to a kiosk he had noticed on the seafront. The sky was clear overhead but cloudy ahead. A helicopter hovered over the ocean, a speck, the constant hum of its rotor sounding like a distant lawnmower. The lane ran to a slow bend; the trees, thickly grouped closer to the cottage, thinned out until there were bare clearings of shortly cropped grass on either side. The land flattened and he caught sight of the distant red box standing incongruously before the sand dunes. It was a fairly warm morning, the breeze had dropped to a whisper and the air was charged with static. Before long, perspiration trickled under his shirt like some fast little insect.

The helicopter swept overhead, a startling roaring blur, close enough to look threatening and fanning the wind his way. It plunged with surprising speed and swooped back to hover before him, keeping pace. Dave could make out the detail of its belly and the two men through its open sides who were taking more than a casual interest in him. For a moment he considered that they were Coddy's men. He hoped they were. It hovered for about thirty seconds – it seemed longer – then soared away inland, across Coddy Hughes' manor, cutting a grey smear across the blue until it became a speck again and then disappeared altogether. The hum refused to fade, a constant intimidation, as though the machine had cut through nature itself and left its mark.

The lane narrowed over a hump-backed bridge across a slow-moving stream. On the other side the grass was coarser and tufted, the earth coloured with stretches of light sand. Pools of black water dotted the area, shrunken so that the rings of dark mud at their edges dried out in stages, the outer layers cracked and lifted in a mosaic pattern of brownish hues.

Dave reached the telephone when the sun was at its peak; it was unbearably hot inside and he wedged open the door with his foot. A minute later he was through to Jimmy Jones.

'You OK, Dave?'

'No, I'm not.'

'Where are you?'

'I'm down on the farm, son, knee deep in pig shit. The smell's so bad it makes my eyes water.'

'Where?'

'It don't matter where. Just tell me what's happening?'

'It's too quiet for comfort, Dave. Something's going down but everyone's being cagey. There's people askin' about you, and it ain't a birthday present they've got in mind!'

'Who's askin'?'

'No names, just faces and a lot of whispers. But there's no doubt about it. It's you they want. What's goin' on?'

Dave ignored the question and asked: 'What do they look like?'

'Rock Hudson lookalikes, my son. Clean cut, thirties, All-American guys, know what I mean?'

'Does the old man know?'

'Tell me something going down in the Smoke that he don't know about?'

'Has he said anything?'

'Only that you're on holiday. It's official.'

'Let's keep it that way. It'll blow over. Don't worry. I'm keepin' my head down for a while. Tell the boys to do the same. If you got problems that can't wait, then get in touch with Ray and he'll let the old man know.'

'We could get hold of these geezers, Dave. Find out who's askin' the questions?'

'Blimey, don't do that! I already know who it is. Just stay loose. I'll be in touch.'

'Take care, Dave. I don't like the sound of this.'

'I'll make out. Just tell everyone to watch their backs.'

'Take care.'

'Yeah.'

'See you.'

It was a relief to leave the kiosk and feel the breath of air. The sounds of the gentle waves washing in enticed him over the bank of fine sand. Dave saw the horse first, about twenty yards from him, its thin reins hanging loosely from the bit, its chestnut coat gleaming across its bare back. It stood head bowed, snorting. Behind the horse a trail of pits in the dry sand created a path across from the damp firmer stuff at the water's edge; here, the prints became more defined and trailed off across the beach.

The girls stood in the sea facing the horizon, calf deep until a swell and then the water lifted to the shoulders of the shortest and to the waist of Patricia Hughes. Dave was to discover later that since her divorce she had reverted to her maiden name. They skipped and splashed. Their girlish yelps and laughter reached across to him. They seemed totally unaware of being watched. The four of them were naked. Their clothes were scattered across the beach. Dave's breath was swept away as he watched, captivated, barely able to move. The bodies spanned perhaps thirty years but he would never have guessed it; the sweet curves were as firm as they had ever been. He could have enjoyed watching them play indefinitely but reserve, maybe a fear that they might discover him, turned him round.

On the road he emptied sand from his shoes and started back. He searched above the distant line of trees for signs of the helicopter but could not find it and guessed that it was retreating from the quickly approaching clouds. The sky had become mottled with tufts of cloud racing in from thicker stuff on the coast, casting moving shadows on the road ahead. He wondered whether he would beat the rain to the cottage. He heard the faint clatter of horseshoes on the road and turned to see the woman, Patricia, astride the trotting horse. She was smiling under the cap of flattened straw-coloured hair flattened further by her spectacles that looked like a butterfly embellished hairband. She had dressed in a short thigh-length towelling robe. She did not speak but looked directly ahead, allowing the horse to walk beside him. There was a look of complacency in her expression, as if she enjoyed the baiting and knew exactly how much it was unsettling him. Her loose leg dangled freely beside him, perhaps a yard away, brushing the chestnut coat of the horse. Her robe, buttoned at the midriff, fell away either side exposing a blue wedge of bikini bottom against her pale skin. Dave pulled his gaze away and glanced up. There was a terrible glint in her eye as she kicked and moved ahead of him. He watched her round the bend, grateful that she had gone.

The first rumblings of thunder rippled behind him, forcing his pace, and when it died it left a hum of singing voices carried, presumably, from a wedding at the village church. Dave reached the cottage just as the first splashes of rain dotted the ground.

The horse was tethered under the awning along the cottage side wall; it backed around, stamping, unsettled by the murmur of approaching storm. Dave felt gutless, adrenalin reached out to every nerve end. He was amazed at his own nervousness. He pushed open the door and lifted the dimness inside. She faced him, framed in the square of brighter light, perched on the edge of the table with her toes barely touching the stone floor, her hands gripping the wooden table-top either side to hold her balance. She was smiling at his expression or at the sounds of 'All Things Bright and Beautiful' that began somewhere behind him. Her wide eyes flickered and widened. The smile fluttered, first in apprehension and then to something else; a dare, almost. The robe was undone exposing her long neck, the valley between her swollen breasts, the faint gleam of down across her midriff and the blue material beneath. Because of her pose, with her back arched over the table, the material bulged, and as she shifted her weight the pathway between her legs was presented to him. Her spectacles lay on the table next to the pile of breakfast dishes.

It was instinctive. From the moment he pushed open the door, from the moment she first saw him in the pub, there was never a real doubt. Her wet salty mouth locked on to his; his hand moved between her legs, bringing a gasp from her mouth that sent hot air into his; her legs clamped around his waist parting his way, dampening the material. He tasted the sea water that trickled from her hair, eyes, nose and mouth, consumed, convinced that she would suffocate beneath him.

It thundered again with an almighty crash that shook every window in the house and lightning cracked out of the darkening sky.

There was nothing tender in this coition and not the slightest kindness shown. Blood seeped from her mouth, thinned by spittle, it flowed by jagged glass embedded in his side, it oozed from broken skin on knees and elbows, it spat across wounded foreskin and mixed and it circled her dark nipples with tiny flecks. They lay, raw, unable to move, against the thick table legs on the cold stone floor tiles. The tablecloth had come down at some stage smashing glass, splattering them with milk and cold coffee and preserve.

She whispered thickly, 'You hurt me.'

'Of course I did.'

Across half a mile of countryside, getting fainter all the time, down the lane, across the garden and through the open door, fading to a murmur before it reached their ears, the vicar said, 'And may God be with you,' and the congregation, 'Amen.'

Bleeding there, throbbing, gazing at floor level past the legs of table and chairs into the dark recesses between cupboards, Dave wondered if their brutish emotions had filtered into the walls and doors, whether the cottage would be a different place now.

She stirred and stood, straddling him, gazing down at him, her blond hair in strands over her face. Lumps of preserve became unstuck from her stomach and fell on to him; spilt coffee and milk found its path southward through the dark curls and down her legs. He looked up at her, at the display between her legs.

'Jesus! They're going to need a space shuttle to get my ballocks back –,' he began but was cut short.

She raised her finger and hushed him. He watched her move, still feeding on her movement, as she stepped across him and slipped on her robe. She picked up her spectacles and without a backward glance went out of the cottage. He waited for the sounds of the horse on the tarmac, visualizing her nakedness on its back, thinking of the wet patch that would shortly stain the chestnut hair as she drained that which he had put there.

While the bath filled Dave cleaned up his side and stuck a plaster to the wound. Her scent was trapped in the dried white flakes she had left behind but this was going to go the way of the preserve and cold coffee. He drank a quarter of the scotch he took from his case and carried the remainder with him to the bath where he climbed gingerly into the hot water. Gradually the stinging disappeared leaving a positive glow and a feeling of drowsiness so heavy that it was difficult to move an arm.

The door opened and cut into the steam.

She stood in the doorway and leant against the frame. An expression of mild apprehension did not match the certainty in her eye.

'I reached the corner and decided there was no way I could present myself like this. I thought of falling off the horse but that wouldn't be convincing, would it? I mean, what on earth did I fall on to cover myself in marmalade and milk and for God's sake, love bites? Look!' She swept back the robe to show a mark just below the elastic at the back of her briefs. 'Not that I need an excuse, but it might raise Daddy's eyebrows. He's very old-fashioned. Anyway, I didn't expect any of that. I look as though I've been hit in the teeth!' Her top lip was swollen and there was a red patch on her chin caused by his stubble. 'Anyway, it's peeing down out there.' She moved in, dropped the robe and wriggled out of her pants. 'Move up,' she said and climbed in, tap end. The water flushed over the side before it settled below the overflow. He noticed the bruising beginning to darken around her dark nipples.

'Here.' She handed him the flannel. 'You do it. You caused it.' There was a look in her eye that spoke of affection. He hadn't noticed it before.

'You caused it Patricia. I had nothing to do with that part of it.'

'Maybe,' she countered. 'But you didn't seem to object.'

He grinned.

'What did you expect me to do?'

Sunlight tumbled in from the small square window above the basin, shafting through the steam.

'The storm is over,' she said.

'It could easily start again,' he said.

Her eyes narrowed.

'I saw you on the beach earlier, with the girls.'

'We noticed. We saw you arrive.'

'They're all yours?' He smiled. 'You're in good nick for three kids.'

'I'm in good nick period, if you don't mind.'

He nodded agreement.

'What happened to their dad?'

'We fell out.'

'Does he see the kids?'

She shook her head.

'He's never seen Tracy. She's six. We haven't seen him since then.' Her glance flashed over the small room then settled back on him. 'This room has a certain primitive charm but there's a definite smell of mould.'

'That's the laundry basket under the basin. Someone must have been keeping old socks in it.'

'Now you've ruined the picture. Why not the smell of the thatched roof after the rain?'

'What am I? A poet?'

A smile lit her face. She crossed her arms around her knees and leant back with her head between the taps. Beads of water collected on her forehead.

'In the pub you were staring at me.'

'You looked out of place,' he said.

His feelings were intense, sharpened by knowledge yet tempered by guilt. Or rather, he felt that he should have felt guilty. He felt that he had abused Coddy Hughes' hospitality.

She touched her breast, flinched, then examined the small nipple and the bruising.

'You did that,' she said thickly.

'Yes.'

She laughed and reached for the bottle. The scotch burned and she coughed.

'God, I hate that stuff,' she said. She eased her legs down between his, pressing him with her toes, her knees lowered sufficiently to reveal her hair broken by refraction. He grew against her foot.

'Tell me about you?'

'I'm not married,' he said.

'I know that much.'

'I'm in the family business.'

'What else?'

'I've got a flat in London, above one of the clubs, and I've got a room at home.'

'What about girls?' she asked.

'You're very beautiful, you know that?'

'So are you. What about girls?'

'Nothing about girls.'

'I've heard differently.'

'Who told you that?'

She smiled. Her front tooth was slightly crooked.

'What happened to the kids?' he asked.

'They took the short cut home. I had to bring the horse the long way. Tracy, Jackie and Karen. Karen's the eldest. She's twelve. Tracy is the apple in granddad's eye. She always has been. He makes up for absent fathers.'

Dave nodded reflectively. 'I can't picture Coddy Hughes with kids crawling all over him.'

'You'd be surprised how domesticated my dad is. I took them all to London once, to see the shows. About two years ago. Tracy was too young really. We stayed at the Hilton.'

Dave studied her thoughtfully, wondering whether she was telling him that she knew all about the American and the trouble that he was in. She had not once asked what he was doing up here and it was the obvious question.

'Daddy takes us away twice a year,' she continued. 'But he can't get around like he used to.'

'You've not thought of moving away? Getting a place of your own?'

'I've got as much freedom as I need. I'm thirty-four. Daddy accepts that. No questions. No restrictions. Discussions centre around the girls, their schooling and so on. He likes me to get out. He'd like me to meet someone.'

'He doesn't like James.'

'Oh, I know that.' She raised her eyebrows. 'James is all right.'

'Only all right?'

'He's safe. He's very rich, legitimately so, and he's not likely to end up in prison or in some gutter with a knife in his back.'

'Nor am I, sweetheart.'

'Huh! You're about as safe as safe sex! That's how Tracy arrived!'

She shivered. Perhaps the conversation had cooled her.

Dave pulled the plug and led her to the bedroom to hunt out the softer towels. She stood head bowed and let him dry her. He was gentle, particularly around the cuts on her knees. He knelt behind her, patting the towel against her legs, then drawing it apart like a pair of curtains to reveal her trim behind. He felt an urge to bury his face between her as if devouring her would be the final satisfaction.

'You leave my bum alone,' she said. She turned around inside the towel. She held her legs closely together; her slender hand did not entirely cover the extremities or the parting between. He let the towel fall. She moved her hand.

'You're looking from a purely aesthetic point of view, of course?'

'Yeah. What's it mean?'

'It means that I'm going to fall over if you keep doing that.'

He picked her up easily and carried her across to the bed.

She drew her legs apart. He reached across to kiss her and it lay between them, throbbing, threatening to burst. He felt her tremble.

'Be tender with me this time,' Dave said.

They spent the following few days together. Even in that short time she seemed to have changed. She radiated; her complexion and her character smouldered as though fired by some inner furnace. It was impossible not to recognize the sparkle, the confidence, the added spring in her step.

On Thursday she couldn't make it; she was taking the children into Lincoln. Dave found himself in the bar of the Royal Oak again. He knew that it was a mistake and that he was going against the expressed wishes of Coddy Hughes but things had moved on from there. It was lunchtime and the bar was empty. The balding man served him and then went out to his cellars. He stood at the bar and considered finishing his drink quickly and getting out before any damage was done. The door opened. It was too late. And as soon as he recognized James Osbourne he knew it meant trouble.

Backed up by two friends, Osbourne walked directly up to Dave and said, 'I want a word with you.'

Dave turned to face him.

'What can I do for you?'

'I want to make it clear to you that Patricia and I have been seeing one another for quite some time and that we have an understanding.'

'Fine,' Dave said. 'That's quite clear.'

'I want you to keep away from her. You have nothing in common; you do not fit in. Is all that clear to you?'

Dave shifted his glance to Osbourne's friends who stood just behind. He gave them his best effort at a conciliatory smile. He didn't need this. Coddy had warned him. He was suppose to be lying low, keeping out of trouble. Backing down went against the grain. That upset him more than anything else.

'There's no need for all this,' he said.

'I want your word that you'll leave her alone.'

Dave sighed.

'I'm sorry, pal, but you're talkin' to the wrong person. If you have a future with Pat you should be discussing it with her.'

'I'm not your pal, Dave. I never will be. And the discussion is with you. If you don't mind we'll leave Patricia out of it.'

Dave shrugged and turned back to the bar. He lifted his glass. James Osbourne prodded Dave's arm and some of the drink spilt. A dark veil drew across Dave's eyes. Osbourne prodded again.

'I'm talking to you,' he said threateningly. 'Do we have an understanding?'

Dave's beer glass exploded on the side of James Osbourne's face and sent him sprawling across table and chairs. Before he had landed firmly on the floor and before his friends had moved, Dave's shoe had sunk into his groin. It was over in seconds. Osbourne lay paralysed on his back as frothy blood poured from his mouth and nose.

Dave turned on the others. 'Any arguments?'

They shook their heads.

The barman appeared from the back and made suitable threats. As Dave left the bar the others rushed to aid their friend.

Dave anticipated the next move. He knew that the police wouldn't get involved and he guessed that James Osbourne would cause no further trouble – Coddy wouldn't allow it – but he knew also that Coddy wouldn't let it rest there.

Dave was in the orchard when he heard the car. The sun had just cleared the treetops and begun its dissipation of the early morning mist. Two men armed with shotguns left the black Rolls and called him over. The rear door was pushed open and Dave found Coddy Hughes sitting stiffly in the seat, his cane held upright between his knees.

'Morning,' Dave said while he tried to gauge the man's mood, wondering whether his daughter was to be the subject. Suddenly he felt nervous at the possibility. Even though he hadn't seen Pat since the fight her scent was still about him; he drew it in with every breath, the musky scent of female sex, unmistakable and yet personalized, unique. It was in his nose and throat, in his hair. Coddy couldn't fail to recognize it.

'David, get in a while,' Coddy said calmly.

Dave watched the two armed men spread out either side of the car, guns no longer broken, and he knew there was a problem. He climbed in and sat beside the diminutive figure.

'What's happened?'

'You've happened. You've arrived in my village like World War fucking Three!'

Dave studied his new adversary. 'I'm sorry about what happened. Let's not beat around the bush.'

'I'm sorry too, Dave. You let me down. You seem to have some kind of death wish about you. My feelings for your father are holding back what I'd like to say to you, but I'm surprised he hasn't taught you self-control.'

'Is he all right?'

'James? All right? Well now, apart from his nose being about three feet away from his mouth, and his front teeth chewin' on his arsehole, I'd say he wasn't too fuckin' happy.'

Dave held on to his smile.

'I know about you, Mr Hughes,' he said. 'And I know that it's only these last few years that have slowed you down. If someone came in and started pushing you, you'd have killed the guy.'

'We've got nothing else to discuss,' Coddy said.

'Yes we have.'

Coddy sighed.

'I know what's been going on. I'm not stupid. Even Patricia's mother thinks that she's sniffin' glue or something.'

Dave's mouth was dry. Without realizing it he was digging his fingernails into his palms.

'I know that Patricia has obviously found some qualities in you that are attractive. Frankly, I have not. You don't actually inspire confidence, Dave. You came here with a heavy reputation, and your actions since then have given me no reason to doubt it. The reason you were sent here in the first place is because you think with your dick. Down south, apparently, there's a joke that Dave Smith would fuck anything in a skirt including the odd Scot! You heard it? You think it's funny?' He paused for a moment and then said: 'If only one tenth of your reputation is right then you're not to be trusted within a mile of any woman. That certainly includes my daughter.'

'These things are always exaggerated. It would take some kind of superman to do some of the things I've been accused of.'

'Maybe,' Coddy said. 'But when all this is over I'd like you to go back to London, put some space between you. If in three months you still have feelings for one another we can take it from there.'

'I can't do that. Patricia isn't a girl anymore. She knows what she wants. If she doesn't want to see me then I'll never bother her again. But she's going to tell me. Not you, Coddy.'

Coddy raised his eyebrows in surprise. Suddenly he smiled and there was something approaching affection in his eyes.

'I'm going to leave it there for now young man. There'll be no more wandering down to the village. Is that understood?'

Dave nodded.

The affection vanished. Coddy sighed. 'I'll speak to my daughter,' he said.

Dave climbed out of the car and watched Coddy's men get in. Moments later the car roared off.

It rained through the afternoon and the weak light barely found its way into the cottage. Dave bathed early and towelled himself down while watching for Patricia's arrival from the bedroom window.

He was nervous at the prospect of meeting her again. It came down to violence and whether she thought his treatment of her ex was uncalled for. It came down to her attitude over the use of violence to settle an argument. He wondered how much she knew about her father's line of work and whether she accepted that it hadn't been his refined manners and his persuasive abilities over the conference table that had led him to the top. He wondered whether she accepted also that some men could never be pushed around.

He heard the car before he saw it. A metallic BMW. It flashed past the short expanse of lane that he could see. A moment later came a screech of brakes. Two men in dark suits appeared at the entrance to the drive. The drizzle didn't seem to bother them as they looked around before walking almost nonchalantly toward the cottage. The black automatics they held seemed to cut a hole through the dripping grey.

Dave was stunned. The implications were still sinking in as he saw the men duck for cover behind a low hedgerow, their attention directed toward the orchard.

Two flat explosions rattled the window. Dave leant closer to the glass to bring the orchard into view. Joe Daley stood under the trees, his raised shotgun smoking. He had already broken it and was bringing fresh cartridges from his pocket. He was standing there as if taking part in a grouse shoot. Dave mouthed the words, 'Get down for Chrissakes!' But even as the last word silently emerged he heard the clatter of automatic fire and watched Daley sink to the spongy ground. Bullets smacked into the mud around him. Tree bark ripped open. Daley lay still. His gun stuck in the earth and pointed at the low sky. A sow nearby had her belly torn out. She squealed and slipped then slowly hauled herself from the mud and lumbered away, barely concerned.

Dave moved. He put his weight against the old dressing table and pushed it against the door. He pulled his case from under the bed and tore into it, throwing his clothes aside until he found his .38, a black Smith & Wesson.

The front door crashed open. Glass smashed. He moved to the window. A dozen coats of paint held it firm. The thump of footsteps sounded on the narrow stairs. He put his shoulder against the frame. The window cracked, the wood splintered, and it opened. The bedroom door thudded into the back of the dressing-table. The opening in the window was barely wide enough to take him but he made it, and landed on the awning that ran along the side of the cottage.

The dressing-table slid back and the door crashed open. A gun roared. The window smashed and showered him with glass. Dave fired one shot into the room before he lost his footing and skidded on the tin roof. Timber cracked as the awning caved in. He rolled over the lip and landed flat on his back on a freshly turned border. For a moment he lay winded, unable to move.

One of the men had remained at the cottage door and now he came charging around the corner. He was blond, about six-three. Jimmy's description flashed into Dave's mind. He was still lying on his back as he pulled the trigger. The man's blue eyes widened as he realized his mistake. The bullet caught him in the knee. He yelped, spun round and fell backwards, away from Dave. His 12-bore Spatz flew into the air. Dave fired again and saw a neat hole appear in the sole of the man's shoe.

A clatter of fire came from above. Bullets smacked the earth just a foot from Dave's head.

He struggled to his feet, shouting out loud as slivers of glass cut into him. The rain washed blood across his pale body. Keeping close to the side of the cottage he ran to the back.

An old fence ran from the side of the cottage across to the outhouses. It was rotten in parts but just about adequate to keep the pigs from wandering. Moving in a crouched position Dave splashed his way to the sheds. The goon who could still stand up was going to have to make the same crossing to get to Dave and that wasn't going to be easy for him.

He crawled into the end shed and wedged open the door. It gave him a perfect view of the cottage.

The rain grew heavier. He began to shiver. Ten minutes went by.

'You hear me mother fucker?' The voice came from the cottage. 'There'll be another time, you can be sure of that!'

Minutes later he heard the distant car doors slam and then the engine. He stayed put for half an hour, until dusk began to fall, then he left the shed and keeping to the line of trees he circled the cottage to the road.

It was the better part of another hour before he chanced the cottage and in that time he examined it from every angle. Eventually he crawled in. He had just finished checking the place over and was still naked when he heard another car draw to a halt. His heart sank. He pressed himself against the larder wall and held the gun to his chest.

'My God! My God!' Patricia's voice carried through the open door. She had seen the smashed glass, perhaps even sniffed the cordite that still soured the air. She threw on the light. As she saw him her face drained of colour.

He winked. 'Hello, sweetheart,' he said. He dropped the gun to his side.

'Are you shot? There's so much blood.'

He glanced down. He was covered in mud, head to toe, but in a number of places the dirt had turned red.

'I don't think so. Most of it is cuts from the glass. But I'm hurting all over so I wouldn't really know.' He moved forward. She stayed motionless by the door. He switched off the light and peered out into the darkness. She sensed the danger and moved out of the doorway.

'What happened?'

'I don't know. I think Daley's had it. He's under the trees. Go and fetch your dad, will you? He'll know what to do. I'll cover you from here.' He steadied himself against the wall.

'You're coming with me,' she said sternly. 'If you think I'm leaving you like this you must be joking.'

He nodded, too shattered to argue. 'Give me a minute,' he said. 'I'll put some clothes on.'

'You better. Daddy's very particular about that sort of thing.' She turned up her nose. 'You could use a good deodorant, as well.'

Dave moved into the manor house. A doctor came out to check him over. Once he had gone Coddy admitted sheepishly, 'There's a squealer. North or south I don't know. I'll check my end. I imagine your father will do the same. It must be someone pretty damned close. Apparently they had a fucking helicopter out.' He glanced up to see the surprise in Patricia's eyes. He rarely used the word in front of the women. 'Sorry, sweetheart, but you can't trust anybody nowadays!'

Patricia filled Dave's glass with malt. She ignored her father's.

'You were lucky,' Coddy said, obviously upset that security had been breached on his manor. 'I told you to stay low, didn't I?' It was the closest Coddy could get to an apology.

The attack spurred Dave's father into overdrive. He gave the Americans a foothold in the London casinos where they could clean up their dollar bills – something they had been hankering after for years. Two days later Coddy came down to say: 'I've heard from your father. He's had to make concessions to get you off the hook, but it's done. The contracts are cancelled. He wants you home.' He finished. That was it. He walked past the two of them into his study and closed the two large doors behind him.

Patricia turned to him. 'I went to see James at the hospital. Before I came to the cottage that night. His jaw is wired up. He looks dreadful. I decided then that I didn't want to see you again. I was coming to tell you.'

Dave nodded. 'What changed your mind?'

'Daddy spoke to me while you were with the doctor.'

Dave couldn't hide his surprise.

'He told me that James got what he deserved, that there were three of them, that he wouldn't have been pushed around either.'

She carried her glass across to him and sat on his lap. She stroked his hair back and kissed him. The drink she held up threatened to spill. 'I must be mad getting mixed up with you,' she said lightly. 'Daddy told me what you said to him. About it being my decision and not his. Not many people stand up to my father.'

'Well, is it down to you, or not?'

'Of course I make my own decisions.'

'Well, I'm running out of time up here so you've got another one to make.'

'I wondered about that. It would be like the marriage of two Royal Families. You know, two manors.'

'Who said anything about getting married?'

'I did,' she said. 'You don't think I'd live with you without a ring, do you? Daddy's very particular about things like that.'

He reached forward to touch her glass with his.
'Well, in that case . . .' he said. '. . . Here's to two manors.'
She tasted the malt. 'I hate this stuff,' she said.

Chapter 4

1986

The Americans had lived in England long enough to have been forgotten by the society they left behind but barely long enough to feel accepted by the new. Their absence was no longer conspicuous. Sharon's parents were dead and Tony had lost all claim to whatever rung of the ladder he had been on. Cocaine had been his downfall; that and booze, and it had led to him being sent to England to work under O'Connell, even though O'Connell was old enough to drop. Tony considered it a punishment. A kind of exile. If he was remembered at all then it was as an example to young upstarts: 'You don't let personal matters jeopardize business', and, 'If you don't control your temper you'll end up like Tony Valenti!'

In the UK, the capital of the Old World, he was still an outsider. He paid the taxes and the rates and was generous to strange charities. He attended the local church and the small community fêtes. In some ways the quieter pace of life suited him. The feeling of safety was in itself a rare pleasure. But he was still an outsider. There was an unspoken complicity between the English that other races were inferior. Their ancestry had left them with an aloofness, a discipline, an orderliness; even the down-and-outs in Central London had more style, certainly more manners, than their New World contemporaries. Even the down-and-outs queued for Chrissakes! The English had a magnificent capacity to ignore anything remotely disagreeable – and to them foreigners were just that. The English were . . . insular, of an island.

Approaching the UK at the rate of one mile every two and a half seconds, O'Connell raised his voice to counter Concorde's continuous roar.

'We've lived here five years, Tony, and you still don't know what the place is famous for?'

Valenti's sharp features remained blank.

'Rhododendrons,' he offered.

O'Connell sighed and said disappointedly, 'Magna Carta. Runnymede! The Magna Carta!'

'Oh yeah. Remind me what that is again.'

'It's serious shit, Tony. Trial by jury. All that political crap.'

'Yeah, I remember.'

'Lemme tell you somethin'. We've got a lot to thank the barony for. You can't get to judges like you can get to juries.' The old man chuckled. 'King fuckin' John didn't know he was signin' us into power!' He paused before adding, 'The grandchildren were telling me all about it. They're doin' it at school. Those kids give me a lot of pleasure in my old age.' He turned to the scarred leathery features of Tony Valenti. 'It's a shame you never had kids, Tony. Everyone should have kids.'

The old man knew only too well why Tony and Sharon had remained childless. After Sharon had been caught cheating Tony had knocked her about. The finest doctors in the world agreed that she would never conceive: the damage was too severe. O'Connell himself had tried to talk Tony into a divorce but he wouldn't have it. Valenti was besotted with his wife, children or no children. Just so long as she didn't do it again.

'It was good to see the old faces again,' O'Connell said.

Tony Valenti didn't agree. He had been acutely embarrassed by the knowing looks, the smirks, the way in which old friends had pointedly ignored him. They had treated him like so much shit on the sidewalk and given him the widest possible berth. If the truth was known he was relieved to get back on the plane.

O'Connell went on, 'I wish we could have stayed longer. When you get to my age whenever you leave New York you wonder if you'll ever see the place again. That's something you can promise me, Tony. If I die in the rain over there . . .' He indicated forward. '. . . I want my body freighted back to Manhattan.'

'You got it,' Tony muttered but his thoughts were racing back to the meeting they had attended earlier in the day.

As it was with the majority of families, relationships were occasionally strained. In this respect the Americans and their relatives in Sicily and Naples and Calabresia were no different. And as with most families the patriarchs – in this case they were out of the Cosa Nostra and Camorra – showed their issue tolerance and understanding. In return they expected loyalty and respect. They received both in large measures.

The Europeans had reached an agreement with the Colombian cocaine cartels by threatening to kill all their couriers. When the body count reached double figures, El Papa had agreed to talk. The link gave the Mafia exclusive rights to the two billion annual trade and their American relatives were given the job of handling it. With the increased supplies and vast fortunes tied up it was imperative that new markets were found. Mainland Europe was the obvious target, especially with the opening up of the Common Market frontiers already on the drawing board. Eventually their attention turned to the UK.

The Americans were already established in England. They had been drawn by the wide-open gambling laws. They owned houses on the banks of the river at Runnymede. Their business in the UK still centred on gaming and its associated money laundry which cleaned enormous amounts of US and Canadian dollars. Heading up the UK end was O'Connell and he was summoned to meet the heads of the families in New York. He took Tony Valenti along for the ride, and to carry his bag.

Concluding his report to the leaders, O'Connell had said, 'Under a thousand kilos were seized last year, mostly by Customs, mostly from the assholes on the continent. They're not even touching the surface. The imports are basically split into four: through Liverpool, mostly from the Crescent, and that's handled by a local gang, the Scousers, run by Vic Hannington; through the main airports, Heathrow and Gatwick, by John Bracey. A guy named Stafford Carr runs Hull. That's another port on the other side to Liverpool. He imports through Holland, and then the freelance, mostly dropped off the top of Scotland around the islands and then picked up by the trawlers. That's the import situation as near as damnit. As far as the distribution is concerned the place is split between southern England run by the Chinks, and Mick McGovern who runs Scotland. Between the two is a buffer zone controlled by various smaller gangs. The Chinks deal under the protection of the main London gang, the Smiths. There's an agreement between them that goes way back. My feeling is, that in ten years or so, when the heavies move out of Hong Kong, the

Chinks will want to expand. That's the picture but it ain't the whole story. Things are pretty unstable over there at the moment. Mick McGovern who runs Scotland is keen to expand southward. One of the guys he wants to move in on, Coddy Hughes, is related to the Smiths. His daughter married the eldest son. The Scousers from Liverpool are making noises and threatening to join McGovern. The whole situation is likely to blow, maybe turn in to a full-scale war. If it does then someone is going to have to pick up the pieces.'

From the shadows a voice of authority spoke quietly.

'The Smith's organization is best suited for what we've got in mind: a nationwide distribution. We need to pressure them into ending their agreement with the Chinese. Stafford Carr can be closed down easily. His shipments from Holland will be cut immediately. The Liverpool end is more difficult. We'll work on it. It might be that Vic Hannington takes a long vacation. For the moment we'll live with the airports and Bracey. At the end of the day he'll fall in line. If we open up negotiations with McGovern and make the Smiths aware of it, then they'll come around to our way of thinking. Is that a problem?'

'No problem,' O'Connell said.

'What about you, Tony? I know it's a long time ago but these things don't go away.'

Tony Valenti nodded sullenly.

'I had a run-in with the Smith's eldest son. It was ten years ago. You all know what happened. He screwed about with my wife. I don't hold any grievances. Business is business. I put my wife in the picture and she ain't likely to do it again!'

The room filled with muttered approval.

'Business is business,' Valenti repeated. 'And if you consider that the Smiths are good for us then that's good enough for me.' He lied, of course, but he was totally convincing.

'That's a wrap then,' the leader said softly. 'Let's get to work.'

Roaring towards Heathrow at over twice the speed of sound Tony Valenti thought about the meeting. His expression did not alter as he considered the irony that after all this time his family wanted to embrace the people he hated more than anyone in the world. And yet behind the insult lay a flicker of hope. It was just possible that in the ensuing struggle for control of the UK underworld – World War Three, Goddamnit – he would find his chance for retribution.

He glanced at the old man beside him.
'What is it?' O'Connell growled sleepily.
'Nothin',' Valenti muttered. 'Nothin' at all.'

Chapter 5

Some three-hundred and fifty miles north of Heathrow where the Americans were landing, men waited at another airport. They wandered down queues made ragged by a jumble of luggage to scrutinize the features of unsuspecting men, yet in their search they remained anonymous, hardly noticeable. Anonymity was the mark of their profession. They heard the roar of planes dropping from the low bank of dense cloud and they heard distorted voices heavy with Glaswegian accent resounding from the speakers, unclear in the vast ringing hall. The various sounds of engines and vehicles and nervous chatter did not distract them.

Since mid-morning they had waited. They had watched the queues shorten and lengthen, seen the small family dramas played out, seen a man argue with his wife, seen a dozen children thumped for getting in the way, seen a lost child consoled by a couple of WPCs, seen porters making their tips and plastic cups fill every available surface, and now, under the stark fluorescent strip they watched the cleaners mopping between the groups of night-time travellers, the holiday-makers doing it on the cheap. Bedraggled, fatigued people dossed down in makeshift beds, small children lay limply in the sagging arms of their parents or lolled in their pushchairs and eyes became sore and vacant and less excited. The planes kept arriving and departing, the automatic board kept flicking and the tannoy voice kept ringing.

Men waited and watched, drank coffee out of plastic cups and smoked endless cigarettes. Eventually they made a telephone call. They heard that he hadn't been found in any of the stations or depots or car-hire firms and they guessed that he had found a lift south. All was not lost, however, for men were now watching the motorways and waiting at service stations as far south as the Midlands.

All morning a great mass of cloud had moved in off the North Sea, drawing a darker colour across the land and, by mid-afternoon, the ceiling was low and dense, bringing forward the dusk. At first the rain was heavy, blurring the dark shadows and the arcs of light thrown from the street lamps; now it was gentle and constant, filtering into the spongy earth.

The weather suited Tommy Smith; no one was going to notice a man with his lapels pulled up to hide his face. People became anonymous in wet weather, heads down, collars up, hugging shop doorways for shelter, even the colour of clothes and hair darkened to a likeness by saturation. His problem was the scarcity of other faces. Now that the pubs and clubs were closing the weather was forcing the stragglers indoors. It would not be long before he was a lonely figure on the road, easily seen and just as easily picked up. The police stopping him would be bad enough for Mick's influence had probably reached the northern cities, but if Mick's people got to him first then he was finished. His options were disappearing. In the next half hour or so he had to get a lift or he had to steal a car. And stealing a car to drive the length of the country all in one go was going to be pretty chancy even on such a night.

Tommy glanced again at his watch. The articulated lorry that had roared down the M6 cutting through the surface water had dropped him ten minutes earlier. Since then he had smoked two cigarettes while studying the bright entrance of a service station from between the comparative shelter of two tightly parked container lorries. Beyond the lorry park where the two giants stood in isolation, bathed in a veil of rain and darkness so that only their massive silhouettes were visible, a row of cars parked neatly in the white painted rectangles, shiny skins glinting in reflected light as the water droplets collected together and zig-zagged in crazy patterns across them. Four powerful bikes decked in superfluous chrome, angled on their parking rests, were parked haphazardly next to the cars and immediately outside the entrance, parked in the no-parking area, an empty motorway patrol car stood with its doors unlocked.

The wind increased and swept water from the top of the containers. For a few moments Tommy was pelted with heavy drops and he was conscious of the rain seeping through to his shirt. He started from the darkness between the lorries just as the overnight coach from Glasgow pulled in and he was glad to mix with the stream of passengers as they filed from the coach, stepping between the deeper pools of spitting water, to the welcome of the unflattering white lights of the cafeteria.

Tommy moved along the ragged queue towards a cluttered stainless steel counter. In front of him people were stretching as they shuffled forward to order their teas and coffees. The queues in front of the toilets grew around the edge of the room; people danced from one foot to the other. He made the counter.

'An all-night breakfast, please. And coffee.'

A woman serving half smiled, perhaps at his accent. London, born and bred.

'Can you wait a minute, love?' she said and indicated the queue from the coach. 'I'll do your coffee.'

She was pleasing, something special, her spotless wraparound parted occasionally hinting that she wore no skirt beneath. There was a promise there, one that would never be kept.

He nodded silently and took his drink to the stand-up counter. The tables were full.

The queues for the toilets dwindled, those people who needed to use them again lined up again, hoping to make it before the coach driver got to his feet and, in a few minutes more, the vast room had all but emptied. Chairs blocked the gangways between tables full of empty crisp packets and brimming ashtrays and spills of tea and coffee. A couple of youngsters appeared and began to clear away. Coach parties: twenty quid spent between them and the place left looking like the England football supporters had held a stag night.

Tommy noticed two uniformed policemen as they moved from their corner table.

'See you, Liz,' one of them called to the woman behind the counter. She waved at the swinging door. Tommy watched the policemen run through the rain to their car. In a moment a plume of smoke put-putted from the exhaust and the headlamps produced two explosions of light in the dark. The rain fizzed in the beams.

Tommy turned back to check out who was left in the cafeteria: half-a-dozen leather-clad youths, three couples, one with a sleeping baby, an old man, two drivers and a skinny girl who looked like she was on the game.

The waitress weaved toward him carrying his breakfast. She wiped over the surface of a table and laid down the food.

'OK?' she asked as he sat down.

'Looks good,' he said quietly.

She stood by his table for a moment and unconsciously patted the back of her hair which was neatly clipped under a white cap. Her breasts rose against her smock. He smiled at her, almost knowingly, and she hesitated.

'Cheeky sod,' she said. 'Sauce?'

'No, this is fine, thanks.'

He watched her nod and make her way back to the counter. She had coloured slightly, knowing that his eyes were on her. He concentrated on his breakfast. He hadn't eaten anything for over twelve hours. Lunchtime seemed a lifetime ago.

A tall young man who had arrived on his own picked up his cup and turned to find a table. He chose one close to Tommy away from the Hell's Angels, and set his cup carefully before pulling back his chair and setting himself down.

He was gaunt and pale, his eyes were sunken under a mop of limp, brown hair. Tommy noticed the frayed cuffs and the scuffed and holed shoes. He saw the cup lifting unsteadily and the man's frightened eyes on the fried bread that Tommy had left at the side of his plate.

'You finished with that?'

Tommy's blue eyes narrowed before losing their steel.

'You want it?'

'If it's all the same to you. Ain't eaten a thing since breakfast, kind of shaky.'

'It's bad for you. Full of cholesterol.'

'So's starvin', but people still starve,' he said and wiped egg yoke and grease from the plate before stuffing it into his mouth. He wiped his lips on his sleeve and gulped some tea.

'Saw you drive in; bad night for travellin'.'

'I ain't doin' it for pleasure.'

'Goin' south?'

'Got to.'

'Birmin'ham?'

'Further, maybe, if the petrol holds out.'

'Out of dough?'

The man nodded.

'Outa luck, outa fags, outa dough.'

'Times are hard.' Tommy tossed over a cigarette and stretched across to light it. The thin man drew smoke deeply and coughed.

'Ta,' he said and sniffed. 'You from the south, right? London, right?'

'Maybe.'

'That's where I'm goin', if the petrol'll get me there.'

'Car might not make it. What is it? Seventy? Seventy-one?'

'Two point three, seventy-three, goes like a pissin' bomb. Trouble is she eats the juice.'

'Still hungry?'

'Naw, I'm all right now.' He drew on the cigarette again and coughed again.

'Could you use some dough?'

'What's your game?'

'I'm lookin' for a lift. I'll pay you.'

The man frowned. 'What, you break down or somethin'?'

'Yeah, somethin'.'

'Well, what about the petrol?'

'I'll get that.'

'That'll do me then, pal.'

'There's somethin' else.'

The thin man scratched his forehead with dirty nails, waiting for the catch.

'There's a geezer sittin' in his motor at the back of the car park. He's lookin' for me. Wouldn't want you to get hurt.'

'A cop?'

'No, just a geezer, but he could turn nasty. If you went to your car, made to pull out then stop at the entrance, I'll hop in and off we go. It's gotta be worth a ton to me if you get us to London.'

'A hundred quid?'

Tommy remained expressionless. He lit another cigarette.

'Hundred quid,' the other repeated. 'I don't need trouble but I can't turn that away. All right.' He looked up suspiciously. 'Half now, so I know you ain't goin' to leg it. What's your name, anyway?'

'Tommy Smith.'

'The footballer, right? Liverpool, right?'

'Leave it out. I'm not that bleedin' old!'

'Give us another fag then, and tell me what to do.'

'How much petrol you got in the tank?'

'About two an' a half, maybe three gallon.'

'Stone the crows! That won't get us half way to Brum never mind

London.' He reached for his wallet. 'Here, here's twenty notes. Fill her up. What about oil and water?'

'She's all right. I checked her this mornin'.'

'OK. You know what to do?'

The other nodded. 'Right. My name's Roy Alexander.'

'I'll buy some more fags and a couple of rolls for you. When I see you outside the door I'll make a move.'

He counted out five tens and added them to the twenty.

'I'll give you the rest when we reach the smoke.'

'Right,' Roy said. He took the money and stood up. 'Be ready then,' he said excitedly. He reached the door before he stopped and called back: 'Cheese n' tomato.'

The others in the room looked his way.

'Eh?'

'The rolls, cheese n' tomato!'

'Right,' Tommy smiled. He watched the car splutter into life and the wipers arcing across the glistening windshield. The headlamps, one dimmed, glared as the car moved off toward the garage. Tommy walked to the counter and paid for his meal. He bought the rolls and cigarettes and stuffed them into his leather pocket. He left the shrapnel out of a tenner on the counter.

'Come again,' Liz said and gave him a smile she reserved for her drivers.

'I'd like to,' he said and returned the knowing glance that meant nothing at all.

'Cheeky sod,' she said.

Chapter 6

Starting at Carlisle the great M6 cut a deep concrete groove through the Lake District and Forest of Bowland and snaked its way through the counties of Cumbria, Lancashire and Cheshire, slicing through the buffer zone of the divide and, on it, the dipped headlamps flashed in both directions boring through the incessant wall of rain. Bonnets and exhausts steamed, engines rattled and tyres whined as they sent up curtains of spray.

Roy Alexander was a good driver, alert, steady and fast. He unwrapped one of the rolls from its cellophane cover while his other hand remained firmly on the wheel. He kept at a steady sixty and cruised twenty yards behind a BOC tanker so that the spray fell before he was on it. The windshield-wipers worked overtime against the flood. Tomato juice filled with seed trickled down his chin and he wiped it on his sleeve.

'Don't know if he's followin' or not,' he said with his mouth full.

He studied the flashing lights in the mirror.

'Just concentrate on the road,' Tommy muttered.

'Been up here long?'

'Couple of days.'

'Come by train then, eh?'

The answer came with the flare of a cigarette lighter. 'You want one of these?'

Roy finished the roll and took the cigarette. He kept his eyes on the road while he bent to receive a light.

'Naw, I motored up on Sunday. Had to leave it.'

'Accident or busted down?' Roy seemed to jump at the idea.

'Neither.'

Roy's disappointment was obvious even in the dark. After a moment he said, 'Well, ain't none of my business. If you don't want to talk about it, fair enough. Should know what we're up against, though. If that bloke's followin', I should know, that's all.'

Tommy sighed. 'My old man's got business interests up north. Been up there to sort things. He got ill earlier in the week and yesterday they got wind of it, that he was rushed into hospital. With him out of action they're tryin' to opt out of the deal.'

'Business trouble! When you said about gettin' hurt I thought you meant like, really hurt.'

Tommy chuckled but there was little humour about it.

'These Scottish bleeders have been known to cut up rough. They take their business seriously.'

'What kind of business you in?'

'Entertainments, mostly. Consumer goods and entertainment.'

'Luxuries! Ain't much call for luxuries up this way, not any more. That's why I'm goin' south. Got to. No choice.'

'How long you been out of work?'

'Three years now. Got a wife and kids – two kids. Never thought anyone would go hungry in this country. Didn't think they allowed it. This month we've been hungry. The kids are startin' to get ill 'cos of it. They get school meals on the social but they're cuttin' them back and, anyway, they don't help during the school hols. I've already cut everythin' out 'till there ain't no more to cut. An' you have to choose between hot water an' food. What we had before an' what we had to sell kept us goin' along with the handouts. But it's three years an' what we had before is all gone now so I got nothin' else to sell. An' things is wearin' out, all together it seems. I know you don't have to have a washing-machine or a fridge, but Christ, things ain't geared up to not havin' 'em. Not today. Now the heatin' in the house is buggered an' I need a new tank. The bastards ain't goin' to give me one either. They say the insurance should cover it and the insurance people say it don't. Who the hell do you fight?'

'Could sell up.'

'You're jokin', right? There's millions in the same boat as me. Don't tell me you believe these bleedin' figures on *Out of Work*?'

'Never given it much thought. Never did believe anything the politicians said.'

'House prices have hit rock bottom up here. If I sold out now I'd owe more on it than I'd get. An' where the hell am I goin' to put the family? Council don't want to know. They got people camping on their doorsteps. Not only that, they'd have the bleedin' kids off you soon as look at you. We've got no rights today, nothin'. The right to starve, that's all. I've got to get a job. That's why I'm travellin'. There's work down south. Anyway, you got your own troubles. Your old man's ill.'

He sensed Tommy's nod.

'Hope it's not serious. I remember losin' my old man about five years ago. Heart attack. Went over in the middle of Sainsburys. We all said it was the bloody cost of food that caused it. Bloody government takin' us into the Common Market. What a con job that was. Never went shoppin', my old man. Mum always did all that. But she was a bugger. Moaned and groaned after him to give her more housekeepin', said he hadn't got a clue how much she spent on the weekly shop. So this day, Saturday it was, 'cause he was goin' to go on from there to see Carlisle play Oldham, she went off to buy some cheese – he liked his old cheese on toast in an evening – an' left him lookin' at the meat counter. When she came back there was a crowd there an' he was on the floor. Went over just like that. One minute himself, the next gone. I'm glad he ain't alive today to see us like this, though. He would have gone spare thinkin' of my girl goin' out with great holes in her shoes. I think that would have killed him anyway!'

The next few minutes were coated in thoughtful silence. The rain was easing a little and through the shroud the orange glow of small village street-lights decorated the darkness.

'People in work ain't got a clue how we're livin'. That's the trouble. The highlight of the week is the *TV Times* comin' out on a Wednesday. Our TV's busted now an' I think that's what broke the back of it. My old girl's been pretty good. She's been cleanin' and takin' in washin' an' she ain't moaned but when that TV busted she just sat there an' cried. She put up with the shit 'cos I can't afford the decoratin', she put up with the hand-me-downs an' not goin' no place but when that screen went dead she folded up. It was then I decided to get on me bike. I left her with a few quid, enough for a week, put a tenner in the tank an' took off tonight. I'll send this hundred quid to her all right, an' that'll cheer her up. By Christ it will! I'll send it first post tomorrow. I'd like to see her face, mind. Got a good mind to drop you off then turn 'round an' hand it to her personally, so I can see her.'

'Put it in the post, my son. You'll be all right.'

Roy felt warmed by the conversation, lifted from his isolation. 'I hope you're right, mister, 'cos I'm running out of ideas.'

The road ahead began its sweep between the two giant cities of Manchester and Liverpool. The tanker blinked and moved across to the slip road and Roy edged the Victor slowly up to the back of a container lorry. Spray splattered the windshield, fanning off the giant square of rippling canvas in front. He eased back slightly and considered overtaking, instinctively glancing in his mirror. Two pools of light, full beam, exploded in the glass and slid to the right as the car behind accelerated to overtake. Roy pulled back into his own lane and glanced sideways as the dark sinister shape of the Jaguar slipped by.

'That him?' Roy grunted.

'Yeah.'

Roy eased into the fast lane again and watched the tail-lights of the Jaguar growing dimmer until they vanished into the curtain of rain and darkness. He slipped back behind the shelter of the lorry.

'Looks as if he's lost interest.'

Tommy grunted, suddenly alert, feeling the gut reaction to the adrenalin rushing through his body.

'It was better to have him behind. While he's up front he could lay something on for us.'

'Glad I'm not in the entertainment business,' Roy said. Without understanding it he sensed the danger. 'There's another exit coming up. Shall I take it?'

'No. If we tuck up behind him he'll have less chance.'

'They cut up rough in the boardroom then?'

Tommy grinned.

'Course, I always knew there was no difference between the big businessman and the criminal. Come to think of it, the politicians too. That much stands to reason. They're the criminals because they have the power to do somethin' about it an' they don't. But what can you do? When the kids are starvin' you gotta do somethin', right? Don't let the bastards get you down, right? But there's too many bastards in this country now; everyone's lookin' after number one. How do you fight that?'

'I'll tell you how, son,' Tommy muttered quietly. 'You break some heads. It's the only thing anyone understands. I'll tell you this, my kids ain't starvin'. I ain't got no kids. But if I did an' they were because some official bastard wanted it that way, then I'd climb over their counters and tear their bleedin' heads off!'

'I believe you. But some of us ain't strong enough to do that.'

'When you get mad enough you'll do it.'

'Maybe, maybe not.'

'Listen, there's trouble all over. There's always going to be someone who wants a bigger share, and if he has more it stands to reason that some poor sod is goin' to get less. There ain't no difference in it to the way countries act movin' across borders. There's only one reaction you can have, whether you're a country or whether you're guardin' your own front door. You fight back. You hurt the bastard so much that he ain't never goin' to come back again. And if that means some arse'ole neighbour, or some stupid inspector with your insurance claim, or the bleedin' social people that ain't payin' you enough, then it makes no difference. You simply make 'em realize that if they even think about upsettin' you they ain't never goin' to look the same again and neither is their family. And if you can make them really believe that, you'd be surprised at how accommodatin' they suddenly get.'

'Does that include the police?'

'The filth? Yeah, kozzers included. Even the Queen of bleedin' England if she comes round to threaten my family. We're very reasonable people. I don't condone anyone gettin' hurt that don't deserve it. But some people are born different, they want to make trouble, they want what's yours.'

'I hear it but I don't like it. I ain't into violence an' I don't want my kids to be. I'd sooner walk away from trouble. There's gotta be some other way.'

'Let me know when you find it.'

The night grew darker as the meter ticked around and the air in the car became dry and clogged. Altrincham, Crewe, Stoke, Stafford, came and went, the great sprawling metropolis of the Midlands, Birmingham, was negotiated and that was the M6. They skirted Coventry and Rugby and joined the M1 and the new signs flashed Northampton and London.

The small hours crept by, the unreal time when noises seemed duller and moves made in slow motion. The traffic had dwindled and most of it consisted of heavy goods lorries and coaches. The speed limits became irrelevant and plumes of spray hung behind the roaring wheels. Out of the eastern sky a pale ghost of iron grey cloud touched the darkness.

'Maybe he's packed it in,' Roy said as he fought for concentration and accelerated past another flapping canvas. His passenger stirred. The further south they had come the safer Tommy felt. He had considered the various possibilities a dozen times.

If Mad Mick had been going to hit them then he would do so on the M6 and when that hadn't happened it would be before Northampton, and then Newport Pagnall, and now it had to be before Luton. Even Mad Mick wouldn't venture to the steps of London. That meant that at some stage in the next few minutes, in some form or another, the move would be made. He lit two cigarettes and passed one to Roy. Roy sensed the sudden alertness in his passenger and gripped the wheel tighter. His body coiled slightly, expectantly.

'You thinkin' this is it?'

They passed the slips to Bedford and then Dunstable, examining every vehicle they overtook. The sky was fingered with greyness and without them realizing it the surroundings had picked up a monotone form. The pale light intensified so that things found their drab colour and the low cloud that stretched in every direction was a blanket of mist and drizzle. Luton went by and for the first time in over twelve hours, since the moment he had watched the news on the television in his room, Tommy allowed himself a moment's relaxation. For some reason Mad Mick had called off his men. The exits for St Albans and Watford were quiet.

'I'd like to get to see the studios,' Roy said. 'See 'em making the films, eh? Maybe get some work there. That would be somethin'.' He had seen the Elstree sign. He glanced at Tommy and winked. 'We made it. You're home. Told you she'd make it. Goes like a pissin' rocket, don't she?' He rubbed his neck and swallowed sorely. 'I could murder a cuppa.'

'You're right, son. You done well. Take the next slip. There's a place we can get a drink and a wash just off Apex.'

'I never had any doubt that she'd make it. She might rattle a bit, some of the body falls off sometimes, but she's got as much heart as a Rolls.' A large sign approached indicating Mill Hill and Edgware. Roy sat up behind the wheel.

'I get quite excited at seein' London, like a kid.'

'You're been before?'

'Came down for a weekend as a kid. Seen the Palace and the Planetarium.'

Tommy grunted his disapproval.

'They say the world's gettin' smaller but for some people it ain't. You can fly to New York in the time it's taken to drive from Manchester and you've never even seen the Smoke.'

'Done The Tower an' all. Saw the jewels.'

Tommy shook his head.

'Well, that's it then. I mean, even I ain't seen the jewels!'

A three-inch hole appeared in the windshield; crystals of glass sprayed in with a sudden rush of cold air and water; the remaining screen milked in a crazy jigsaw and then broke into a thousand pieces that thudded into the car. Wind and rain lashed in and almost lifted the car. Instinctively Roy's foot was on the brake; the wheels screamed, the car slewed sideways and moved inexorably toward the cavernous underside and monstrous wheels of a huge articulated lorry. The nearside rear window shattered and Roy heard something crashing about his head. Something ripped into the metal in front and raised sparks from the bonnet. A burning sensation swept down his side and his gasp for breath doubled him in agony. His left arm, limp and useless, dropped from the wheel, and the car lurched toward the truck. The rear end touched and the kick-back sent the Victor out of control. It spun behind the lorry and rumbled and tore at the metal barrier dividing north and south. Lorries and coaches swerved to miss them, sparks flew and tyres screeched. Tommy released his belt and grabbed hold of the wheel. He screamed above the roar of noise.

'Get her over! Don't stop!'

Roy understood and ran the car into the slow lane. He kept his head low to keep the rain from blinding him.

'Keep her at twenty,' Tommy shouted. 'There's a turn about a hundred yards ahead.'

The Victor didn't make it. The rear wheel had buckled and they ran on the rim. The shaking bonnet bent upward at a crazy angle and threatened to fly off altogether. They ground to a halt twenty yards short of the turn, on the hard shoulder. Vehicles thudded past.

'We've got to get out of here,' Tommy shouted. 'You all right?' He saw the red stain spreading out on Roy's shirt.

'I don't know. I'm shakin' like a leaf. I think I'm going to throw up.'

'Save it 'till later. That wasn't a stone that hit us back there. We've got to leg it.'

He opened the door, stepped out on to the wet surface and peered up the road between the oncoming vehicles with their pale orange headlamps bearing down, at the deep ridges cut into the barrier. He ran around the front of the car and caught hold of Roy as he staggered from his seat. A streak of blood trickled from Roy's hairline and thinned with the rain to run quickly down the side of his cheek. Tommy pulled Roy's jacket together and buttoned it over the deep red flood at his waist.

'I can't stand up. I can't!' Roy's face contorted and his legs buckled. Tommy helped him back to the seat. Roy gasped again and let out a long groan.

'Roy, I gotta go. The filth'll be here any second. I'll look you up. You ain't seen me. You ain't seen nothin', understand?'

Roy looked up helplessly. He trembled. His eyes began to slip.

'I'll make it up to you. I'll find you and you'll be all right.'

In the distance a siren wailed above the general clatter of traffic, and a flashing blue light blinked like a sapphire on a pool of grey.

Tommy glanced down again and saw that unconsciousness had relaxed Roy's features. He pulled up his coat collar and began to run, splashing through the dancing puddles, across the oil stains that had created their own palettes, then he was turning his back on the rush of traffic and he was racing along the darker surface of the slip road toward a built up area where cars were parked end to end on either side, where milk floats clinked and postmen wandered. He walked by silent shops while the rain blurred the orange light thrown from the street lamps and splashed from the glistening surfaces of black and grey.

He found the narrow alley he was looking for and walked between the walls of brick and concrete. He side-stepped an overflowing gutter and fiddled with the rusty latch on a battered green gate. Beyond, across a tiny square of concrete, he recognized a red back door and banged it until his fist hurt. He smacked on the mottled glass until lights were switched on and the sound of muffled voices came from within. Bolts were thrown back and the door opened and he looked into the astonished face of a heavy set man dressed in blue striped pyjama bottoms and a white string vest who said: 'Jesus!' And then he began to fall.

The heavy set man reached out quickly to stop his fall and all but carried him into the hallway. The door slammed shut. The wind increased in strength and drew more rain from the low cloud and sent it forcefully up the alley, pelting and rattling the green gate, lifting it over the fencing in a curved spray to collect and run down the glass of the back door, collecting the light from within as it zig-zagged its way southward.

Chapter 7

The pre-war three bedroomed terrace was built to a similar format across the length of the country. The back door led to the kitchen which in turn led to the hallway and the stairs to the bathroom and bedrooms. When Tommy awoke it was in the curtained back bedroom. His clothes had been piled neatly on a single chair and his watch faced him from a small MFI bedside locker. It was ten o'clock. He could hear the hum of Radio One and the playful chattering of sparrows on the outside guttering. He swept back the duvet and examined a dark bruising that began on his ribs and swept down beneath the elastic of his shorts. He left open the bathroom door while he used the pan and sluiced his head in a basin of cold water. He borrowed one of three tooth brushes upended in a plastic beaker and cleaned his teeth then considered using the razor but decided against it. There were some things you did not borrow. Not today in the age of AIDS and Aquarius. He walked back into the bedroom and sat on the bed while he fastened his watch. Shadow filled the doorway and he glanced up. A woman stood framed in the light from beyond, arms folded, shoulder leant against the post, the questions on her face wanting some answers.

'You've been on the radio. Least, I'm guessing it was you. A shoot-out on the M1, some guy full of holes, coppers all over the place.'

'Don't know what you're on about girl.'

'You bleedin' well do!'

She was in her mid-twenties, darkly tanned, half-Middle-Eastern with large black eyes and shiny cropped hair. There was a touch of rouge on her cheeks. Or was it anger?

'Where's Pete?'

'He's gone to bleedin' work, where do you think?'

It was anger, he decided.

'And the kid?'

'Round next door. I made out I wasn't feelin' well. And that wasn't a lie, seein' you here!' She moved into the room and drew back the cotton curtains. 'I'll go and make a drink. I want you out of here by lunchtime.' He watched her walk back across the room and noticed the trim figure working beneath her pencil-line black skirt. Suddenly she stopped and turned and looked back from the landing through the open door.

'Don't you get any ideas, Tommy Smith! You're gettin' coffee and naff all else!'

Tommy raised his hands in mock surrender and grinned. He lay back on the bed and tried to recall what had happened. He remembered the strong arms of Peter Hough setting him on the couch and then a phone call, but that was all.

A few moments later she returned with a mug of sweet coffee. He sipped it and watched her move back to the window to gaze out at the wet tiled rooftops and the chimney stacks expelling the white wispy strands of smoke from the 'smokeless' fuel.

Against the light her blouse became transparent and through it he could see the curve of her bra.

'Who did he phone last night?'

'Last night? It wasn't bleedin' last night. It was five o'clock this morning. He was goin' to call your brother but he couldn't get through. I don't know what the neighbours is goin' to think with you bangin' on the door at that time.'

'Sod the neighbours. Come and sit over here.'

'Piss off Tommy,' she said and continued to gaze from the window.

'That's nice.'

She half turned toward him and her eyes narrowed fractionally.

'You're trouble, Tommy. You always were. You're like a magnet and bother is drawn to you. You can handle it most of the time, but other people can't an' they get hurt. Now you might care or you might not care about other people but it makes no difference 'cos they still get hurt whether you do or not. Pete wanted to stay and help and get involved like a few years ago but I don't want you near him. That's why he's gone to work. And when he comes home tonight he won't even ask what happened, 'cos nothin' happened. You were never here.' She hesitated and drew a deep breath. 'Do you understand what I'm sayin', Tommy? The past is gone. It never happened. You shouldn't have come. I wish you hadn't. Pete's tryin' to make a go of it, and he's tryin' hard for the sake of the kid. He ain't got your brains and if he follows you he'll end up inside again. That's all I've got to say to you, Tommy Smith. Next time you get hurt and you come past this house, I want you to keep walkin'. For you and your family it don't exist!'

He nodded and gulped at his coffee. His eyes had dulled at the rebuke. He leant across to the chair and fished in his jacket pocket for his cigarettes. He lit one and lay back, his head sinking into the soft pillow, and watched a jet of smoke stream up to the artexed ceiling. She noticed the sudden flicker of his eyes, the sudden steely dullness that came down like an inner eyelid as the sparkle went out, and she shrank back immediately. Her recoil could not have been more pronounced had she stepped on something evil and repulsive. The fear drained her face of colour and her hand half hid her features as she pinched her quivering lower lip. She knew that she had overstepped the mark. One word from him and she would be back on the meat rack at King's Cross again. One word from him and her efforts over the past few years would count for nothing, her plans for the family totally irrelevant. She owed Tommy and his family and she knew that the debt could never be repaid. You gave them whatever they asked for; offer them anything less and you offended them. They were not the sort of people to take for granted or threaten or voice an opinion about and now, after all this time, she had allowed her temper to overshadow her self-preservation. The thought and her fear showed on her face.

Tommy turned his head on the pillow and looked at her, still mildly embarrassed.

'I didn't mean all that, Tommy,' she said, turning toward him. She looked at the floor, refusing to meet his gaze, knowing the cruelty she would find there.

'Leave it out, girl. You meant it all right. Forget it.'

She glanced up, surprised.

'You won't tell Pete what I said?'

'Not a word.'

She nodded briefly while the relief softened her features.

'Well, shall I get in with you?'

'Naw, you do what you want to do.'

'I want to, Tommy, but if I got the choice then I won't.'

He grinned. 'You were a slag, you know that? Now you're a lady. If you an' the kid ever need for anything, just let us know.'

'Is Pete included?'

'Can't be, can he? He left the firm. Once you leave, if you're allowed to, then you lose all fringe benefits.'

'I left.'

'No you didn't. You're just on temporary leave of absence. Extended maternity leave.'

She looked at him thoughtfully, considering the implications, and they didn't worry her.

'You're not like the others.'

'A lot of people say that. You can't blame me for what other people think.'

'I don't want the kid hurt, that's all. I want everything for him.'

'Is he Pete's?'

A moment's hesitation destroyed the possibility of a lie. 'He looks like your elder brother but Pete thinks he's the spittin' image of his dad.'

'Might as well go along with that then.'

'I think so,' she said softly.

He finished his cigarette and reached for his clothes.

'It's time I was on my way.'

'I hope your dad's all right.'

'It's got around then?'

'It's been in the paper. An emergency op and all that.'

'Stone the crows! Sounds like we've been advertisin'.'

'Does it mean a lot of trouble?'

'We could do without it.' He shrugged and added, 'A bit of bother, that's all.'

She walked across to him and straightened his tie and looked into his bloodshot eyes.

'If it had been you I wouldn't have left.'

'If it had been me I wouldn't have let you.'

She followed him from the room, across the landing and down the stairs.

'I want to make a quick call,' he said.

She pointed into the living-room.

'Through there.'

He found a small neatly furnished room, a leather three-piece, a wall unit housing a shelf of books, another of photographs of a young child, a drinks unit, a television and video, a stacked music centre, pale grey wall-to-wall and dralon curtains over uPVC double glazing, the smell of lemon-scented polish and a gas fire. It was a hideaway and he felt like a trespasser. He punched six digits into the push-button telephone and listened to three guttural burrs before he heard a familiar voice. He looked across at the girl while he spoke and although his thoughts were on the call his eyes delighted in the curve and movement.

'Dave? It's me boy. I'm home. Be about thirty minutes. How is he?'

For a few seconds he listened and then he replaced the handset.

'Is he all right?' she asked.

He shrugged. 'They're seein' the consultant later.'

She nodded. At the door he brushed her painted lips, a platonic kiss that reminded him of a thousand broken promises.

''Bye Denise,' he said and stepped into the yard. She had closed the back door before he had stepped across the puddles to the gate.

The day was brighter. The rain had stopped and the cloud had become feathery and broken. He stepped into the alley and closed the gate behind him, conscious of the dripping surrounds, the overflow snout still trickling and the ground beneath it washed clean and glistening. The air was chilled and fresh and tinged with the smell of wet grass and the fumes of the city. He was home. The thought added a spring to his youthful step.

To the left of the darkened alley entrance a navy blue Lada stood idling on freshly painted double yellow lines. It idled on the fast side and it rattled as most Ladas do, put-putting gently from its nervous exhaust. Its squareness and heaviness of shape reminded passers-by of a fifties' style. The driver they saw, with his collar pulled up, the roll-up suspended from his lips, his face a mask of concentration, was instantly forgettable, nondescript, and the passenger in the back seat was hardly noticeable either, perhaps because anonymity was his trademark and, as with the driver, a necessary part of his profession.

Chapter 8

Theca, the Star of the Veldt, glanced up expectantly as her elder brother walked in from the hall. Her features were classically English, her pale skin emphasized by her dark hair. Even when she was tired and drawn, her loveliness was still evident.

'It was Tommy,' he said quickly and saw the relief in her large brown eyes.

Every time the telephone rang it was a heart-stopping moment. The door was purposefully closed on it, so that the conversation was private. When the door opened again the same troubled questions were written in the strained eyes.

'He's back. He'll be here in half-an-hour.'

'Thank God for that, at least,' Sally said as she lifted her china cup from its saucer and fought to control its shake. 'Where is he?'

'Over in Mill Hill. He's taking a cab.'

'What's he doing over there?' Worry made her voice quiver. She shook her head. 'Did he sound upset?'

'I said we'd explain everything when he got here,' Dave told his mother. He was a big man of thirty-nine, balding prematurely, fighting a weight problem, but losing. His eyes, brown and large, were dulled and sore through lack of sleep. They reflected his sister. As he sat down heavily at the dining-table he glanced across at her as if to share some secret message. Theca saw it and looked at her mother. Sally was stunned like the rest of them. The feeling of nausea from her fluttering stomach showed on her face.

The knowing glances, the lowered voices, the door closing on the telephone calls: none of these things escaped Sally but she was too tired to argue.

She finished her tea and stood from the table.

'I'll go and get ready. When Tommy comes in I'll make some lunch and then we'll go. What time is it now?'

'It's ten to twelve. We've still got two hours!' Theca shrugged, irritated at her mother's fussing.

Sally turned to her son.

'David, I'll have to get some shopping on the way. I need some things for your dad.'

'I'll go and get the shopping now,' Theca said, grasping the opportunity to get away for a while. 'Write a list.' She turned to Dave. 'When Tommy gets here you can tell him what's happening.'

'Sounds OK.' Dave nodded. He left the two women busily making a list and checking the cupboards and went back into the hall. He dialled a number and spoke quietly into the handset.

'Tommy's due back. Look out for him. Theca's going to do some shopping. She'll use the Mini. Two of you go with her. Who's at the hospital now? Right.' He hung up as Theca appeared and opened the cupboard for her jacket.

'I'll call in and collect Ted on the way back,' she said, then quietly added, 'I think we should have someone in to help Mum out, just for the time being.'

'I don't know, Sis. It keeps her occupied. I don't think we should change things at the moment.'

Theca saw his point and shrugged. She opened the front door.

'There'll be two guys behind you.'

'Why?' She turned sharply.

'Because I told them to, Sis. Until we know what's happening out there we've got to play it safe.'

'I don't want anything to do with it.'

'That's beside the point. You're a Smith. Start acting like one. Until things are sorted out we've got to watch ourselves.'

'I don't like it, Dave. I don't like to be followed. I don't trust them and they make me nervous.'

'You won't even know they're there. Now go on, get the shopping.'

She closed the door, her slight heaviness of hand indicating her anger. Dave smiled. In the kitchen Sally asked, 'What was that about?'

'You know the Star, Mum. She's got a temper at the best of times but at the moment she's a bit emotional, tired like the rest of us. She flared up at the thought of a couple of minders.'

Sally nodded, understanding more than Dave knew about her

daughter's dilemma. The women in the family were not involved in the business and when it threatened their freedom, they felt hostility towards it.

'She thinks you ought to have someone in to help out, while you're visitin' the hospital.'

Sally smiled quickly. 'No, that wouldn't do.'

'I know, Mum.' Dave reached out and put his arm around her shoulders. 'Go and get ready. I'll put the kettle on. Tommy will want a cuppa when he gets in.'

As he filled the kettle he watched his mother walk stiffly from the kitchen past a calendar hanging by the door. It showed the month of May 1986 and the date of Friday 23rd was circled in black ink, marked because his parents were supposed to be flying out to the Continent for a fortnight's holiday. Dave sighed at the irony. The pressure of business, especially the noises of hostility emanating from the north, had weighed heavily on his father and much persuasion had been necessary to stop him postponing the holiday.

Dave heard the back door close and saw Tommy sneaking through the kitchen. Although he had tried to clean his clothes there were still signs of dust and grime and the watermark on his blue collar had dried to a white ring. Stubble on his chin darkened his tanned features even more. His bloodshot eyes lent a sparkle to the steely blue. He had the same colouring and characteristics as his mother. Both David and the Star of the Veldt took after their father.

Tommy's grin was reflex, a sigh of relief at being home and seeing a face that he could trust.

'Where's Mum?' he whispered.

'Upstairs,' Dave countered quietly. 'Christ, you look rough.'

He moved to pour some tea. Tommy sat down.

'I could have done without the advertisin'. I had some bother gettin' back.'

Dave nodded over the steaming teapot. He replaced the china lid.

'I guessed as much. I saw the news and put two and two together. I thought about sending you an escort but you'd already left the hotel.'

'I couldn't hang around, Brov,' Tommy said seriously. 'As soon as I heard it on the one o'clock I was on my bike. Mick had his army out and they didn't want to talk no more. I couldn't ring you from the hotel!'

Hotel billing systems automatically logged outgoing calls and there was no way Tommy wanted his whereabouts recorded.

'What happened?'

'I thought we'd made it.' He sipped his tea gratefully. 'Just relaxin' when they hit us comin' off the A41. The geezer givin' me a ride took one in the side. It looked bad. I ended up in Hough's gaff overnight.'

Dave frowned.

'Pete Hough?'

Tommy nodded.

'He's not one of us, Tommy.'

'Had no choice, Brov. Anyway, I got away with it.'

'Denise there?'

'Yes.' Tommy laughed in order to cover his thoughts. 'She kicked me out this mornin'. Gave me a right ear-bashing.'

'It was still dangerous. You should have come straight home.'

'At the time I could hardly stand up and the filth was all over the shop.'

'What happened?'

'Shotguns. They hit us four or five times. Fucked up the paint work good and proper.'

'Christ! It sounds like you were lucky. But so far south! It's a bit fuckin' naughty.'

'It doesn't make a lot of sense, though.'

'Go on?'

'Think about it. The good shot was aimed at the driver, not me. And they saw me gettin' a lift. They knew I wasn't drivin'.'

'What then?'

'Thinkin' about it now, I have to ask whether they were serious or just puttin' the frighteners on. Know what I mean?'

Tommy lit a cigarette and blew smoke out with the question: 'How's Pop? Is he safe?'

Dave's grunt was almost contemptuous.

'You know he was bad at the wedding? Went early?'

Tommy nodded, remembering it well. His father had looked ill.

'He went to The Tower on Monday still moaning about his gut. His foot was playing up too. Wouldn't see Noddy. Spent Tuesday in bed with Mum fussing around him.' Dave paused while his younger brother put out his barely touched cigarette. 'Tuesday he started throwing up. Bad. Theca came round, took one look and called Noddy. Noddy took a look and said hospital. Teddy was over the Castle so Theca drove Pop to the hospital herself. Panic ain't the word. She rang Jimmy and he got hold of me. It was theatre that same night, no messing. The girls were in a helluva state. It was questionable whether he was going to pull through the operation. They didn't think they'd see him again.' Dave waved a dismissive hand. 'Anyway, some bastard over there squealed to the press and the next thing we know the BBC were camped outside. That's when your trouble started. By the time I phoned, you'd already legged it. We went up last night but he was still shaky. I don't know whether he recognized us. He's got tubes coming out of his arm and a catheter or something stuck in him but they've eased the blockage. That's all they would tell us. We're seeing the consultant at two.'

'How's Mum takin' it?'

'Hard. Tearful. Theca stayed here last night.'

'What about the hospital? Is he safe?'

'Don't talk to me about that. They've got him in an open ward. Wouldn't hear of going private. You know him and his NHS. I'll have another go today but I know the answer before I start.'

'You've got people there?'

'Christ yes. Mind you, it's probably unnecessary. Half the filth in London is camped out over there.' Dave grinned. 'Still, you should see our guys. They're going to kill some poor sod with a trolley before long.'

For a few moments Tommy considered all that he had heard then he glanced up.

'They're suppose to be flyin' out today. It's a shame this didn't wait until next month.'

'I know what you mean, Brov, but just think if it had happened next week with him in the middle of Portugal.'

They heard the sound of a light step and turned to see Sally. Tommy was on his feet immediately and went across to hug her. She seemed small and fragile against him.

'Oh, Tommy,' she sighed and pressed the side of her face against his chest. She shook away her emotion and said, 'Some of your clothes are in the back bedroom. You better go and change. And shave. You can't turn up at the hospital looking like that.'

Tommy released her.

'David has told you everything? I'll make some sandwiches. You go and change now. We haven't got long.'

He examined her face for signs of strain.

'Isn't Star back yet?' she asked.

Dave called in from the dining-room: 'She's calling in to see Ted.'

'Oh yes.' Sally's thoughts were elsewhere: in the hospital, in the past, in the fearsome future. She turned to the work-surface and began on the sandwiches.

They were almost ready and Sally was just adding garnish when the back door opened and Theca led Ted into the kitchen. She lifted a bulging Marks and Spencer bag on to the side.

'Hello, love, hello, Teddy.' Even as she spoke Sally barely glanced up. 'Did you get everything?'

Theca nodded and began to unpack. Ted kissed Sally's cheek and hugged her quickly, silently, before joining the brothers in the dining-room.

'All right, Teddy.' Dave said. It was a greeting, not a question.

Ted nodded. 'How did you make out?' he asked Tommy.

'I'm in one piece, but lucky. Explain later,' Tommy said in a whisper.

Ted glanced over his shoulder through the open door at the girls busily unpacking the shopping. His curiosity would have to wait until they were alone. He was shorter than the brothers and carried much less weight. He was forty, greying, and had about him a studious look stressed by silver rimmed spectacles positioned slightly low on his nose. He wore a pin-stripe with a hint of white handkerchief in his top pocket.

The women carried in the sandwiches and fresh tea.

'Did the children get to school all right?' Sally asked.

'No problem,' Ted said. 'Jean came in early to look after them.'

'Will they let us see Dad this afternoon?' Tommy asked.

Dave frowned for a moment and then smiled at his younger brother.

'They'll let us do anything we like, my son.'

Ted chuckled.

Sally's glance was sharp. She had heard it before, from her husband, but always in jest. He didn't really believe it. Yet there was an intrinsic truth in what her eldest son had said. They did get their way; people fell over themselves to help. But it wasn't out of love or kindness. It was out of fear or respect. Perhaps the two were related.

Now that her husband lay seriously ill some of that respect would disappear and in its place would grow hostility and revenge. Keeping her family safe until the crisis was over was not going to be easy and the responsibility rested on David's shoulders. She was not sure whether he was ready for it. She looked at her elder son and saw her husband and when he spoke she heard her husband.

'Are we ready then?' She heard and watched Dave lead the way. 'Theca, you had better take your motor. Mum and Tommy can come with me.'

Sally brushed a hair from her suit jacket and followed the others into the kitchen.

Although the house would be empty, they didn't lock the doors or windows when they left. They never did. There wasn't a villain in London who would step a foot on the road without an invitation.

As the two cars pulled from the kerb, the Star's red Mini and Dave's black Rover, another car with darkened windows pulled out in front of them. Before they had gone fifty yards yet another car with similar windows had pulled up behind them. From the upstairs windows in various houses men watched the convoy move slowly to the corner and they sat back to continue their watch, feeling some relief that the family had left their patch without incident.

The great concrete and glass office buildings had emptied and the lunchtime crowds filled the pavements and burst into the roads. The cafés and restaurants and pubs were full. The convoy joined the stream of traffic and slid on to the North Circular. The four-storey red-bricked hospital loomed, the entrance canopy fanned out before them. Down-at-heel men carrying cameras and microphones leapt from their places and made for the slowing cars. As the family left to push their way through the press of reporters, two men appeared and slipped quietly into the driving-seats of the cars and drove them to the park. Dave led the family to the glass doors of the lobby entrance, searching Fleet Street's faces for one that he recognized. Passers-by turned to watch the commotion, wondering who the celebrities were. People inside looked out sternly, upset by the intrusion and wondered in turn who it was getting the media attention. One or two officials shook their heads in dismay and muttered about the hospital being turned into a circus.

The wide entrance hall, smelling faintly of disinfectant, housed a shop, a café where the seats were uncomfortable and the fixed tables cluttered with empty cups and saucers, various receptions, clearly marked and signposted corridors radiating from both sides and, at the far end, a bank of lifts. The family went swiftly across the tiled floor, passing the brisk, white-coated receptionists and people being comforted, fatigued faces in the stark light. They passed a bank of trolleys and wheelchairs and screens. Their footsteps seemed loud and urgent. Tommy put his arm around Sally's shoulders and Theca flashed a secret message to Ted. They reached the lifts and stood aside as a couple of specialists came out laughing. In the enclosure of the lift Tommy asked, 'Was it like this last night?'

'Worse,' Dave said flatly. 'The TV people had a van outside but we had that moved, at least.'

Each of them made quick glances toward Sally, wondering how she was bearing up.

The lift halted abruptly and the doors jarred open. They moved out to the third floor reception and stood by an area of seats and a drink machine while Dave went across to the desk. Moments later he returned and told them, 'He'll be with us in two minutes. Let's sit down. Dad's comfortable.' They sat tensely, straight-backed, watching each movement. Tommy lit a cigarette. A group of passing nurses flashed significant glances.

'You shouldn't smoke in here,' Sally admonished, thinking perhaps that was the reason for the dark looks.

'Look, there's an ashtray,' he said in defence.

She saw it and nodded.

'You shouldn't smoke anyway.'

They watched a tall, slim man, dressed smartly in dark blazer and flannels, lean over the reception desk, glance their way after talking to the girl sitting there, and then approach. Under his rich tan his gaunt good looks suggested something in the region of forty-five. He smiled briskly, put a folder under his arm and rubbed his spotless hands together. There was an honesty in his square features. He looked at the five people and chose Sally.

'Mrs Smith?' His voice was touched with a French accent; deep, quiet, flattened vowels that were both slow and elegant.

He sat down opposite and shuffled some papers from his file. His knowledgable, almost sad eyes met Sally's and moved to Theca, and then addressed the others.

'It's not very good I'm afraid. It doesn't look good. As you know we operated to remove a blockage but . . .' He shook his head. 'It's not very good at all.'

'Is it cancer?' Sally blurted out the question, fighting for control.

'There is a growth that is widespread and we've taken a section for examination. I'm unable to identify it and it will be a few days before we know whether it is malignant.'

'What are you saying?' Sally asked. The others looked resigned, fixed and stony.

'A few weeks, a month.'

'A month!' Sally faltered, horrified, and the thought grooved its way across her forehead.

'Maybe longer,' the Frenchman added quickly, gently.

Sally was numbed, unable to speak, unwilling to comprehend.

Theca asked: 'If you don't know what it is how can you tell it's a month?' Her voice was slightly hostile.

'You've always got to remember,' the consultant went on, 'that while I speak to you in medical terms there is someone up there who has the last say. And he might decide he doesn't want him, maybe, for a year, maybe two . . .'

'Have you spoken to him?' Dave asked.

The consultant nodded.

'Yes, we talked this morning.'

'How is he taking it?'

'He is a very strong man. We've managed to ease the immediate blockage and obviously he's a lot more comfortable. We won't do much more until we get the results back.'

'If he'd come in earlier would it have made a difference?' Dave asked.

The consultant shook his head. He had heard that question so many times before.

'Even a year ago would not have made a difference.'

Tommy remained motionless, absorbing, angry.

Ted said: 'When can we take him home?'

The consultant seemed taken by surprise and his guard slipped momentarily.

'Oh, oh, well . . .' He shook his head to give himself time. 'Not for ten days at least. We must wait for the results then we can talk of that.'

'It's important for us to get him home,' Ted insisted.

'I can understand that.' The sympathy hushed his voice to a whisper. 'Let's wait for the results.'

Sally asked quietly: 'Can I go in and see him? I've brought some things.'

'Of course. Of course.'

'I'll come with you,' Theca said.

'No!' Sally said firmly. 'I'll see him on my own.' She stood up and picked up her bag and walked, a lonely figure, toward the ward entrance.

The consultant got to his feet.

'You must watch out for her,' he said and collected his notes. 'I'll see you again.' He moved off toward the reception. Dave caught up with him and the others watched although they could not hear what was said.

'You know who you've got in there, Doc. What can we do to give him a better chance?'

The pause was long before the answer came with what sounded like contempt: 'This is something that cannot be fixed. There is not a thing in the world that you can buy, or a surgeon or a hospital that will give your father a moment in the world longer than he will get here. And that is not very long.'

Dave's expression hardened.

'Out of respect for my old man we're seeing you here; we've come to you. He's a great believer in the Health Service. Don't get carried away with the idea.'

The consultant studied Dave out of narrowed eyes. Tight-lipped, he said: 'It was mentioned to me that your family has, how was it put? A certain influence? Let me make one thing quite clear to you. Your family will receive the same response from me and from my staff as any other family in similar circumstances. Do I make myself clear? Exactly. No more and no less.'

'Did I ask you for any favours?'

'If you didn't ask, then you haven't been turned down. Is that not so?'

'That sounds like a good place to leave it.'

The consultant nodded briskly, turned on his heels and left Dave looking thoughtfully after him. Dave felt neither anger nor calm but thought that one day, after the event, he might hurt the man, just a little, just to make a point.

From the starkly lit waiting-room where they sat and waited for Sally, where Tommy fed a coin into the drinks machine to obtain coffee for the Star of the Veldt, a corridor led from the lifts past the reception desk, past the ward sister's office on the left-hand side, past the sterilization room and the toilets, to an open-planned ward which housed two rows of neatly made beds. All but two beds were occupied and an attendant and a nurse were busily making ready for visiting hours. Two of the beds were screened and, from the others, patients read quietly or watched, curious that a woman had been let in early to see the patient in the left-hand bed at the far end of the ward. They saw her bending over the patient, saw their lips move as they spoke, saw her clutch his hand in hers, his face tug into a huge grin and then her tears sparkling in the fluorescent wash.

Chapter 9

Shortly after getting married, Dave had moved into a five-bedroomed detached house on The Ridgeway. Since he had inherited three children from his wife's first marriage and later added two of his own, he needed all the space he could get. Things would get easier now that Patricia's eldest daughter, Karen, was married. The weekend just gone, the marriage and her flying off to Tunisia seemed an age ago.

The house stood back from the main road, guarded on all sides by a high brick wall. The front garden was surrounded by tall trees and thick bushes. A gravel drive reached its end around a massive oak which rose above it all. At the rear of the house was a modest indoor swimming pool with a sauna enclosure built into one end.

Soon after leaving the hospital Dave's Rover crunched on to the gravel. He checked the time and knew exactly where to find his wife. Patricia was on a health kick; the necessary worry that mothers experience during the run-up to a daughter's wedding had led to overeating and an increase in the waistline. Dave found her in the pool. She had completed thirty laps but her breath was barely raised. She saw him, gave a little wave and using the metal rungs she climbed out and reached for a towel.

'You really don't need all this. You look in good shape to me.'

'Ugh! Look at this.' She pinched an inch or so of fat around her middle. She slipped a robe over her bikini. 'What happened?'

Dave repeated what the consultant had said and watched her face fall. Her spectacles, when she put them on, slightly enlarged her eyes and seemed to increase the compassion in them.

'Sweetheart, I'm so sorry.'

'Theca's staying with Mum for a few nights. We're going to see him tonight. Mum wanted to be alone with him this afternoon.'

'That's understandable. God, she must be feeling wretched. I'll get across to see her. The kids' half-term starts tomorrow so I can go up most afternoons.'

'I'm not stopping,' Dave said. 'But I wanted to let you know.'

She nodded gratefully but her look was touched with disappointment.

Another car rolled over the gravel and moments later Jimmy Jones peered through the pool window, acknowledged Pat's wave and Dave's nod and walked nonchalantly to the open door. Jimmy Jones was Dave's right-hand man. It was not uncommon to find him at the house. He had become one of the family. His dark visage and sharp looks were trusted and totally accepted by the children. He was a stocky, good-looking man of part-Indian or Pakistani extraction. Being a bastard child he was not sure, for his Welsh mother had never bothered to ask.

'How did it go, boss?'

For the second time Dave recounted what the consultant had said. They said goodbye to Pat and made their way back around the side of the house to the cars.

'Find out about that consultant,' Dave said. 'A French geezer. Levy or something. He's got an attitude problem.'

That was enough. Jimmy Jones knew exactly what was required. Perhaps not this week, or this month, but at some time in the future the Frenchman would meet with a little misfortune. If he had children it might be that they disappeared for a day or two. They would turn up totally unharmed and none the worse for the experience, but in the horror of those two days a parent can learn a lot of respect.

Dave continued: 'Better send someone to Tunisia to keep an eye on Karen and John. And make sure someone keeps an eye on Theca's kids as well. A discreet eye. She'll go loopy if she finds out.'

'What now, boss?'

'The hotel first,' Dave said without changing his expression. 'I'll be about an hour. Keep an eye on the foyer for me. I've got to make the hospital about seven. I'll see you in the club after that.'

Jimmy Jones followed Dave across London to Park Lane and took up his station in the hotel lobby. If any unwelcome face showed up and that included any press photographer who wanted faces for the Sunday supplement, he had plenty of time to warn Dave.

For Dave Smith the last couple of years had been coated in

lethargy. He had gone through the motions, hiding his sense of increasing languor from all but his wife. His feeling of detachment was fed by a growing suspicion that the old days were finished.

The period of enforced idleness, the security that had existed for over a decade, had dulled the essence of his motivation. But things were stirring again and Dave recognized the old feeling; something deep within him was beginning to spark. The trouble was one thing, the threat from Scotland sharpened his senses and pushed anger back into his eyes, hooded them so that his look was vaguely contemptuous, but Sharon Valenti had a part in it too. After all this time she remained a challenge. When her eyes flickered his way they seemed to question his masculinity; appreciating, certainly, but querying also. In a peculiar sense he felt that he had to prove something. That it was forbidden made it all the more exciting. The feeling was extraordinary and mixed now with the danger, the threat to the family, it was inseparable. He was suddenly alive, heady with old sensations, and his instincts were being recharged by the moment.

Before Dave had properly closed the bedroom door Sharon Valenti had flown into his arms. Her négligée parted on the way and flashed him a nipple and a quick peep at pukka blond curls.

'Oh darling! I thought you weren't coming. You're so late!' The words, wrapped in accent, came breathlessly, between kisses.

She didn't stop to hear his excuse or to find out about his father. Those things would keep. She was all that he could have wished for. Being unable to bear children had kept her vagina duck-arse tight and she held him inside her and rippled against him, and he was drawn out, stretched, and the sensation was almost unbearable.

And yet there was something mildly detached and adrift about it all, a sensation of familiarity, that he felt at once comfortable and yet faintly disappointed. As he lay against her, he experienced a sense of panic, an unreasonable fear that gripped his thoughts, mocking him. In that moment of introspection he felt that his time was running out, that something was creeping up on him and that sooner or later he would have to turn and face it. But there was no holding back. His release was urgent, vital, and when, through clenched lips she murmured, 'Oh God! Oh my God!' a little smile played with his expression. It was not out of satisfaction, more than that, it was out of victory.

The guilt that Dave felt, that he should be indulging while his father lay close to death, lent an edge to his violence and he hurt her.

While they made up afterwards, she in foetal position, he pressed against her cool behind, she said, 'Tony's got somethin' going down. He's been makin' quite a few trips lately.'

'Oh?' he said.

'A couple back home. Thank God he didn't take me. It would have stopped me seeing you.' She squeezed his hand against her breast.

'He's back now?'

'Oh yeah. But he's buzzing. He's up to something.'

'Like what?'

'If I get anything you'll be the first to know.'

'Any visitors?'

'Just the usual crowd. No one I don't recognize.'

'Anything about charley, South America maybe?'

'No.'

'What about the word "distribution". Heard that in passing?'

She shook her head.

'What then?'

'He sings. He gets up earlier.'

'Fuck me, that does sound serious.'

She punched his arm.

'Don't make fun of me,' she said.

'I wouldn't do that, sweetheart.'

'On the other hand. I love it when you talk dirty.'

She moved her behind gently against him and snuggled in closer. He kissed the back of her neck. There were striking similarities between Sharon and his wife that had not gone unnoticed. He often toyed with the notion that the likeness gave him a certain security.

'Christ, I'm exhausted,' she said. He smiled grimly. 'Every time with you it's the same. I feel stretched to a pulp. It hurts. In a nice kinda way. It shouldn't, but it does. Somehow it's like the first time over again. Every time.'

'Whaddaya mean?'

'Well, I dunno. I mean I love you, you know that, but it's somethin' else too. I need to feel some pain. I like it. Not in any warped sense, but in the sort of submission, the layin' waste, the feeling like a tom, almost, whose trick has just been a part of the rent, it's an act of vengeance, pure and simple.'

'Vengeance?'

'Yeah, against Tony. Can you understand that?'

'I think so. I'm not sure.'

'I hate him more than anything in the world. I detest him. But I ain't stupid. I know I'm tied to him for life. There's no way he'd let me go. He'd kill me before he'd do that. So, takin' in his sworn enemy is a small consolation. Got it?'

Dave grunted. 'That sounds like serious shit. How long have you felt this way?'

'I ain't usin' you, Dave. This is just an extra. I've loved you for ever. You musta known that.'

'It can't do any good to hate someone so much, not all the time. Anyway, if he don't know about it, you aren't doing him any harm.'

'I know that. But the feelin's for me, not him. Lemme tell you somethin',' she said. 'I shouldn't, but what the hell. After leaving you I don't bathe or shower. I'll go back and tell him that I'm kinda horny. He used to be a regular little rabbit. I'm talkin' three or four times a day. Not that he was any good, but he's lost it altogether now. I know he's seen doctors, the lot, and they put it down to drug abuse. He was in and out of hospital dozens of times. I think the episode with you started it all. He got rid of all the mirrors in the house. We're talkin' serious psycho problems here. A regular Norman Bates. But that was ten years ago.'

Dave gulped.

'Anyway, his addiction was one of the reasons they sent him over here. If he couldn't sort himself out, then he couldn't go home. The old man O'Connell took him in hand, got him off the junk, gave him back some kind of self-respect. But it was too late for his dick.'

'What's it got to do with you not taking a shower?'

'Whoah! Don't rush me. I'm comin' to that. Even though he can't get it up himself he still feels he has to look after me. He doesn't, of course. He hasn't got a clue. But I let him think he does the trick. He uses his fingers and his tongue. While I'm still tinglin' from your touch the old fool thinks he's suckin' out my own release. He don't realize he's getting his mouth full of you! His nose has been shot to hell by the coke; he can't smell the difference!'

Dave smiled.

'You don't mind?' she asked. Her back was still to him.

'No. In a funny way the thought of it gives me quite a kick.'

He reached to the side table for his Rolex and said, 'It's time to make a move.'

As he headed for the door he said, 'I'll have to bell you, sweetheart, and let you know where and when. I need to stay close to home for a while. At least until I know what's happening to Pop.'

She nodded her understanding and blew him a kiss before he closed the door.

Dave found Jimmy Jones near the lobby telephones in a position that gave him a good view of the entrance. No mention was made of Dave's diversion or the fact that he had kept Jimmy waiting. It was accepted, a part of the job; it was questionable whether Jimmy Jones had even thought about it.

As they walked through the lobby Dave glanced through the glass wall partition into the bar and his step faltered. The years were peeled away and for a moment he was flat on his back and looking up into the lifeless eyes of the blond man.

He caught Jimmy's arm.

'Clock the fair-haired geezer chattin' up the barmaid. Have you seen him before?'

Jimmy Jones peered through the glass. The tall blond man was perched on a bar stool, his elbows resting on the bar surface as he talked to a woman behind the bar.

'Yeah, I've seen him around,' Jimmy said. 'He came in about twenty minutes ago. Do you know him?'

'We met before. A long time ago. He had more hair in those days.'

They reached the entrance when Dave paused and turned to Jimmy. 'Look, I don't believe in coincidence. Get a make on that guy will you. How long has he been in town? Where he's stayin', what his name is for fuck's sake.'

'OK boss.'

'Make sure Sharon gets out of here OK. Make sure he doesn't follow her. If he does, then get a couple of guys together and get in his way. It shouldn't be difficult. One of his legs is shorter than the other.'

Jimmy nodded. If he was surprised at the request he didn't show it.

'I'll catch you at The Tower later,' Dave said.

A short detour took Dave to the river and he pulled up on the Embankment. A grim sky reflected its depression on to the water. There was something belittling about the river, perhaps its history, that drew him back time and again. The ebb and flow, its heartbeat, contained his ancestral blood; it whispered to him and turned his thoughts to the past. His grandfather had died in the thick waters and, more than that, those same waters had washed across his father and poured into his father's heart.

Chapter 10

'Dad! Dad!'

The old man shook away his dream and glanced at the three people in the cubicle. A curtain had been drawn around his bed. A translucent tube running into his right nostril tightened and he moved his head forward to release the pressure. Another tube ran from his left arm and looped upward to a bottle of glucose. He felt tied up, bound. His sleep had been too deep. Slowly the shapes that moved before him found their form.

Theca, his Star of the Veldt, sat close, leaning forward, holding on to his mottled right hand with both of hers. Her eyes were sore, yet wide, begging for his attention. Sally sat to his left, fussing in her bag, bringing out a bottle of orange juice and fresh, neatly folded pyjamas and newspapers. Ted, Theca's husband, stood near the end of the bed. It was his first visit to see Tom and he was shocked to find how ill he looked. Beside the apparent weight loss the skin on his neck was grey and loose and his brown eyes were dull and speckled. His thinning white hair was ruffled and his normal imposing frame seemed somehow fragile and weak.

' 'Ello darlin's.'

His eyes flicked to each of them in turn and rested on his daughter. Although glazed they appeared to caress her gently.

'Hello Dad,' she said bravely.

'My, you've turned out so beautiful,' he said weakly.

'What have they done to you?' she whispered.

'I'm happy, baby. They're shootin' me with so much dope that I can't feel a thing. And it's all legit. Paid for by the NHS. Half the town could score on the shit they're pumping into me.' He chuckled.

Theca looked across at her mother.

'They said he was ill,' she said, 'but he looks great to me.'

Tom looked from the girls to his son-in-law.

"Ello Teddy boy!'

'All right Tom?' Ted said thickly.

'Gawd! Glad to see you're wearin' your best suit to come and see me.' Tom grinned and turned back to Sally. "Ello darlin', you been all right? They been takin' care of you?'

'Everything's fine. I've got the photographs back.'

'Did they come out? Let me see.' He reached for his spectacles, careful not to knock the tubes or the glasses on the cluttered side table.

Sally handed him one photograph at a time.

'Look at little Alan, and there's Mark, and there's little Tommy. Here's one of the girls together.'

'Ah, love 'em,' Tom chuckled. 'Have you heard from Karen and John?'

'They 'phoned last night. It's too early for a postcard from Tunisia. Maybe tomorrow.'

'He'll be too busy to write postcards.' Tom laughed. He finished looking at the photographs. 'How many came out? I was having trouble with the camera. Ted, count 'em. How many are there?'

Ted took the photographs and began counting. He lost it at fifteen and began again.

'Dave and Tommy are outside,' Sally said.

Tom nodded. 'Well, boy, how many?'

'Twenty-six.'

'Well, done 'em, didn't we? Twenty-four film, twenty-six shots. Nothin' wrong with that camera.' He turned back to Sally. 'Frenchie saw me just before opening time. Told me he'd seen you all this afternoon. So now you know.'

Sally sniffed.

'It'll be ten days before the results are through,' Ted said. 'We'll take it from there.'

'Don't be bleedin' daft. It's all over, boy. They had a look and there's nothin' they can do.'

'That's not what he said, Tom. He said he didn't recognize it.'

'Bullshit!'

Ted shook his head.

'Sorry about the holiday, luv.' Tom squeezed Sally's hand. 'Should have flown out today. Would have been sunnin' on the Algarve by now.'

'Sod the holiday,' Sally said. 'I just want you to get well. I just want you to come home.'

Tom turned to Theca.

'How's my Star? Been helping your mum?'

'They all have,' Sally said.

'What about the kids? They're not missin' school, are they?'

Theca shook her head and grasped his hand tighter.

'Take your mum out for a cup of coffee,' Tom said gently. 'Send in Dave and Tommy. Ted, you stay a while. I want a few minutes with them. Then you come back and hold my hand again. I like you holdin' my hand, darlin'. Even when I doze off you keep holdin' it. I've been so tired lately. It must be the stuff they're puttin' in the drip. Now, go on both of you. Go and have a cup of coffee.'

Sally leant across and kissed his cheek. 'I'll see you in a minute love.'

'Go on then,' he said.

The girls left Ted looking down into Tom's tired eyes.

'There's been other things, boy, over the last few months. I wasn't born yesterday.'

Ted nodded.

'Blood. Gut aches that wasn't fuckin' wind.'

Ted looked at the floor, not wanting to meet the old man's searching gaze.

'I had a diabolical time back there,' Tom whispered. 'They didn't put me out proper, you know. I was strapped up and saw myself hangin' over this bath – a white bath – while they cut me.'

Ted nodded, forcing calm features.

Dave and Tommy walked in and took seats beside the bed. Expressions were fixed.

'All right, Pop?' Dave asked.

'Blimey! You look cream-crackered, boy,' Tom said to his youngest son.

Tommy flashed him a grin.

'I was up most of the night.'

'Gather round then,' Tom said and waited for the others to lean forward.

'First things first, Pop,' Dave said. 'I want to move you to a private ward. We're got to make you secure.'

Before he had finished speaking Tom was shaking his head.

'You're not havin' me in bleedin' BUPA. How many times do we need to talk about this, eh? I told you, boy, every time someone pays for private health they accept there is a second-class service for everybody else. The poorest geezer in this country should get the same health care as the Queen of bleedin' England. Anything else is criminal!'

'I ain't talkin' about the rights and wrongs, Pop,' Dave insisted. 'I'm talkin' about security. Things are warming up out there and it would be easier for us to take care of you in a private ward. I can't have soldiers marchin' in and out of here, can I?'

'What's all this then? Soldiers? You think this is World War Two? With all this lot in here no one's goin' to try nothin'. The place is crawlin' with local nick. I'm safer stayin' put. Anyway, show me where it's written that I've got to make it easy for you?' He chuckled. 'Now, quickly, let's get down to business. Tell me what's been happening?'

They began to whisper.

The Italian-Americans, known sometimes as the Mafia, sometimes as wiseguys, with their supplies of dope from Central America, wanted to organize a nationwide distribution, with their gaming clubs and other business interests fronting the operation. Because of his arrangement with the Chinese, Tom was against the deal and Coddy Hughes was against the trade altogether. Coddy's point blank refusal to deal with dope was fuelling the current situation. Mad Mick who ran most of the Scottish cities was not only prepared but savoured the idea of taking over Coddy's Midland territory. Coddy had grown old and soft and his organization lacked its previous strength. People no longer feared him and when that had gone so had respect.

'Coddy won't change his mind,' Dave whispered. 'Not today, not next year. The bottom line, Pop, is that Mick is going to hit Coddy. In order to do that he's going to hit us. If we're forced into an open war we'll all come out of it so weak the Yanks will move in without raising a sweat. Christ! The Godfathers already own Runnymede and it isn't US gun laws that are keeping them over here. They are sitting there, waiting, sensing a future. Their kids have already got their names down for public school!'

Tom nodded grimly. He opened his hand and relaxed, swallowed loudly against the tube.

There was a savage irony in what his eldest son had said. The

Wops had got their foothold in Runnymede because of Dave. Concessions to get him off the hook, to have those contracts cancelled all those years ago. Of course, the injured party had argued long and loud about letting Dave get off scot-free, but he had been overruled. It was business. To the men who controlled the business that was all that mattered. Tom remembered how he had agreed to launder American funds through his clubs and allowed the families inroads into the capital's gaming.

He sighed. 'So, how did you get on, Tommy?' he asked his youngest.

Tommy shrugged.

'Never got to see him, Pop. Went through the prelims, had a long chat to McLachlan, Mick's banker, who seemed pretty enthusiastic and was tryin' to set up a meet. I was waitin' for the call when I heard about you on the one o'clock.'

Dave interrupted: 'He was waiting to talk to Mick, Pop, explain that we'd negotiate with Coddy, but as soon as Mick heard about you he moved against Tommy.'

The old man examined his youngest son.

'You all right, boy?'

Tommy grinned.

'You be careful.'

'Tried to take him out,' Dave continued. 'Look, it's headlines.'

Tom scanned the newspaper.

'I've seen it already. It's well out of order. Who's this other geezer?'

Tommy shrugged.

'He was giving me a lift.'

'Find out where they took him. Look after him.'

'That's all in hand, Pop,' Dave said. 'Ted's takin' care of it.'

Tom glanced at Ted for confirmation.

'I've got his wife coming down, got her and the kids booked into the Savoy. It looks like he'll be off work for a few months. I figured maybe a grand up front and two-hundred a week. After that we can use him. Tommy rates him as a driver.'

Tom nodded.

'That's good. Mind, should have used your bonce. She isn't going to feel at home in the Savaloy, is she, poor cow? Get one of the girls to take her out and buy her some clothes, eh? Dresses and stuff.'

'Anyway, we've had our problems.' Dave was eager to move on. 'Mick's a mad bastard. We haven't faced anything like this before.'

'Who hasn't?' Tom chuckled and his eyes sparkled. 'Who hasn't?'

'Even our friends are getting jumpy. The coast is holding back, Liverpool who knows? They're comin' to see us tomorrow. I was thinking of postponing it.'

'Don't do that, boy!' Tom grunted. 'These Scouse gits only come down here once a year and this year they'll be lookin' to see that we've got it under control. They'll be lookin' for weaknesses. As far as we're concerned it's business as usual. There is no problem. Problem? What problem? A few murmurs from north of the border, call that a problem? That's what I want them to think. Confidence, boys, that's the ticket. Give them their leg over and send them home thinking we're stronger than ever. Make sure you've got it all in hand Ted, like last year.'

Ted nodded.

'Dave, I think you better go and see your father-in-law,' Tom went on and sighed. 'See how the land lies. I think, maybe, it's time he thought about retirin'. See what he's got to say. You better get up there in the mornin'. After that we'll be in a position to talk to these guineas. I know they'd prefer to deal with us. They trust Mick even less than we do.'

He shifted his position on the bed then glanced at his youngest son.

'Tommy, you better get some kip, boy. After that help Ted to sort out Liverpool. If we can stay friendly with them it might keep Mick guessin' and give us some time.' He turned back to Ted. 'Teddy boy, I want you to stay close to The Tower as a link. I don't want no business goin' through the house, understand? There might be a cashflow problem before long, especially if we have to buy some extra muscle. You better see our bankers, let them know we might need some heavy withdrawals. Sell a couple of properties. They'll sort it out. And safe houses, stock 'em up, get 'em ready, make some promises.'

Tom leant back on his pillow. 'I'm getting so tired. You better get on with it. Send the girls back in. Be careful, all of you. Take care of your families. Take no chances. Make sure there's someone with your kids. Dave, you better send someone to Tunisia to keep a discreet eye open. Wouldn't want to spoil their honeymoon.'

Dave didn't tell him that he had already sent a minder to look after Karen and John. Instead he said, 'Karen 'phoned last night. She knows you're ill, that's all.'

'That's good. I don't want them worryin'. I don't want no one to know the truth. I'm here for investigation and that's all.'

The boys nodded gravely.

'Send in the girls,' Tom ordered.

While they waited in the waiting-room to go into the ward – two at a time the rule said but the staff stretched it to three – the family had barely noticed the old man in the corner and if they had they were not sure whether he was a visitor or a patient. Dave had glanced his way but instantly dismissed him as harmless. He was old, well over retirement. His tall, heavy-set frame was emphasized by a thick navy-blue overcoat that reached down below his knees. In the heat of the hospital the coat was absurd and Dave disregarded the man as a dimwit.

The old man waited hours until the family left the hospital, until the sister and the nurses called for an end to visiting time, and then he made his move. His movements were purposeful, plodding almost, with the stiffness of arthritic joints, yet a power was still evident. Skin had folded and pulled away from his dull grey eyes, cheeks had sunken and become blotchy. A circular brown scar on his temple fed a ragged hairless tributary across the side of his head. Age had opened up his pores and mashed his nose and what once might have been a physical attribute could now have been a spongy embarrassment. But age had also diminished all feelings of vanity along with all other such profound thoughts and what was left was an automaton.

A petite Chinese nurse moved from her desk to stop him. 'Excuse me, sir,' she began and put her small hand on his arm. He stopped and slowly turned to face her. Her pretty eyes widened fractionally as she recognized danger and her step back was instinctive.

'Just a few minutes then,' she said and walked quickly away.

From the middle of the aisle he watched her go and remembered a conversation. Chinese women walked like men; there was no hip swing. Flat arses. Slant-eyed rubbish. All women were full of crap! The next one who even looked at him was going to get her eyes poked out. As he watched her hurrying away the shadowy image of another girl ghosted into his head. She was Chinese too. He was tearing at her clothes. She was screaming. There was blood everywhere. He shook away the memory and smiled inwardly; there was no change to his expression.

He knew that at least two men were watching him closely as he approached the corner bed. A porter and a man in the bed opposite were both on Dave's strength. Dave had paid the Registrar a small fortune to get his men into the hospital. The old man saw how Tom Smith waved away their concern with the slightest movement of his hand. The porter continued stacking his trolley and the man opposite buried his face again in the *Daily Mirror*.

If the old man was surprised at how ill Tom looked he did not show it. The grey eyes softened as he settled back in an upright chair. The plastic creaked as it took his weight.

'My old friend,' Tom whispered. 'You're looking good.'

'Crap! I look like shit. And you?'

Tom gave a faint resigned shrug that hardly troubled his shoulders. He touched the translucent plaster that held the tube to his nose.

'It's been a long time, Scratch.'

'You're right. Too long. I remember the old days, Tommy. I dream about them.'

Tom Smith nodded slowly.

'I know what you mean.'

'Ain't no harm in it, is there? At the end of the day that's all that counts, ain't it? Memories. That's all we got left. We sure as fuck can't take anything else with us, eh?'

'I ain't gone yet.'

'I didn't mean that.'

'Tact never was your strong point.' Tom smiled.

'We fought some fuckin' battles, though, didn't we? Remember the South Coast? Bryant? The look on his ugly boat when we told him to walk the plank? And Chinatown, now that was a cracker. The tart, eh?'

'I wasn't there.'

'No, you weren't. I was.' The old man's eyes glazed in reverie, getting off again.

Tom studied his worn features.

'What have you been doing lately?'

The big man grunted down his nose.

'Waitin' for your call.'

'Well, now you're here.' Tom nodded. 'Are you ready to help me out for one last time?'

The big man's eyes had moistened. He reached forward and put his huge hand over Tom's, careful not to knock the drip that fed into his forearm. He felt the cold clammy flesh of Tom's hand and read into his words.

'You ask me as if there's a question. You've never had to ask yourself whether you can count on me.'

'I know that, my old friend. I know that. In forty years I've counted on you more than anyone and no one ever knew it. We've hardly met a handful of times and there's been no recognition for you.'

'That's the way I wanted it.'

Tom looked saddened.

'It's a waste.'

'It's not!' The old man trembled in a sudden burst of anger. 'It's not a waste!'

'Well, my friend, I am in trouble. And I need your help again.'

The grey eyes flickered enthusiastically.

'But what of afterwards?' Tom continued. 'There will be no more calls. What can I give you?'

'Forget the future. Who cares? There is no fuckin' future. Look at me. I'll even have to hurry on this one or I won't make it. Tell me what you want?'

'Lean closer then. I'll whisper. This lot could be wired.'

The grey eyes took on a slyness, momentarily searching for the hidden devices. He nodded and moved forward so that his ear was only inches from Tom Smith's lips.

Shortly after the old man had gone another man in an ill-fitting white porter's jacket that stretched at the seams across his broad shoulders, lumbered forward across the linoleum floor and manoeuvred a trolley full of books into the ward. He was what they called a volunteer worker but in order to get the job for just an hour it had been necessary to threaten the regular volunteer with a choice of castration or an hour-long cup of tea at the hospital café. The charity worker had thought for quite a time before he decided on the tea.

Totally ignoring the calls from other patients, grunting an apology to a small nurse he almost flattened, he pulled up beside Tom's bed. Beads of sweat ran from his grooved forehead over his craggy tanned features. His path through the ward was marked by a trail of paperbacks on the floor. He mopped his face with a huge white handkerchief and his determination eased. Mike Mountford had been with Tom, on and off, for thirty years. While Raymond Jones had been the most famous, and probably the best, cat-burglar in the country, Mike Mountford had established his own reputation as the fireman, the torch, equally at home with explosives or matches.

'See you haven't passed your driving test,' Tom joked.

''Ello boss,' Mountford said in a deep breathless voice. He turned up his hearing-aid. 'That's better. Now I can hear you.'

Something in his small green eyes offered affection. Nothing else about his looks did.

'Mike, boy, how are you?' The speckled hand raised and beckoned him forward. 'Come closer. You can guarantee the filth is listening.'

'This is goin' to be difficult then 'cos I'm having trouble with the old hearin' lately. How are you with the sign language?' Mountford smiled. 'How are you boss? I've been hearin' some diabolical rumours about your health!'

'Tell the bastards that I haven't gone yet! What's been happening?'

'Dave's copin' pretty well. Bit heavy-handed but that's to be expected. He never was a ballerina, was he?'

'I hope not, Mike. I think you'll find that ballerinas are all women.'

'Ugh? What about that big geezer with the long hair? Nuri somethin'? Nuri Gella?'

Tom grinned.

Mike Mountford waved at the warm air.

'Now Tommy's back Dave will calm down,' he said.

'Tommy was lucky,' Tom snapped. 'Fuck me, it sounds like the Royal Family on one of their pheasant shoots. This is England! London! Not the fuckin' Falls Road. I mean, shotguns for fuck sake!' He shook his head in dismay.

'You knew Mad Mick in the old days, didn't you?'

Mountford nodded slowly.

'Yeah. Smart arse little toerag even then. He dropped out of Edinburgh University to join the Marines before endin' up in London and hittin' it off with the twins.' The fireman snorted. 'As soon as they were banged up he pissed off north again. No one heard from him for a couple of years and then he surfaced in Glasgow . . .'

Tom Smith knew Mick McGovern's history by heart. He changed the subject.

'The Scousers are comin' down tomorrow. Will they line up with us?'

'Doubt it,' he said earnestly. Ass'oles have been waitin' to spread out for a long time. See this as their big chance.'

Tom's eyes hooded. 'Will they go it alone or will they line up with Mick?'

'That's a tricky one. If Mick made 'em promises, who knows?'

'I'd hate to see any trouble on The Barge.'

'They ain't that stupid, boss. The best they could do is Ted. He's the only family that's goin' to be there.'

'No. I told Tommy to help out.'

'Still, they ain't goin' to cause trouble with Dave on the loose. It's Dave they're scared shitless of. You and me know different, or at least we think we do, but the faces out there, and that includes north of the border, think he's a fuckin' psycho!'

'I'd still like to have a few people in reserve.'

'I know what you mean, boss. Leave it to me.'

Mike Mountford stood up to go. 'Do you want one of these books? Got the Godfather here somewhere.'

'Naw,' Tom sighed. 'Saw the film. Can't be bothered with fiction.' He chuckled, then he looked up and said seriously. 'Take care of my family, Mike. This thing could escalate. Let me know what goes on.'

'OK boss.'

The trolley rumbled on its way to the double doors and was left blocking the lift entrance.

Alone again, Tom lay back with his thoughts. His main concern was his eldest son and whether, given the present climate, Dave would keep the lid on his temper. Dave had always been impulsive, his fiery temperament had often got in the way of reason; violence had all too often been his first resort. This flash temper was a sign of immaturity. To an extent age had brought it under control but it was still there, just a little deeper beneath the surface. When he looked at Dave he saw a cold hatred, an impatience; there was about him a mark of fury.

He exuded danger like some people exuded sexuality. Tom's world was full of heartless men, their cruelty was legend, yet even they feared his eldest son. In the whole of the Smoke, a Smoke filled with the violent, the uncompromising, the most dangerous of men, Dave held the position of dubious veneration. It was largely undeserved; it had grown from rumour, that he had been involved in this and that, particularly the Chinese wars which left a dreadful scar in the hearts of many men. But it was there nevertheless, this respect, this reverence. Tom Smith thought of these things and hoped that his eldest son would remain in control. Dave's short fuse was the one variable in his careful plan.

Chapter 11

The Eagle Public House had been partly hit in the blitz but they had rebuilt it. It was here that Tom Smith had first set up in business. It was gone now for the property developers and bent councillors had destroyed the old city far more effectively than bombs ever could. They worked from the inside, like a hidden cancer, and just as deadly. They had destroyed a way of life, a history, and in its place they had put something else, something superficial, as far removed from Old London Town as the Prince of Wales from reality. In place of the Eagle a multi-storey office block towered over the surroundings and the locals called it The Tower. The gymnasium next to the Eagle had gone too, for boxing was a thing of the past – some people did not believe it – but the land had stayed with the family. On the site a nightclub took its neighbour's name and under quiet green neon spelling out THE TOWER a doorman welcomed the visitor. The Tower Casino with its nightclub and restaurant had become a London landmark and was frequented by celebrities from the studios and the castles. Together with its sister clubs, The Arsenal, The Moat, The Fortress and The Castle in London and The Martello on the Kent coast, it was the legitimate end of the Smith family business. The Barge on the river was their latest acquisition but The Tower remained special. It had been their first to open and it remained their headquarters. In the offices behind the restaurant, away from the casino's gaming tables and the noise from the nightclub, the business was conducted. Adjacent to the offices was a four-roomed flat and it was here, in the private bar, that the brothers and Ted would meet.

The Smiths had a workforce of some two hundred and twenty people and that figure did not include the part-timers and the cleaners and the vast army of small, independent businesses that relied on the Smiths, nor did it include the businesses that the Smiths part owned or had capital invested in; even that was just the tip, the up-front, insurance-stamped employees; beneath the surface at least that number again relied on the Smiths for their living. The accounts department along with payroll was stationed over at The Castle where Ted spent most of his time but it was here, in these offices and the flat next door, where the decisions were made.

Tommy's role was still incidental. To a large extent his father had kept him clean. With regard to much of the family business, he was left on the periphery. It had come as a surprise to both Dave and Ted that Tom had chosen his youngest son to make the Glasgow trip. They decided it was a ploy to make Mick think that their father's regard for him was insignificant, sending his least experienced emissary. For the most, Tommy was shielded, certainly from the collections and the potential violence that they entailed. He stuck closely to his father, away from the running of the business for that, on a daily basis, was passing more and more to Dave and Ted.

Dave thought that it was a good thing. He recognized a compassion in his younger brother and that was dangerous. If not a weakness, exactly, it was certainly a handicap. Their business was war, it was fought on the capital's streets, and compassion meant anarchy; that simple. Criticism, differences of opinion, even voices raised loudly, were put down swiftly and clinically. Anything else would mean government by the people – no government at all.

In the business the problem was and always had been what to do with the cash. A bent bank was helpful and there were quite a few of those, but dummy businesses were essential, businesses that relied on cheap raw materials and consumables but heavy overheads. Marine salvage was always a good bet, insurance another. They produced a service or an expensive nothing at all that the retailers could sell. But most of the laundering still took place in the gaming clubs, no questions asked, where proof of wins and losses was all but impossible to obtain. The Tower Casino earned annual profits of over eight million pounds, but more importantly, its laundry service was invaluable. Together with the Ritz and Casanova it made London the most successful square mile outside Las Vegas.

Dave made The Tower in the late evening and met Barry Theroux, his manager, in the lounge. A group of minders in dark suits sat at one end and acknowledged him in a friendly relaxed way. Theroux was in control; quiet, unassuming, thoughtful and unruffled, he had been with the family all his working life. A handsome man, spotless and manicured, his dress was immaculate. His voice was level.

'Evening, Dave. The others are upstairs.'

Dave nodded. 'Anything going down?'

Theroux shook his head. After the attack on Tommy he had tightened up security and brought in more muscle.

'Pretty quiet,' he said. 'This trouble has kept some of the regulars away.'

'We could do without it,' Dave muttered.

They paused at the Showcase Restaurant to watch a few scantily dressed girls kicking at the air. The place was half full. Waitresses in short black skirts weaved between the tables looking for work.

'All this fuckin' aggro makes you lose your appetite,' Dave muttered.

'It's the same upstairs,' Theroux said. 'Plenty of street punters but the heavy rollers are giving it a rest.'

They walked across the deep royal-blue pile to the lifts. 'Establishment, ain't we?' Tom used to quip about the carpet and that knowing glitter would sparkle in his eyes. A cover-girl receptionist smiled brightly with promise as they passed her counter. Dave left Theroux at the lift and made his way up to the office.

'Well, Brovs, it's all over,' Dave told the others. 'I'm not sure we can wait any longer before making some pretty heavy decisions.'

'Like what?' Tommy asked sharply.

'Like giving some of it back, Tommy. There's an army on our doorstep. Maybe you hadn't noticed. Unless we start dishing it out they're going to march in here!'

'That's well out of order, Brov, and you know it. We do what he tells us, right up until the time comes that he can't tell us anymore. After that he'll leave us some instructions.' Tommy was adamant. He shook his head angrily. Somehow Dave's suggestion was an insult to his father. He turned to Ted for support. 'What do you think?'

'I go along with you, Tommy. I think we can afford to leave it a while.'

'Fair enough.' Dave knew he was on a loser. 'But don't forget that the people who dealt with Pop aren't necessarily going to deal with us.'

'He knows that. He won't leave us in the air. You're underestimating the business, Dave. They'll deal with us.'

A knock at the door interrupted them and they turned to see Jimmy Jones peer around the varnished wood.

'Sorry to barge in,' he said in his Welsh accent.

'All right, Jimmy?' Tommy asked.

'Peter Hough's outside. Wants to know if he can have a word?'

Dave cut in: 'He can have quite a few. They all start with F.'

Tommy turned to the others. 'He did me a favour last night, Dave.'

Dave nodded. 'Yes, that's true. You come in too, Jimmy.'

Jimmy whispered into the corridor and was followed into the room by Peter Hough. Peter stood by the door shuffling his thick frame from one foot to the other, nervously rubbing together sweaty palms.

'All right, Pete? What is it?'

'All right everybody. Dave, you know I left the company? Left on good terms, basically for the kid's sake. I done two years and I thought that was it. Now I hear of your troubles and I can't stay away. Take me back, Dave, you won't regret it.'

'Hang on a moment, Peter,' Tommy said. 'What about Denise? She don't want you back in this game.'

'I know that, Tommy. Christ! I know that. But there ain't another way. I've given it a crack but it ain't me. Eight to five, fuckin' around, doin' the same thing day in and day out, pressin' this button and that. It ain't me.'

'You did Tommy a favour last night and I'm grateful for that, Pete. If you want a few sovs to hold you over it's yours.'

'Naw, Dave. I ain't beggin'. Fuck that. I want you to take me on again. I ain't takin' nothin' I don't earn. Never have. As for last night, let's just say I was glad to help.'

Dave looked from Tommy to Ted. 'All right, Pete,' he said eventually. 'Stick with Jimmy. He'll use you.'

'Cheers, Dave. You won't regret it.'

'I better not.' He nodded. 'All right. Wait outside.'

Once the door was closed Dave turned to Jimmy Jones. 'Watch him, Jimmy. I ain't sure about him.' Dave's eyes narrowed as he wondered whether he had made the right decision. Jack McVitie had introduced Peter Hough soon after Hough's release from High Point. Dave never had much time for Jack the Hat but until booze got the better of him he was a useful source of information on the twins. It was to keep McVitie sweet that Dave had taken Hough on in the first place.

'There was a time when he was useful,' Dave went on. 'But he was nicked for a garage load of dodgy videos and the toerag never said a bleedin' thing to us. Free enterprise ain't trustworthy, so watch him. I'm not even certain he wasn't fuckin' around with more than a bit of puff. Those silver bins he used to wear always hid his minces from the day. Know what I mean?'

Dave paused and made sure Jimmy caught his glance before asking: 'What did you find out?'

Jimmy shrugged and said matter-of-factly: 'A Yank. His name's Herman Tartt. Been over here two months. He works for Runnymede, drives for Clough and Valenti. He had a couple of drinks and left about half-an-hour after you. You were right about the limp. He uses a stick. No problem. He wasn't interested in anyone else.'

Dave understood and nodded.

'What's that, Brov?' Tommy asked.

'Nothin'. A face from the past.' Dave changed the subject and addressed Jimmy again. 'Business. Scouse is coming down tomorrow and I want you on The Barge. Is your end sorted?'

'All tied up, Dave,' Jimmy confirmed.

'Teddy will sail with you like last year. It's important for us that it goes right.'

'Right then, I'll see you tomorrow night, Ted. I better get back. I think Barry's got more minders down there than he's got customers.'

'Know all the faces?' Dave asked.

'Yeah, no sweat.'

'See you, Jimmy.' Before Jimmy Jones closed the door Dave added, 'Watch him.' Jimmy nodded and pulled the door shut behind him.

Chapter 12

Theca had been named after a wild rose. Her parents were visiting South Africa when Sally was pregnant. Food poisoning put her into hospital. Tom turned up with some local flowers called Theca, the Star of the Veldt. He kept the label and when his daughter arrived he had a ready-made name. He still called her his Star.

Knowing that Dave had put minders on her, Theca took special care to lose them in the traffic build-up around Marble Arch then used the next ten minutes to confirm it before parking her car in a cobblestone Victorian courtyard in Grosvenor Gardens. She didn't notice the pale blue Escort parked opposite on a yellow line, or the two men in the front who seemed to take not the slightest interest in her. Once she was inside the mews flat the men relaxed, finished their animated conversation and got on with the serious business of watching the street. The two men didn't know it but they were employed by the family. Beneath their seats were loaded revolvers that they would use without compunction. They were minders, top class, selected by one man, and paid accordingly.

It was a quiet corner of London, a spit from the palace and the tourist hordes, a place where celebrities could live in comparative seclusion. Birdcage Walk was a few hundred yards away and the Star and her lover had spent many hours during the spring amongst the courting couples that poured from the packed offices, as if the Walk offered them privacy or at least immunity, during their stolen lunch hours. Hand-in-hand the couples went across the greenery, the secretary and her boss, the junior buyer and the copy typist, the lovers, feigning affection, excited by the mystery, moving through the ritual of deceit and exaggeration. If the Walk offered Theca and her lover respite it was in his flat above the courtyard where, uninhibited, the restraints of marriage cast aside, they wrapped around each other with intensity and delight. They fucked until they were sore and shattered, until they fell into a post-coital sleep. And then it had been like a dream, until the next time.

'God! I've wanted to see you. I've thought about ringing you a thousand times. I needed to know that you were all right. Coping.'

He closed the heavy door behind her and they embraced in the wide hallway.

'Hold me, please. I'm not all right.' She dropped her Chanel handbag on to the polished floor.

He sighed. 'Bad news?'

'My father's dying.'

He nodded quietly. 'What can I do?'

'Hold me,' she whispered and began to cry. Her tears marked the wool of her grey jacket. He led her by the hand into the lounge.

'You need a stiff drink. Come and sit down.'

Theca broke free and moved into the kitchen. 'I'll make some coffee. I can't face a drink.' She found a tissue and wiped her eyes. Since the start of this she carried a pocket full of them. He stood aside and let her get on with it, knowing that she would tell him in her own time. 'They operated and found . . . they couldn't do anything. He's got a few days, possibly a month.' Her dark eyes brimmed. He watched a tear splash on to the Formica surface.

'Well I need something stronger than coffee,' he said and walked into the lounge.

A few moments later she found him standing by the open veranda doors studying the skyline, his features drawn and worried. She watched him lift a brandy glass to his lips. She had a fleeting memory of his bed and glanced toward the bedroom door. She had been naked on top of the quilt, on Friday because Dave's eldest was getting married on the Saturday, and she had heard: 'This city could be called igneous'. He had spoken quietly, deeply, in a voice still thick with sex. 'It was raised from the Great Fire, and then again in the blitz, and now it is on fire again. Look!' He had pointed to the window, at the dusky skyline that blazed with the dying sun. The colours tumbled through the high windows and turned her body into gold, the gold around her neck into liquid fire. She had turned to look, arching her back so that her pointed breasts rose irresistibly and he had reached across to their tips. 'As long as you remain a part of this city,' he had said. 'Then I will love it.'

That was when she had reached her decision. The leaking sun had helped. 'I'll tell Ted next week,' she had said quietly. 'After the wedding. I'll speak to Dad first.'

Seeing him now, somehow smaller, it was difficult to imagine the scene.

'It's all so unreal,' she said. 'Noddy came to see Mum – the doctor – and he was devastated by the news, had no idea. He said that Dad must have been hiding the symptoms for a long time. It was just like him. Stubborn. Wouldn't let them mess him around. He is such a . . . dignified man!' Theca used the tissue again. 'And now there's trouble. I don't know the details but I know the signs. Everyone is being so secretive.'

She glanced around the tidy room and took in the dark leather upholstery, the glistening spider tables, the audio equipment, the unit holding a collection of exquisite glass ballerinas they had picked up in a small village in the New Forest. For a fleeting moment she thought the place was cold and masculine. There was no sign of family or history, no photographs – although she knew he had one of his kids next to his bed, no silly paintings that the children had brought home from school. It was like an expensive hotel room before the suitcase was opened. It didn't matter. In due course she would change it all.

It had been almost a week since their previous meeting. Her weekend had been filled with the wedding and since then . . . Perhaps it was fate, she thought. Perhaps God was punishing her. She shook the absurdity away. Suddenly all of it was in perspective. The future would have to wait. Only her family mattered.

Theca sat straight backed on the edge of the couch, knees together, formal, holding a china saucer in one hand and lifting a cup to her lips with the other. There was no way for him to embrace her. He sat opposite in a wide armchair and placed his glass on the spider table.

'I have to tell you this,' she said seriously between sips of her coffee. She looked at him earnestly, trying to gauge his reaction. 'You've seen the newspapers and the television reports so you know what they're calling him. They aren't spelling it out but sooner or later one of them will, and anyway, the implication is there all the same. Gangster! Hoodlum!'

He nodded.

'Some of what they say is true,' she went on. 'Some of it is not, and some other truth is probably far worse. Some of the papers are even suggesting that the shooting in Mill Hill had something to do with him. They talk of gang war breaking out. You have never asked me about my family and I have never volunteered the information.'

He held up his hands, palms outward.

'I don't want to hear this, Theca. I'm interested in you, not your family.'

'I am my family,' she said timidly.

'Even so –,' he began.

'Whether you like it or not I am part of their world. There is no way that they would break the tie and no way that I would want them to.'

'I wouldn't ask you to do that.'

'I realize what they mean to me. How much they mean. You would have to accept that. My family.'

'Perhaps they wouldn't want me.'

'I want you and they will respect that.' She spoke surely, with authority.

He shrugged weakly.

'I want you, Theca. I wouldn't ask you to give up your family. That wouldn't do at all.'

She stared at him in silence, wanting to tell him more but finding it impossible. For one thing she knew little about the business. It was the unknown, the lack of confirmation, that frightened her above all else. She heard the stories, the gossip and innuendo, but all her father had ever said was to take no notice, that some people would always find fiction to explain success in order to excuse their own failure. And when, later, she had asked her brothers, they had terrified her with such tales of terrible butchery that her father had been furious and since then neither of her brothers had ever mentioned the business again. Even Ted would not confide in her, fobbing her off with the idea that he was only on the periphery, dealt with the books, that sort of thing. Even today she had no idea whether the stories were true or not but her curiosity had turned to anger that she should be treated so differently from the boys. Shielded. Perhaps it had been necessary to keep it from her mother, even Pat to an extent, but Theca was different, stronger; her father's blood flowed through her. Perhaps because she was younger and had come of age in an era of equality, she would never accept those places reserved exclusively for men. More than that, those places had become a challenge to her, there to be scorned, their doors battered open. She had a right to be taken into his confidence, as much right as the boys. Now it was even more imperative. If there was a real danger, and since her minders had been increased she guessed there was, then she ought to be told. But more than that, there were vast areas of her father's life that remained a blank and now she needed to fill in those details before it was too late. She needed a tie that was unbreakable, a bond that would reach beyond his death. Only an understanding of his life would achieve that.

'Obviously you didn't have a chance to speak to him?' Lewis interrupted her thoughts. She shook her head.

'All of a sudden things look pretty impossible,' she said.

'We'll work it out,' he reassured her. 'Let's take one day at a time.'

She attempted a smile.

Theca spent the early evening at the hospital with her mother. They sat on either side of the bed, Sally holding one hand, Theca the other. Sally spoke, or whispered, and Theca listened and clung on to every glance that her father offered. Inside she was dying and needed to fight to hold back her tears. Her stomach and her chest felt so heavy and yet empty, nauseous, a bereavement even before the robbery. If her father didn't figure in the future then she wanted no part of it either. For an absurd moment, in that chair beside the bed, she wanted to die with him, and she thought that she could.

She was staying with Sally for a few nights but could not bear the thought of the same conversation suffered these last few hours, nor could she stand a prolonged visit to her own home. She wanted to see her children although for the moment even they had become of secondary importance, but she did not want to see Ted.

Theca pulled up at her parents' house, conscious of the car that pulled up twenty yards behind her.

Her mother made no attempt to get out. Instead she said, 'The nurses, especially that little Chinese one, said he is such a kind man, always asking if it's too much trouble for them to bring something. A real gentleman they called him. I told him, you tell them, I said. That's what they're there for, but he won't.' She hadn't stopped talking since leaving the hospital. 'Fancy saying sorry about the holiday. I told him not to be such a silly sod. As if I care. And did you see what he put on the form, the consent form? Under hobbies he wrote grandchildren. But he looked well, didn't he?'

'I was there, Mum.'

Sally unbuckled her seatbelt and opened the door.

'What time will you be back?' There was a touch of anxiety in her voice.

'I'll tuck in the kids and make sure Jean's all right. Say eleven.'

'I'll still be up. I can't sleep.'

'See you later.' Sally watched the Mini pull out and gave a tentative wave and noticed the dark Rover pull out behind it.

Theca checked her mirror and swore under her breath as she saw the other car drawing up behind her. She drove quickly across to The Tower, hoping to catch Dave.

It was mid-evening and Dave felt physically exhausted. His day had been spent making the security rounds, tightening up his forces, ensuring that the safe houses were armed and stocked. Getting hold of weapons was easy enough, even a civilian with two hundred nicker in his pocket could pick up a revolver in a couple of hours simply by asking around; Spatz pump-actions and self-loading Brownings were still favourite with the robbers and they were more expensive, but just as available. Having a stock of them in the right places was a major factor in an underworld war. Faces on the streets were even more important. Security was everything. First priority was the family safety, and then the clubs and collection points. They needed watching around the clock; visitors and punters and even employees were scrutinized on their way in and out. Every face was clocked. Anyone acting remotely suspicious was pulled aside and finger-fucked. Like Heathrow. The attack on Tommy had surprised Dave, infuriated him, made him realize just how vulnerable they were. Years of peace and, to some extent, appeasement, had led to a run down in their forces. Even when his father had got wind of Mad Mick's increased activity he had done little to balance the scales. Dave had argued with him that it was necessary to increase their strength but the old man had seemed apathetic, not wanting to appear aggressive. His father listened but, as the weeks went by and Mick continued to strengthen his forces, he did nothing. And now it was probably too late. Mick was breathing hard on Coddy's doorstep and as a final insult – a challenge to fight or run – he had hit

Tommy. Without his father's backing there was only so much Dave could do on his own. Even his brothers wouldn't act without the old man's say so. Yet. The time was approaching when Dave would have to take over and he wasn't at all certain how the others would react.

He lay on the couch in the back room drinking vodka and looking through the two-way mirror at the early punters, watching the graceful and not so graceful women moving about the bars and tables, enjoying their movement. It used to excite him to watch and although it was still a pleasure it no longer led to other things. When Theca found him he was two-thirds into a bottle and looked tired and drawn.

'You drink too much,' she said haughtily.

'You might not know this, Sis, but vodka stops the clap. You drink enough and you can't do it!'

He was honestly pleased to see her. There was a warmth between them not shared by the others. Only her father was closer.

She mixed a scotch with dry at the bar, dropped in some ice and carried it over to the window.

Around them the city landscape had turned into an electric galaxy; a billion lamps burned orange and white. London! The Smoke! Somewhere he was out there. She wondered what he was doing now, right this moment. Was he thinking of her? She shook away the moment of yearning, that horrible, gutless insecurity. London! An island, she thought. A world of manufactured light moving through space.

One hundred and fifty feet below her, bathed in the street lights, the streets seemed unreal, the night traffic and pedestrians miniaturized, moving in slow motion. The city made her shiver.

'This royal throne of kings, this scepter'd city . . .' she murmured quietly, playing with *Richard II*.

'I think England comes into it somewhere, Sis,' Dave said.

'I know that.'

She turned back to Dave and sat next to him. For a while she sat drinking and watching the customers then she turned to him.

'I'm leaving Ted,' she said and her nervousness made her voice cold.

Dave lifted his eyebrows and pretended to be shocked. For some years he had watched her relationship with Ted disintegrate. He had heard about her small circle of friends and the time she spent with them in the Kensington restaurants – on the second floors, of course

– or in the bowels of Annabel's or Tramp's. A small circle of disillusioned women who were clinging hopelessly to a youth, a time when all things were possible, letting alcohol draw its dizzy veil on reality. And six months ago he had heard about her affair. He had hoped that it would fizzle out. He believed that there was no way his sister would hurt her children. He had been wrong but he was not surprised. Theca was as headstrong as he was; passion and physical contact were important. At one stage he had considered talking to his father about her but had decided against it. There was no point in upsetting the old man if the thing had died a death anyway. It was going to blow open now, though, for Ted was family. He was as involved as any of them in the business and the business could not afford any ill-feeling. Especially not now. Not while the world and God knew who else were against them.

'What's happened, Sis?' he asked and for a moment she saw herself in his round eyes.

She raised her hand in a throwaway gesture. 'We've been bad for some time and I met someone else.'

'Who is it?'

'Does it matter?'

'I suppose not.'

'I love him, Dave. I love him. All I want to do is be with him.'

'What about the kids?'

'They're resilient. If there was another way. But there isn't.'

'Christ! They'll be devastated. They might get over it but they might not.'

She shook her head and gulped at her drink.

'I've been over it a thousand times. Do you think I've arrived at this decision without thinking it through?' She seemed helpless and fragile. 'I can't go on any more, Dave. Obviously I'm not going to do anything until . . .' She left the sentence hanging.

'Has Ted got any idea?'

'I don't think so. He should have but I honestly don't think he's noticed. Or he doesn't care. I've come in later, I've not been interested, I've treated him badly, flaring up at the slightest thing. I don't think he's noticed.'

'Is there any chance at all?' He paused, filled his glass again and said, 'What about a holiday, Star? Couldn't you and Ted go away for a few weeks to sort things out?'

She smiled quickly, without humour.

'You're not listening to me, Dave. I don't want to be with him any more. It's over. I don't love him. I don't desire him. I can't bear him touching me. I want to be with . . . someone else. I'm not going to change my mind. Not now. Not ever. I can't live without love.'

'Love dies, Star, you know that. It fades away and dies, like people. In the beginning it's wonderful and exciting but it won't always be that way. What happens then? Will you find someone else?'

She pulled a face.

'Maybe I will, if that's what it takes. But I don't agree with you. Love only dies if you let it die. Look at Mum and Dad. Has their love died? There's more there, after forty years, than we have ever known. Anyway, this is beside the point, Dave. I'm telling you now and I'm going to tell Ted after . . . when Dad . . .' Her mask slipped and a tear glistened.

'You'll break Mum's heart, Star,' he said heavily.

'I know,' she nodded sadly.

They sat in silence for a while drinking, fixed gloomy expressions watching the customers without seeing them. Brother and sister, a yard apart with a light year between them. She was thinking about her father and whether love was strong enough to keep him alive; he was thinking about her lover and whether death would save her marriage and, more importantly, save a split in the family, save an interruption to the business. Love, the only thing worth living for, and death, the only real alternative.

She glanced up, wide eyes curious.

'How do you think Mum is coping?'

He shrugged. 'She's stronger than you think. Grief is no stranger to her. Nothing's going to hurt her as much as when Mick died. She'll handle it.' The vodka was speaking and he could not help himself telling her something else. 'I'll tell you something now that nobody knows, not even Mum and Dad. When I was thirteen and you were six, before Tommy was born, Mick was three. They always told you that Mick died in a traffic accident, right?'

Theca's brow ridged in concern.

'He didn't,' Dave said and shook his head. His eyes glazed, not in the Smith veil of anger, but into confession. 'Remember the railway track that went down the bottom of the garden? I was with a couple of mates in the back garden. Mum told us to play with Mick. We didn't. We took off over the track. Must have left the gate open because Mick followed us. It was one of those electric lines. I never told anyone I saw. They took Dad to the hospital. They wouldn't let Mum see the body.'

Theca reached forward to grasp his hand but it was not enough and she knelt beside him and put her arms around him.

'Oh David, why didn't you tell us?'

'They blamed me. Of course they blamed me.'

'No! No!' She shook her head.

'It never goes away, not entirely.'

'Well it's about time it did. You couldn't know. How could you? Kids of that age don't think. You should have told us.'

For the first time in her life Theca understood what had eaten her brother's soul. For a moment she felt incredibly close to him.

A vodka tear brimmed in his eye and he flicked it away angrily as though his emotion was something to be despised.

'When Dad came back from the hospital I was waiting for him in the front room. I watched the door open. I was frightened to death. I'll never forget the way he looked. His tie undone, his collar all over the place. His eyes so red they were almost bleedin'. When he walked up to me I thought I was goin' to get it. Suddenly his great arms came around me and he whispered, "I love you, boy. We'll never speak of it . . . again." ' The last word was almost lost.

Theca buried her head into his warm lap. 'Oh Dave, what's to become of us?'

He stroked her soft hair.

'I feel so defenceless,' she said.

'I know, Sis. It's like being cut off, lost at sea. Maybe it's seasickness we're all feeling.' Gently he raised her head. 'I've got to get some sleep,' he said, wanting to be alone. 'I'm going to see Coddy first thing in the morning.'

'Just tell me one thing. Does Pat know all about this?'

He shook his head. 'No one knows.'

'Well, I think you should tell her.' Her eyes glazed reflectively.

He looked at her, looked into his own eyes, at his own features, beautiful on Theca, and he realized just how much he loved his sister and how, before long, he was going to break her heart.

Dave drove home without an escort. He drove carefully because of the booze. The conversation regarding his father's past, his final admission – something he had decided he would never divulge – left him dejected and self-critical. He needed the comfort and familiarity of Patricia, the security of her gentle breasts and the warmth of her breath. Only then, wrapped in her protecting embrace, could he sleep.

Chapter 13

Dave left the Smoke as the dawn ghosted out of the darkness. During his drive north to meet his father-in-law he recognized the places and yet he had that strange feeling of detachment, as though he had seen them before but only in his dreams; his sense of isolation was acute. He thought of Coddy and his father, old men now, broken. The end of an era was drawing in. The men, the legends, were dying out or were shut away, effectively dead. Things were changing; today's villains were international: bankers, politicians, presidents for Chrissake! The day of the odd fire-bombing, the leaning on an occasional shop-keeper, the messing up of a pimp's front teeth, those days had gone. Karen's marriage was not yet a week old and he had spent a long time with Coddy and the family at the reception but they had not discussed business. It was a rule unlikely to be broken that at such times such things would not be mentioned. No matter how pressing the problem it would keep.

Some places seemed to unlock memories; they brought them together like a treasured collection and imbued a sense of familiarity and comfort, even a false, illogical security. For Dave, his father-in-law's manor some way north of Skegness was one such place. He found an easiness there, an intimacy that came from the past, and an acceptance also. In a strange sense he had come to share his wife's roots and he looked upon the place as a second home.

Whenever he approached the manor his thoughts turned to the girl he had married, as she was, the long-limbed pale nymph rising from the water or that fleeting view when she had stood over him in the tiny kitchen. Shadows now, laughing ghosts. His thoughts turned to Sharon and the grief she had caused and the way he had gone back to her time and again, addicted. After a long absence she had contacted him five years earlier and they had been meeting regularly ever since. Sharon Valenti. His perfect fit.

He shook away the thoughts and concentrated on the present. He didn't give much thought to how he would approach his father-in-law. That could be played instinctively. But only God knew what Coddy's reaction would be to the idea of retirement. Dave's gut feeling was that the old man would start World War Three; certainly that would have been the way of the Coddy Hughes of old. He would have marched into Glasgow on his own. And taken it apart. But time was the enemy of passion, of strength too; he had seen it in his own father.

Security had tightened. Two men came out of the brick building and gave his Rover a close examination before recognizing Dave and opening the cast-iron gates. They waved him through and closed the gates immediately behind him. The guards had obviously telephoned the house for Coddy Hughes was on the steps to meet him. He was wearing his neck brace again; he had left it off at the wedding. In faded jeans and blue shirt Coddy looked younger than at the weekend.

As it began to rain, Dave parked in front of the silent house. The vines and creepers that climbed up beyond the ground floor had darkened by saturation; the stiff leaves danced, shot by heavy drops. Dave dashed up the steps to the sheltered porch where Coddy waited, ten yards perhaps, but his lightweight, V-necked sweater had changed to a darker shade by the time he got there.

'Come on in, Dave,' Coddy said in his gravel tone and put a close arm across Dave's shoulder to guide him to the door. The physical contact and the serious expression gave Dave the feeling that Coddy had been primed about the reason for his visit.

'Do you want to brush up?'

'No. I'll have a drink first.'

'Mother is out so we've got an hour.'

Dave relaxed in a leather armchair while Coddy poured some coffee. He carried one across the parquet and handed it to Dave then went back for his own. Eventually he sank into his own chair and raised the footrest. He sighed as the weight was taken from his back. He balanced his stick against the arm and leant back with his drink, toying with the cup, studying Dave out of an amused expression.

'That's a relief,' he said. 'Simply to sit down after standing gives me considerable pleasure. When your body begins to fall to pieces it doesn't take much to please you.' He lifted his coffee. 'I'll drink to your old man,' he said.

'I get the feeling I'm here under false pretences. Which one of us has got the news, Coddy?'

Coddy smiled craftily.

'Tom told me all about his gut last weekend. It was reaching crisis point then. He knew it. For some months he has spent a good deal of his time putting his house in order.'

'I'm not with you.'

'You will be, don't worry. Your father has known for some time how serious his condition is. You don't get so close to death with gut cancer without certain symptoms. You think you have come all this way to tell me that Tom is dying? You think he sent you up here to ask me to retire and hand that Scottish bastard everything I've built up?' Coddy smiled affectionately at his son-in-law. 'Dave, you have a lot to learn about me, and about your father.'

'What are you telling me?'

'We guessed that Mick would make his move as soon as your father went down. That's one of the reasons he held off the hospital so long, to give Tommy a chance to deal or at least to get back safely. As it happened, Tom couldn't hold out long enough. But it ended well. Unfortunately he didn't get the chance to talk to you and once he was hospitalized he couldn't take the chance of being overheard. You're up here to meet Mad Mick and these guys O'Connell and Valenti from Runnymede. We're going to listen to what they've got to say.'

Dave's look was stony. His eyes became slits. 'For fuck's sake! Valenti! He was the guy that caused all the grief before.'

Coddy waved a dismissive hand. 'He's just a voice. He's so old he's probably forgotten. But Mick wasn't open to negotiation unless we had the Yanks here. It was your father's idea.'

Dave felt mildly hurt that his father had chosen to take Coddy into his confidence in preference to the family. Hurt and surprised. He finished his coffee but his eyes betrayed him.

'Family doesn't come into this,' Coddy said as though reading his thoughts. 'Once you're in the picture you will understand what I mean. What I'm going to tell you now goes no further than this room. It will become a burden to you. You can't even discuss it with members of your own family. When your father is dead only you and I will know about it. And sooner or later, when I am dead, you will have to find someone else. Someone on the outside, someone you can trust with your life. And you've got to start looking for that person now. Grooming him. Getting to know him so well that there can never be any doubt in your mind. Maybe someone already springs to mind. Who knows? I don't want to know. No one must ever know who you choose.' Coddy sighed. 'So, it was not about my retirement. I'm too fucking old to retire!'

Coddy's wife arrived home earlier than expected and made a fuss of Dave then fed Coddy his medication and insisted that he took his morning rest. Coddy had given up arguing about such things long ago.

'You'll have to wait a little longer. We'll talk later,' Coddy assured Dave as he went stiffly from the room with his wife right behind him.

Dave showered and changed in time for lunch. They took up the conversation again later, in the drawing-room. Coddy let Dave pour the malt and light the forbidden cigars. He looked comfortable in his slightly raised armchair with his footrest six inches from the floor – lord of his manor. His eyes were fiery and alert, watching Dave's every reaction, the scar between them paler than Dave remembered. His thick bald head, held by the pink brace, barely moved as he smoked his cigar or flicked the ash or lifted the crystal glass to his lips.

'Every organization needs muscle, you know that. Occasionally a job comes along that is so delicate, or maybe dangerous, that members of the family cannot be involved. Neither must they know anything about it for if they knew, not only would it worry them but they might want to get themselves involved. Equally there are times when members of your own organization need minding and sometimes it's best for an outside agency to do this. It saves recognition and so on. Take your sister, for instance. She has a problem handling such things. If she doesn't know she's being watched because she doesn't recognize the men watching her, then there's no problem.'

Dave wondered whether Coddy and therefore his father knew about the Star's affair. Could it be possible? His thoughts raced.

Coddy continued: 'Occasionally, and I can't remember the last time, one of our own people goes off the rails and needs putting right. If we use our own people it leads to tension on our own doorstep, it builds mistrust, insecurity. You know what I mean? At such times an outside firm is required. But the only way you can trust an outside firm is if they work exclusively for you. It is even better if they don't know they are working for you. If only one man, someone perhaps, who owes you his life, someone whom you can trust with yours, if this man is sent to recruit his own muscle, then you are reasonably safe. Your father has such a man who has such a firm. He uses him when it is necessary and when there is no alternative. It's your father's secret weapon. Only one man, the man who put it together, is known to us, and that is Scratch Fox. Sergeant Scratch Fox.'

'Dunkirk,' he nodded. 'I remember you telling me.'

'When Fox got back he was in hospital for about a year. From there it was an institution, shut up with the real mad bastards. Half his brain had been blown away in France and what was left was the evil part. It turned him into the cruellest son of a bitch you're ever likely to meet. A real mental bastard. And one that hates women. When he came back with half his head missing his wife and kids did a runner. Fucked off with some Canadian. Anyway, the end result was this hatred for women. All women. But because your father saved his life, and then later helped him at a time when he was totally helpless, when he was going through the agonies of losing the only things that mattered to him, it produced a loyalty second to none. And this was the man your father chose to run his secret army.'

Dave was shocked; his mouth dropped open in amazement and yet even as Coddy spoke certain things began to fall into place. Answers that had never been good enough were suddenly and clearly understood. The surprise turned into a wry smile.

Coddy went into detail about Fox and the secret army. He described how and when they were used, how they were financed. he coloured in the grey areas of the past, secret wars that had been fought to gain control of gaming and prostitution, opposition that had been taken out or brought under control. Dave heard it all, how it started, how it grew. He heard about the Chinese wars and the South Coast wars. He was given a history lesson about things that happened during his childhood, time that he spent in ignorance, before he knew about any of it. And even though he knew a great deal about the present business most of what Coddy told him was new. Suddenly his father was no longer that intimate friend who had grown older as Dave had grown up but something more than that. They spoke for most of the afternoon and again after dinner.

It was approaching midnight when Coddy's wife Mavis interrupted them. They could see immediately that something was very wrong.

She spoke quickly. 'There's been trouble. It's dreadful. A newsflash!'

Coddy half raised from his chair, his rigid expression draining of colour.

Dave was silent.

'People are dead,' she said, breaking into a sob. There was something else. They could see it in her swelling eyes.

'Come on, old girl,' Coddy said gently. 'What is it?'

Her voice grew fainter. 'It's Ted,' she said.

A muscle in Dave's jaw began to throb. His eyes narrowed fractionally and that veil of anger drew across them like an inner lid.

Chapter 14

Hearing about her brother's torment left Theca emotionally exhausted. After leaving him that evening she had no idea where to go.

Without consciously deciding to see her friend she rang the ornate brass bell on Margaret's door shortly after leaving Dave. She felt wretched. Drink on an empty stomach had caused a sickly sensation, tiredness and despair had done the rest.

In a blue silk dressing gown and without make-up, strands of her long dark hair damp from a recent bath, Margaret Caveille was beautiful but in a completely different way from Theca. Brown eyes were darker still, black almost, by the loss of emphasis that eyeshadow usually provided and her skin radiated an olive glow. She was in her mid-thirties, of part-Latin descent. Her eyes asked impossible questions. Ten years previously they had used the same maternity ward and slept in adjacent beds.

'I didn't know where else to go,' Theca said.

Margaret recognized Theca's distress at once. She put her arm around her and led her into the lounge.

'Come on, sit down. John's in Paris, the kids are in bed, so we've got the room to ourselves.'

'I couldn't face my mother again,' Theca explained. 'Going over it all again and again. I couldn't face Ted. I can't stand the deceit anymore. Not now. I don't want to have to worry about every word I say.'

Margaret had coffee on the boil. She poured another cup and set it down in front of Theca.

'There, I've made it strong,' she said.

Theca tried a smile.

'Now, come on, tell me all about it. I've seen the news, but there weren't any details. Is it bad news?'

Theca nodded. She lifted her drink. The tiny cup rattled on its saucer.

'My father's dying. They say a month but I think that was for Mum's benefit. He looks terrible.'

Margaret hid her surprise.

'Have you seen Lewis? Does he know?'

She knew all about Theca's affair. That had been shared from day one. There was little that women did not tell their friends, they delighted in the intimate detail; they shared each other's happiness and sorrow. Perhaps that was the difference between men and women: women listened, and probably cared.

'I saw him earlier. I couldn't go back. I'd never wrench myself away and Mum's waiting up.'

'What are you going to do?'

'I don't know.' Theca's voice was a whisper.

'What do you want to do?'

A despairing shake of the head and then, 'I want to be with him.'

Margaret waited.

'But I can't, not now.'

'One step at a time. You don't have to make decisions. They'll still be there next week or even next month. You don't have to rush anything. In any case, you're not in any state to decide anything right now. Best wait a while.'

'I'm sorry,' Theca said. 'I shouldn't burden you with all this.'

Margaret smiled softly.

'Of course you should. I'd be hurt if you hadn't come to me.'

'What can I do? I feel so weak. I can't think for myself anymore.'

'The most important thing right now is to get some sleep. Can you stay here?'

'No, Mum's expecting me back.'

'I'll ring her.'

'No,' Theca shook her head. 'She needs me. That's the point, everyone needs me. But I need someone too.'

'You have me,' Margaret said gently. 'And I'm here any time you want me. I can come back with you if you like. I can listen. They can talk to me. It doesn't matter who listens, does it? 'Cos all we're really doing is talking to ourselves.'

Theca glanced up and flicked a stray smile. 'That's a bit profound for this time of night.'

'It's no trouble for me to stay with you for a few days. I'd like to help.'

'No. Suddenly I feel better. Just talking to you has helped. I'll be all right now. Maybe that's what I needed. To talk instead of listen.'

Sensing her friend's resolve and fearful of it Margaret said suddenly, 'Theca, what are you going to do?'

'I'm going home to see Ted.'

'You're going to tell him?'

'Yes.'

'I don't know that it's wise at the moment. Can't you wait? Emotions make things so unclear.'

'I am clear,' Theca said. 'I need to be honest with him. I can't handle my father's death while I'm having to watch every word I say. It all needs to be out in the open, then I can take it from there. Best to get it over with.'

'What of the children?' Margaret asked. 'What if they find out? Losing your dad is going to be bad enough. If they thought that you and Ted were splitting that would destroy them.'

'I'll keep them out of it.'

'Can you be sure that Ted will?'

'Yes,' Theca said. 'I honestly think that Ted won't care!'

It was nearly midnight when Ted parked the car in his drive. He had been over to King's Cross to lean on a couple of dealers who had been late with their monthly. He hated the place. It was a shithouse. Argyle Street was littered with raving skagheads (alkies), the urine-soaked doorways were filled with beggars lying under threadbare blankets and newspapers, the stairwells filled with junkies scoring for Glasgow Rangers, and the dealers with their mouths full of cellophane-wrapped shit made their money as openly as the shivering toms who waved at the passing punters. There wasn't any way down from the Cross. It was rock bottom.

Ted was surprised to see Theca's red mini for she had arranged to stay with Sally. Perhaps one of the kids had been ill. The house was dark and he guessed that she was in bed. He hoped that she was awake to explain the change of plan.

Quietly he closed the front door and headed for the kitchen. Her voice came from the lounge.

'I'm in here, Ted,' she called.

He turned on the light, squinted at the sudden brightness, and saw her in the leather armchair, legs drawn up, drink in hand, not changed for bed. She had been crying. Her eyes were swollen and hurt.

'I need to talk to you,' she said.

He sat down opposite expecting that a sympathetic ear was required, that whatever it was had to do with Tom.

Theca took a deep breath, hardening her purpose, and spoke quietly, 'I'm in love with someone else.'

Suspecting something was nothing like the certain knowledge and Ted was stunned. He knew how serious it was from the sudden tears in Theca's eyes. She sobbed into her hands. He stared at the floor, fixed expression, while the implications flashed at him from all directions. Love, she had said. Not affair, not slept with. Love. There was a difference.

'Who is it?' he asked eventually.

Not moving her hands from her face she shook her head.

'It doesn't matter,' she said. 'Does it matter?'

'I suppose not.' He nodded. 'How long has it been going on?'

'Six months.' She looked up. Beneath her cold brow her wide reddened eyes looked frightened and uncertain.

'What do you want to do?' he asked gently. His voice seemed incredibly controlled. She had expected some show of anger.

'I don't know.'

'Are you leaving me? What about the kids?'

Again she shook her head. The things she wanted to say were blocked in her throat.

'You certainly pick your moments, sweetheart. You're going to break their hearts.'

Her Smith eyes flashed. 'It's not me you're worried about, then? It's the kids!'

'I didn't say that. I guessed there was something going on. I didn't want to believe it. I've been waiting for you to tell me. Every time we've sat down and talked these last weeks I thought you would tell me about it. I've already got used to the idea.'

'Do you want me to go?'

'No,' he said quietly. 'I don't want you to go.'

She wiped her eyes. 'I've got to get back to Mum. She'll be worrying.'

'So what are you going to do?'

'Let's have dinner tomorrow. We need to talk.'

'We talk every day. Talking isn't the problem.'

Her lips trembled again.

'OK, it sounds good,' he said. 'But it will have to be lunch. I've got a meet with the caterers in the morning and I'm with the Scousers tomorrow night.'

She nodded.

Ted thought that sleep that night would be difficult but it came with surprising ease. The following morning he looked in on the children before he left. They were still asleep. Jean arrived at eight and he gave her some cash and told her that he would be back late. Theca would come home early. Jean was happy with this. She was glad to help at such a time. The family had been good to her over many years. He wondered whether Theca had spoken to her about their situation or whether she could sense the oppression and made more of it than Tom's illness.

'Don't worry,' she told him. 'I'll stay until Theca comes, and if she needs to go to the hospital or get back to her mum, then I'll stay over in the spare room.'

He listened to the end of the first act of La Bohème as he motored across to Soho. He parked outside the Kowloon House and for a few moments he sat and watched Chinatown wake up and spit until the last notes faded.

Lo Fok was the charley man. He had spent the sixties in Kowloon when the British troops were there and had spent the evenings of his youth in the Princess cinema just up from the Dairy Farm. He therefore resembled Christopher Lee, albeit a foot shorter, but he walked like John Wayne in *Rio Bravo* and he had cultivated the voice of the Chinese interpretation of Peter Ustinov, but not very well for he used Wayne's inflection and paused before he finished every sentence. 'You want fried . . . rice?'

When he first set up in England he imported his dope through the merchant shipping lines, mostly hidden in the boxes of servicemen returning from a posting. It was common knowledge that few army boxes were ever inspected and with the continuous movement of troops it had been a ready-made supply line. When that supply line eventually broke down he switched his imports to the Scottish islands. It made sense for the Crescent was now having to compete with Latin America as cocaine grew in popularity.

Lo Fok's restaurant was in the city's secretive triangle, just off

Gerrard Street. An odorous little place where the Georgian terraces had been converted into rows of restaurants and cinema clubs and supermarkets. Rubbish filled the gutters and the narrow side alleys. At night, after the punters had gone, some appetites satisfied by fried rice and beef and vegetable in oyster sauce, others satisfied by the performance of naked women, and sometimes men, or the still commonplace smoking of opium, especially by the older men, the rats came out to satisfy themselves on the piles of rotting vegetables and discarded take-aways and the occasional pool of vomit. All the tourists had heard of Soho and were marked by a little excitement at the prospect, but the area had been cleaned up beyond recognition. The punters came to be titillated and thrilled and maybe a little shocked but they never found any of that. Only the locals knew where those places had moved to.

Once before, perhaps, the area had been a refuge filled with surprises, little courts and alleys full of curiosities, sinister maybe but then eroticism always had been, but it was a place that pulsated with family businesses and loyalties and it was real. The girls that paraded and gave the place its reputation were up front and human. And now ... Wolfenden had a lot to answer for. The humanity had been replaced by a pretence, simulated orgasms as superficial as the façades that replaced the Georgian fronts, and sex shows and sex shop windows, and the streets had been filled with drunken louts full of violence at being ripped off – ripped off on Ribena and water, and Schloss Boozenberg, a fizzy drink they called Champagne. Ripped off at live sex shows where the only things likely to move were the cockroaches. The Raymond Revuebar in Rupert Street was the glittering centrepiece but even that was stale, like his magazines: ice-cold minge to look at; split figs without the sweetener. Any local football club offered more on their stag nights, and a bloody sight cheaper. And with half-a-dozen exceptions, once these places had been shut and the police force of the capital returned to basic wages, then the heart of Soho had been desecrated. It had become a memory. The paint was already beginning to peel from the junk dragons and pagodas.

Ted watched a Chinese chef working behind his steamy window in a little glass-fronted booth under flattened duck carcasses and strips of pork hanging from a line of hooks. It was a cheap parlour, frequented more by the local Chinese than by the English chicken curry and fried rice fraternity.

He left the car and sniffed at the sickly air as he crossed to the worn stone steps of the restaurant. He acknowledged the musical greeting from the chef in the window, busily chopping his cold meats, and climbed the stairs two at a time, heading for the second and third floors and the dim staleness of the scuffed red flock wallpaper. The top of the building was in three sections. The largest area contained Lo Fok's side line, a couple of quack acupuncturists. Since the quacks were his wife and mother-in-law he had little option even though it would have been more profitable to extend the restaurant. The third room contained his office.

'Ah, my very good . . . friend. I have waited for . . . you.' His thin hands waved the air in front of him. 'You want . . . breakfast?'

Ted shook his head. He lit a cigarette while Lo Fok removed his apron.

'How is your father-in-law's . . . illness?' he asked. Eyes became slits over shining black pearls of curiosity.

'He's poorly but it's not as bad as we first thought.'

Lo Fok's bony hand twirled one side of his weak moustache; the quizzical black pearls never left Ted's face. They did not believe him.

'I hear about the . . . hit. Everyone hears it. Too much worry. Tommy . . .?'

'He's all right. They missed!'

Lo wrinkled his nose. 'Amateurs then.'

'That's what we figured.'

Satisfied Lo turned to the business. 'I have what you . . . want. Six altogether.'

'You had them checked out?'

Lo put on an exaggerated expression of hurt. He muttered in Cantonese then said, 'Of course. No AIDS. No clap. No nothing.'

Ted waved Lo's show aside. 'Chop suey?' he asked. It was number thirteen on the menu. It was the term for thirteen-year-olds. Just a term, for it covered youngsters of any age.

'Yes, yes. All that you ask for. Never before. With mother. What time you want? Need sedating, of course.'

'Seven. No earlier. We'll leave the docks at seven. I don't want them hanging around. What about the others?'

'They'll arrive whenever you require. Earlier, maybe, eh? Number seventy I will hold with thirteen.' Number seventy was listed under the beverage section on the menu. Coke.

Ted noticed the table next to the desk, the scales and test tubes, the wad of cellophane envelopes and the tissues to keep off the dabs. He sniffed the air for ammonia.

'It washes back at over ninety per cent,' Lo Fok said nervously. 'Only the best.'

'Don't give me that shit!' Ted snorted. 'Where do you think I was born? I don't give a fuck how much menatol you use as long as the Scousers are happy.'

Lo nodded like a half-starved pigeon let loose in a pet shop. He moved back on to safer ground: 'You want to see pictures? I have . . . pictures.'

He took an envelope from the top of a battered green four-drawer and drew out some snapshots. Ted took out a handkerchief to handle them. Photographs could photograph your fingerprints. He leafed through them. They were poor quality polaroids. Even so, he saw that the four women were handsome, a combination of hair colours, all pretty, all slim, all in their late teens or early twenties, a Chinese girl was particularly eye-catching. Lo noticed Ted's interest.

'You'd like to give her . . . one? Chinese different,' he sniggered.

Ted grunted. The Scousers would not complain. The youngster was pictured with her mother. She was a skinny girl with wisps of hair, slight breasts, prominent pubis, legs held apart; she had the body of a ten-year-old but her face was older. There was a striking likeness between mother and daughter but about twenty years difference. He studied the mother for a moment. She was in good nick herself. Naked, her arm outstretched, one hand parting her daughter's vulva. Ted felt nothing, neither compassion nor disgust. He did not wonder how a mother could do such a thing. It was money. That simple. Perhaps for coke or crack but more likely heroin. He searched for the tracks but if they were there they were well hidden. He felt nothing. He had seen dozens of them and not one had ever interested him. Ted knew that it was only recently that the Chinese had used European girls. Before that youngsters from the age of six were rounded up in the Far East and sent to visit non-existent relatives in the UK. They came for two or three months at a time and were installed in one of a number of houses across London. It was known as the Bird's Nest Run and had been a hugely profitable arm of the Chinese underworld.

He handed back the photographs. 'Don't put her to sleep. That happened last year.'

'Leave everything to . . . me!'

Ted nodded. He turned to leave but sensed that Lo Fok had something else to say. 'What is it?'

Lo lifted his hands. 'It is nothing. Only . . .'

'You going to tell me or shall I guess?'

'It is the overheads.'

Ted grinned but Lo took a step backwards. Behind the laughing monkey . . .

Another babble of Cantonese then: 'It was such short notice. No time . . .'

Ted waited. The grin was still there but the eyes were dangerous. He had lived with the Smiths too long.

Lo turned away, not wanting to look at the threat. 'I don't know what I can do. I will lose money.' He turned back. The grin had gone and Lo cowered.

'What do you want, Lo?'

'If I can use the young one again . . .' He shrugged. 'Last time it was impossible. Too much dick. Liverpool. Animals!' He began to stutter.

'OK,' Ted nodded and smiled gently. 'You'll get a slice of it. I'll have a word with the accounts department.'

The blood came seeping back to Lo's face. He hurried around to open the door. 'Good. Good. Nothing will go wrong. I'll make personally . . . sure. Everything will be as last . . . time. Thank you. Thank . . . you!'

Ted next visited the restaurant that was preparing the buffet and tied up the delivery times. He wanted the chef and waiters off the boat before she sailed. His own crew would do the necessary. From there he went directly to The Barge.

Chapter 15

The Barge glinted like a jewel against the greys of concrete and water. She was a 136-feet converted US minesweeper bought from the family of a well-known film star who had died a few years previously. In her build she was old-fashioned, carvel built of teak and oak and remodelled to Tom's instructions by Trough Brothers. She had been converted to a pleasure cruiser in 1961 and the actor had made huge alterations. Tom, in turn, had taken out the American ostentation and produced a British Queen. In addition to the pilot house on the top deck, it had both a master stateroom and a guest stateroom each with its own bathroom, a 60-feet after-deck for relaxing and a dining-room that seated ten in comfort. On the main deck were two further staterooms, some lesser bedrooms and a large salon. In the murky daylight, under the canopy of grey drizzle, she looked a picture, but when the night fell and the lights reflected on her polish she became something exotic. Berthed next to the warships and run down pleasure steamers she was the one that immediately caught the eye. She was a symbol and Tom was immensely proud of her. He had personally supervised the workmanship and the involvement in design and decor had been, if not an obsession, then a delight. The Barge was not opened as a nightclub; it was used by the family, of course but, more importantly, for private parties to entertain the people whose business dealings were of interest to the family. Politicians and councillors and architects used it. And the police used it more than most. Extra cleaning staff were always employed after the police had used it. And for six months of the year, Tom chartered it, together with its crew.

The captain, Gavin Weerasirie, wore a nautical peaked cap and dark blue jacket and had four crew members under him including an engineer, a cook and a steward. Weerasirie, the three men and one woman, were all loyal to Tom. Two of them were always on board to look after the stateroom with its leather and Persians and the original paintings.

Ted recognized Jimmy Jones' car as he went up the gangplank and found him in the office.

'Hello Ted,' Jimmy said, trying to judge Ted's mood. Every meeting held a question mark. Had Ted discovered the Star's affair? Since one of his jobs was to keep an eye on the family, Jimmy had known about it from the start.

'All right, Jimmy,' Ted said.

Jimmy decided that he hadn't. 'Yeah, things will go like clockwork.'

'Have you heard from Dave?'

'Not yet.'

Ted sighed. 'Do you think it's possible that the old man knows about chop suey?' he asked thoughtfully.

Jimmy Jones raised his dark eyebrows. 'Tom? No chance. That's why he asked Tommy to help out. Slags is one thing but kids is another. You know the boss and kids. He adores them. Nothing makes him angrier than to see kids hurt. He'd go fuckin' apeshit if he found out.' Jimmy grunted. 'Things aren't black and white anymore. Would the Scousers come down here unless Vic brought 'em? And he only comes for one reason. No questions asked. No chance of his old lady finding out. All the mess taken care of.'

'What about Tommy?' Ted said.

'Dave said to tell him there's been a change of plan. Get him back to The Tower before we sail. Tell him to keep an eye on his mother. Anything.'

Ted nodded but Jimmy could see that he was unhappy.

'It's not gettin' to you, is it?'

'Fuck no. It's business. But things are getting out of hand. I don't like keeping things from the old man, or from Tommy either. They should know what we're into.'

Jimmy's eyes hardened slightly. There was a hidden, unintentional threat in Ted's concern. Dave had been right. Before long Theca's affair was going to blow and how Ted would take that was anybody's guess. And if the old man learned about the extras put on for the Scousers, then Dave was going to be embarrassed to say the least. The possibility was out of the question. And Tommy was too young, too naïve, to understand. He still needed shielding. When Dave got back from seeing Coddy he would have to sort out Theca and Ted and he would have to do it quickly. Jimmy knew that Ted would be devastated by Theca's admission and devastated men act out of character. They get pissed out of the minds, they start mouthing off. The business could not afford to have Ted hurt. Not now. Jimmy would have to sound Dave out as soon as he got back.

'Leave things as they are for now. Talk to Dave when he gets back.'

Ted agreed but his nod did not convince Jimmy. He had a gut feeling that things could go terribly wrong. If only Dave's sister could guess at the consequences of her fling.

'I'll get Tommy off The Barge before we sail,' Ted confirmed. 'You can use Pete Hough to keep the beer flowing on the top deck.'

Jimmy nodded and walked from the office, leaving Ted staring thoughtfully into space.

Tommy arrived a little later and they inspected The Barge together. The band was setting up slowly, methodically, as bands do, whistling through their microphones, finding the note on the keyboard or drum. The family owned them and played them in the various clubs.

'Dickheads,' Ted muttered. 'With the noise they make would it matter if their instruments were out of tune?'

'What's given you the hump, Brov?'

'Well . . . fuck it!'

Tommy peered through one of the portholes. 'Just as well the weather is fine,' he said. 'Remember last year when we had a Force Four?'

Ted grunted. What the Scousers had in mind took place downstairs anyway. It was only their followers and bit players that danced and they knew nothing of what really went on. They brought their own entertainment anyway, secretaries and girlfriends, and boyfriends, anyone they wanted to impress. The Barge and the surroundings generally did that.

They checked the salon where long tables had been arranged to hold the buffet then went back to the office where Jimmy Jones and Peter Hough were waiting.

'Don't forget to take down the oil paints,' Ted told Jimmy. 'Put up the rubbish.'

'Even those copies cost a fortune,' Tommy said.

'On my list,' Jimmy said.

Tommy accepted that he would not be sailing without comment. He guessed that Dave was concerned about his mother and wanted one of them close to hand. Just in case.

'I'm having lunch with Theca,' Ted told him. 'Then she's going to the hospital with Sally. I'll be back here about six. You can take off then. That OK?'

Tommy agreed.

'Scousers will start turning up then, in any case. They'll want to wash and change.'

'And the rest,' Tommy grinned.

'Will you give Pete a lift into town?' Jimmy said.

Ted nodded and glanced at Hough. 'Problems?'

'Nothin' I can't handle,' Hough said. 'Bit of a barny with Denise before I left. I just want to check her.'

Ted shrugged and said, 'Fuckin' women! They're all the fuckin' same!'

Jimmy Jones looked across slightly puzzled.

In the car Ted tried to lift Peter Hough's gloom.

'Don't worry about it. Things will work out.' He grunted at the irony. 'It's good to have you back in the company.'

'I'm glad to be back. I didn't think Dave would have it. He ain't normally into second bites, is he?'

'Dave's all right. How did it all start? You leaving, I mean?'

'Fuck knows. My fault. You know how it is? You can't help yourself.'

'Go on?'

'Dippin'. I been thievin' all my life. I was moved from St Albans to Sparrow Herne in Bushey 'cos of it. Can't get it out of my system, see? 'Till now, that is. It's like a drug. When I was seventeen I was in a boy's hostel in Hounslow. That's where I got involved for real. Two of the lads there went out every night. A middle-aged geezer came in once a week to collect the gear. I remember the first job with one of the lads who showed me the ropes. A milkman's house on a Thursday night. They're not suppose to keep their collections at home, for insurance reasons, but they all do. Leave it all over the fucking mantel. All stacked up neat. There was even a fucking note tellin' you how much was there. We smashed the kitchen window, the fucking key was left on the inside of the back door, what, every burglar's dream, and two minutes later we were leggin' it with three hundred nicker.'

'But you were nicked?'

'Yeah. Grassed up. Three months in Nottingham. Young Offenders' Centre. The DC was run like an army camp but it made no difference. As soon as I came out I was at it again. Couldn't help it. Breaking glass, jam all over a bit of cloth, plumber's plunger, glass cutters, even knockin' out the putty and takin' out the whole window. Brilliant. Broad daylight, windy nights, end of terraces, detached. Keep your eye open for built-in porches and sunhouses – places that muffle the sounds of breaking glass. Know what I mean?'

Ted nodded. 'You still fucked it?'

'Yeah. Everyone does, sooner or later. I done the Scrubs. I can still smell that fucking place even now. Shit and sweat. Shower once a week, food you can't eat. Every bit of taste steamed out of it.'

Ted nodded. 'I heard it was a shithouse.'

'In Pentonville it was fucking mice and cockroaches. The place was full of tramps and fucking weirdos who wanted a bed during the bad weather. In Wandsworth it was dope. I got an extra six months there for havin' a nonce with a six-inch nail. We used to spill bleach on to the nonces and terrorists, sprinkle Ajax into their food without them knowing. Fucking laugh that was. In High Point it was dope again. Parcels were thrown over the fence. All the screws were bent as arseholes. Shit that was confiscated was resold by the screws. You wouldn't fucking believe it.'

'I fuckin' would!' Ted said.

Ted dropped him off and motored across to Covent Garden for lunch with Theca. He parked under a giant hoarding that had gone up to advertise a performance of *Tosca* and he made a mental note of the time, hoping to catch it.

He anticipated a heavy discussion filled with recriminations and was surprised that it developed into something else. It was almost make-believe, a light-headed time. They purposely steered the conversation away from all things important and threatening. They knew fully well that the subjects would be addressed sooner or later but now was not the time. The lunch was boozy and enjoyable; the moment, suddenly free from reality, was a necessary respite for them both.

'Look at this! They've turned it into a Cockney kindergarten,' he said.

The garden had gone, moved west; that little surprise in the middle of all the brick and concrete had been stolen by the dubious authorities.

'Coloured brick and cobble. Covent Garden was a landmark, for God's sake. An institution! Now look at it. Superficial junk to rip off the tourist!'

Theca looked at him slightly amused at his outburst. It had been a long time since she had seen him passionate about anything.

'Anyone would think your name was Prince Charles,' she laughed.

'I tell you, sweetheart,' he went on, 'these people need a little slap for doing this.'

'I was thinking this morning,' she said. 'Reminiscing. I suppose you do when you're thinking of giving it all up.'

He nodded. 'Me too.'

'You were working at Somermedes – Green Park. That's where I met you. I remember you asking Dad for his permission and him saying "I'll think about it".' She sighed. 'It seems such a long time ago.'

'It was. Things change. We change. For fuck's sake: look how Covent Garden's changed!'

With lunch finished, in his heart there remained a glimmer of hope for the family and his future with Theca, but in his head there stayed an anger and a mild, fleeting thought about the authorities that had the power to damage the city.

Soon after Tommy left The Barge, just before seven, the Scousers began to pull up in their shining cars. Ted watched them swagger aboard.

'Why those bastards walk so tall I'll never know,' he said to Jimmy Jones.

'It's the city. The football. The Beatles. Cilla.'

'It's a shithouse, my son. It always was.'

They staggered up the gangway, wide alcoholic grins on flushed faces, hands groping the hard girls who held them up.

Ted turned to Jimmy Jones. 'Where were you anyway? I've been waiting an hour. And where's Houghie?'

'Fuck knows,' Jimmy grunted. 'His missus has done a bunk, or something. Left the kid. He's trying to sort it.'

Ted was thoughtful for a moment. He didn't trust sudden changes of plan.

'Denise pissed off? Left the kid?'

'Yeah, that's what he said.'

'That don't seem very likely. Not from what I remember about Denise. She dotes on that kid.'

'We'll sort it out later,' Jimmy said non-committally.

Vic Hannington had red open-pored skin flared by booze. His eyes, small, round and deep set in a pudgy face were glazed black saucers. He held on to his steel rimmed bins as he looked around. His expensive grey, handmade suit was thrown over his short stocky body, yet seemed too slack for him, bunched at his thickened waist so that the slacks flapped at his side; even the jacket fell forward as if there were heavy weights in each pocket. But he was happy with anticipation. As he stepped unsteadily on to the deck there was a confidence about him or a booze-induced feeling that he couldn't give a fuck.

His history was known to Ted; there was far more than the loud-mouthed piss artist picture he tried to paint. To control the Scousers needed a firm hand. Thirty years ago, when Hannington was twenty, a police dog had growled at him outside Anfield. He had returned ten minutes later with a 12-bore and, in front of a white-faced copper, had blown the dog's head off. That was the story. It had made the papers so there was an element of truth about it. Hannington was still a mad bastard, but the madness was now controlled. Perhaps that is what age and marriage to a Liverpool lass had done to the man.

A thick rubbery mouth widened to the width of his face. His arms spread to embrace Ted in a false show of affection. There was nothing between them that was not business.

'Vic,' Ted said, fixing his smile on the give-away black bits of his eyes. The hug continued.

'Teddy, sunshine, it's good to be here,' he said loudly and put his dark glasses back on to save his brain from exploding. He had snorted his way down from Merseyside and the light was destroying his brain cells. Hannington let Ted go and stood aside while his entourage piled on to the deck. He patted the arse of a woman who wriggled by in silver high heels.

'Dirty cow's been gobbling me all the way down here,' he chuckled. 'Talk about a fuckin' turkey. My dick feels like it's been hoovered up!'

The women's fashions were ten years' old and their make-up even older. They were already smashed; the party had started in the back seats. The drivers, smart men in dark suits, all of them Ian Rush clones, watched from the wharf where they had lined up their cars in neat lines.

Pawing their women, eager to get on with it, the couples headed for their allotted cabins. The few single men left struggled to the bar below. The evening was a ritual. Clockwork.

Ted moved back to Jimmy Jones. 'That gives us half an hour free,' he muttered. 'It'll take them that long to get out of their trousers.'

He saw Lo Fok's van pull up. His girls had arrived earlier and were tarting themselves up in one of the spare cabins.

'Here's Fok,' he said absently, momentarily checking the wharf for any strange vehicles: post-office vans, council workers, that sort of thing.

'That's my bag,' Jimmy Jones said and started toward the gangway. Ted checked his watch, spent a few minutes with Weerasirie then went to the office and the adjoining quarters. It was all in hand now. He would, from time to time throughout the evening, make the odd appearance but, come dawn, the Scousers would not remember whether they had seen him or not.

Traitor's Gate slipped by as Jimmy Jones walked into the office and looked through the open door to the private quarters where Ted rested on the sofa. His legs were drawn up on to the glass-topped coffee table. A bottle of Teachers lay in his lap, the golden liquid inside swinging gently from one end to the other. The liquid in the glass held loosely in his hand, moved in unison. Wall lights set in the oak panelling sparkled in the liquid in the glass and in the bottle. In his repose Ted's mouth hung open and his breath rattled a little. Jimmy Jones smiled gently and his craggy features softened. He removed the loose glass and placed it quietly on the coffee table then turned down the lighting to barely a glow. In the office he opened the horizontal slats of a long blind that concealed a two-way to the master stateroom and leant closer for a better view.

Mother and daughter were in there. Fok had laid out his instructions to the letter. The girl was doped, drooping, a slight, fragile figure in the centre of the master bed. Her wrists were tied by loose cord that looped over each corner of the bed. She had some freedom but no escape. The older woman sat beside her, stroking her hair, reassuring. She was undressed down to her briefs. Her daughter was naked. There was no sign of Hannington.

Jimmy Jones saw nothing but the girl and he felt anger clawing up his gut. He saw the white soles of two small feet, bony knees held almost together, long thin legs, a raised pubis barely touched with hair, a flat trembling belly, the outline of ribs and the protuberance of small breasts with the soft tips hardly defined. She lay motionless on the wide bed, her neck and shoulders propped up on a high pillow. Her mother, kneeling beside her, used one hand to rub oil between the youngster's legs; the other was hidden by the girl's curls as she stroked and caressed.

Jimmy Jones grunted to himself, 'There ain't no way that slag is her mother!' overlooking the remarkable likeness.

'That is her mother,' Ted said from just behind him. Jimmy had not heard his approach and was visibly shaken. Ted swallowed half his drink and leant forward over Jimmy's shoulder. 'What's happening?'

Vic Hannington marched into the room. He wore an open bath robe and his semi-erect penis dangled out like a kozzer's truncheon.

'Get the state of that bastard!' Jimmy whispered as though he might be overheard. 'Look at his minces.' Jimmy nodded reflectively. 'He could turn out the light, I suppose, but then he wouldn't be able to see the damage he was causin' and that would take away the whole point of it!'

Hannington was barking orders, slapping a small bamboo cane he carried into the palm of his hand. The youngster was oblivious to it all, just stared out of wide slipping eyes, but the mother jumped. Hannington looked enormous beside the two of them, the fat on his sagging chest and belly concealed by a mat of greying hair. The older woman half stood up to greet him but he lashed out with his fist, splitting her jaw, and even as she fell back on to the bed her blood splattered the cream cover. Hannington held her face down while he grabbed at her flimsy pants. For a moment her behind was lifted up until the nylon gave and she fell back over the end of the bed. Her knees barely touched the floor. He used the cane, drawing a welt with every swipe. And like an old-fashioned pump, each swish of the cane jacked up his penis. He left the older woman crying. They could not see her face, pressed as it was into the bed, but they saw her entire body shaking as her knees sagged to the floor. Hannington crawled on to the bed, between the girl's skinny legs. He moved his hands beneath her to lift her like a rag doll.

Jimmy Jones turned away and said, 'I can't stand any more of this shit! That bastard needs puttin' down!'

Ted closed the blinds and shrugged weakly. He waited until Jimmy had gone then returned to the other room. He poured himself another drink and flipped the play on the stack. The advertisement in Covent Garden came to mind and he selected a disc. *Tosca* filled the room. He turned up the volume and lay back on the sofa finding his earlier position. The music washed over him. His expression was fixed, tired, almost resigned. He might have been considering the state of his marriage, or puzzling over the accounts; he might have been thinking about the youngster next door and the cries he thought he could hear above the intoxicating music.

Chapter 16

The explosions lifted The Barge almost clear of the water and punched a forty foot long gash into her belly. One man, throwing up over the gunwale, somersaulted off. There were three explosions, remote controlled, instantaneous and, even as she settled back, she was rolling. They were not deafening explosions, more of a loud roar that seemed to rush down the corridors and companionways. Observers from the bank would certainly have heard them and seen the bow lift and roll slightly and glimpsed the gaping hole that settled back below the water line. The black gash would have been visible in the dark because of the red glow and the lances of orange flame that hissed up above the water. On the after-deck the crowd began to panic and shout and scream. The roll had caused the deck to dip and people slipped as they fought to reach the raised starboard. Bow and port were down. The black water crept over the portside railings. A few people jumped and began to swim towards the bank.

Ted thought that thunder was clapping around his ears. He was pitched off the sofa and thrown against the cabin wall. Even as he regained his feet and felt the angle of the floor he knew that The Barge was going under. He reached the door as the cabin rolled. He hauled himself through even as the cabin slipped further. Smoke poured out of the corridor and the stairwell. Above the increasing roar he heard the screams and shouts from the salon below. He peered down the well through the smoke that hissed upward as if it were a chimney and saw the teak deck planks bowing and lifting. The boat shuddered. A surge of water rushed through the corridor and the well became a cauldron. Ted made for the pilot house door and was all but carried through it by the rushing water. Only starboard was still above water. He clung to the railings, waist deep, legs carried almost horizontally by the strong current. The Barge turned slowly on to her side. Most of the people from the upper deck were in the water, clinging to the wreckage and splashing to the banks. On the banks a crowd had mustered. People waded in to help others to the shore. Small dinghies and row-boats moved out to the sinking hull. Jimmy Jones surfaced clinging to Vic Hannington.

'Where is she, you bastard?'

Hannington's naked shoulders caught the light and looked white in the swirling waters. The rubbery mouth was not smiling but there was a grin about it. Under the water Jimmy Jones used his switchblade. He tugged upward into Hannington's gut. The fat man's grin turned to a grimace. He growled and rose out of the water. For a moment he was suspended above Jimmy, hands on his shoulders. Jimmy laughed. His hands were still on the knife, above the water now, slicing into Hannington's ribcage. Hannington embraced him and his weight carried them both under.

The Barge rolled further and began to slide. Her stern was clear, the topside of her massive rudder and propeller appeared. From the hawsehole a jet of steam shot into the air as the bulkhead fractured. For the first time Ted was aware of the cold water. His hands were numb around the rail. He felt as though he was being controlled by another force, that he had no choice of his own. He let go of the railing and slipped back toward the pilot house door. As the water rose he forced a deep breath and ducked under. The first thing he noticed was the silence. Silence except for the clanking of the hull. He kicked forward from the doorframe and swam down to the stateroom, using the fixed partition of the wall for purchase. Incredibly the lights still shone and threw a ghostly green illumination into the water. The water itself was like a soup, full of specks that caught the dim glow. His visibility was down to about two yards but it was sufficient. He dived almost vertically through the narrow width of the master stateroom. The pressure on his ears was almost unbearable. The light became brighter.

The girl was suspended on the loose cords, her body half turned toward him, held from rising by her arms, her hair like a sea anemone curling about her face. The bed was fixed to the floor and was therefore at an angle. It framed the girl like a giant picture. As he approached he heard the music. *Tosca* was etched into his head, perhaps into this tomb.

He felt his breath running out. Even as he struggled to unfasten the girl's wrists he thought of his children and he saw them in the dead face and spindle limbs of the youngster. His body was numb, giving up, his lungs at bursting point as he pulled the girl through the stateroom. He noticed the lights dimming and wondered fleetingly whether it was his consciousness. The opera had played out its last tragic note.

Above the stern swung further up before sliding and disappearing. A life-raft, still tied to the hull, bobbed on the surface for a moment before being swallowed like a fisherman's float. Floating wreckage was all that was left; a few people still thrashed the water; a group of small boats marked the grave. On the banks the police-cars and ambulances and fire-engines wailed and flashed blue and orange and searchlights came on one by one. The lights shone on the wreckage and on the dirty smear of grey smoke against the midnight blue.

Chapter 17

The Chinatown wars resulted from the scramble to fill the vacuum left when two of the major London gangs, one from each side of the river, were locked up in the late-sixties.

With only minor interruptions, the Chinese community in Britain had been quietly going about their business, paying their local dues certainly, but filtering larger payments through Gerrard Street to their masters in Hong Kong. Fuelled by suggestion from these masters to fill the gap left by the gangs and expand their interests, especially in heroin and prostitution, the Chinese gangs in London tried for complete independence. Naturally the smaller London villains were opposed to losing their rake-off from the eating houses and they sent in some unsophisticated muscle to deal with the problem. The masters sent in skilled assassins to counter the threat and two local figures, Reynolds from the West End and Hipkiss from the south, were hacked to death on their own doorsteps. Cleverly the Chinese played off one local gang against another, spreading the rumour that each gang was making separate deals. More killings followed with the small gangs having a go at each other. Public houses were wrecked by gunfire. Before long it became apparent that the Chinese had got themselves a leader and, from the loyalty and fear that the man generated, it was accepted that he was a master sent from the Far East to take charge. The way that the Chinese fought, their victims mutilated by knives and machete, sent panic across the capital.

The smaller gangs were losing the war, their strengths depleted more by desertion than casualty, their financial reserves exhausted and, more importantly, left empty because the various collection points had broken down with the collectors themselves too frightened to venture into the open.

Tom Smith had kept a low profile. His non-involvement in the war had mostly to do with his lack of interest in Gerrard Street and the fact that he felt no great allegiance to the other gangs. He was dismayed at the way in which the twins' organization had turned on them and his time was now spent in confirming the loyalty of his own people. At this stage, though, the gangs approached Tom Smith and asked him to try to negotiate a peace with the Chinese.

At a meeting held at The Tower, Tom listened to the five gang leaders complaining bitterly at the Chinese tactics, explaining how they had never wanted the war, that they had always been willing to negotiate even though it meant giving up huge areas of profit. The Chinese had been unwilling to talk. They described the present situation where their families were afraid to walk the streets of London, where even their friends were afraid to be seen with them. They told how their arsenals and their finances had all but been wiped out and they pleaded with Tom to intervene. His forces were in tact; the Chinese would listen to him. In return they offered him a cut of their future business. In effect, they were asking him to lead them.

'I make no promises,' he told them. 'But I'll tell you this. I ain't all that keen on seein' the streets of London run from the other side of the world. I make no promises, but you all know me. I'll see what can be done.'

The five men left The Tower reasonably confident in their new ally. Any reservations were put aside in a situation that left them few options.

Against the advice of the few men that Tom Smith held dear he had stuck to his guns and distanced himself and his organization from the warring gangs. He had gone out of his way to make it known that he wasn't interested and had no plans to expand. Others, including his son Dave, had argued that if the Chinese were allowed to win the war they would be in a strong position to threaten the Smiths' own interests. But Tom was adamant and ordered his people to keep away from the trouble. At the same time, quietly, unobtrusively, he increased his own muscle. His payments for information and influence were more than doubled. Long before his meeting with the gang leaders he already had a shrewd estimate of the strengths and weaknesses of the various participants. Although the Chinese leader's identity remained a mystery, Tom Smith was not unduly worried. He knew enough about their set up to have identified already some of the key figures.

Dave was young and eager to make his mark. He was not yet ready to lead his own men and, although there were a few that worked for him, their loyalty was first and foremost to his father. This was a source of frustration for Dave. Patience had never been his strong point. He had sat listening throughout the meeting but once the others had gone he turned to his father.

'Pop, let me handle this one,' he said earnestly, almost pleading.

'To do what?' His father asked and smiled. 'The other day I heard a Chinese proverb, about golf. Even if you hit your ball three hundred yards and straight down the middle it will not improve your game if you're aiming at the wrong flag!'

'What's that supposed to mean?'

'It means that before you go in you've got to know where you're going. What are you going to do, eh? Take out every slant-eyed geezer in London?' He regarded his son with affection. 'Don't worry, my son, things will work out.'

Dave was surprised by his father's attitude.

His father smiled and told him, 'Something could happen that would make our further involvement unnecessary. Always remember that when you're thinking of rushing in. And one other thing to remember is that when you've got a point to make, make it with such a noise that no one will ever forget it!'

Few people knew when it was that Sek Hoi first arrived; he had been seen in most of the restaurants in Soho long before his credentials swept like a cold wind through the Chinese community. He was an unassuming seventy year old man with a bent back and short legs that carried him with the typical Chinese gait. His face was criss-crossed with lines and strands of white hair fell on either side of his mouth; a mouth that would open to reveal a line of gold teeth. Each morning at seven-thirty he arrived from Leicester Square underground station and made his slow way around to Gerrard Street. He would stop and talk to a few colleagues standing on the narrow pavements before their grocery shops and restaurants; he might stand to scrutinize the posters advertising the latest crop of Hong-Kong-produced films that were showing in the local clubs and then, promptly at eight, he would enter his son's restaurant that was situated in one of the small alleys just off Gerrard Street.

His son, his son's wife and his nephew were his only family in this cold wet country and each morning he looked forward to seeing them again. He didn't sleep well and the nights were long. They, particularly his son's pretty little wife who had come from Peking and spoke only Mandarin, made an absolute fuss of him and made him wish that he was forty years younger. They were his only comfort in the months that he'd been here. He had left behind two other sons and their families and was impatient to get back to them.

On this particular morning his son wasn't at the door to greet him and he entered the silent restaurant feeling slightly offended. His nephew had started to hang the cold meats. The flattened ducks and strips of pork hung from hooks in the front window. In the dimness of the restaurant he saw the ivory Mah Jong bricks scattered across the threadbare carpet between the tables and chairs and he wondered what had happened. He was considering what degree of anger he should show toward his son and nephew as he made his way to the back of the restaurant. As he neared the kitchen the air grew heavy and damp and held in it the sweet aroma of cooking meat.

He had taken three paces into the kitchen before his old eyes grew accustomed to the bright lights and then he was stopped in his tracks, his mind stunned by the scene before him. First he saw his nephew hanging on a meathook. Blood dripped from his flip-flops and splashed into a pool beneath him. Hardly daring to look further, his neck rigid, the old man's gaze shifted to the torso on the work surface. It might have been his son but since the head was missing it was at that moment just a guess. The deep fat fryer contained the body of his son's wife. She was sitting in it, waist deep, naked except for the batter that she had been rolled in. Her legs dangled over the side. The overheated fat bubbled and smoked. The batter had crisped and given her a golden corset and her small breasts projected over it.

His cry was not a scream but more of a long moan as though it was his very life that was being sucked out of him. The scream came from outside the restaurant. It came to him with such piercing clarity that it pulled him back from the horror, back through the restaurant, stumbling over the chairs, spewing a trail of vomit across the threadbare carpet. At the door he saw that three people had gathered at the window. A woman was screaming, being held up by the two men. One of the men saw Sek Hoi at the door and used his free hand to point to the window. The old man came out into the street and peered through the misty glass at the ranks of hanging meat, at the flattened duck carcasses, at the strips of pork loin and at his son's head. And then his scream was real and no longer the prolonged moan. He screamed and screamed and people ran out from the nearby buildings to see the old man slipping into madness. From that day until the end of his life some said that Sek Hoi never regained his sanity.

No one ever found out who was responsible for the murders but a lot of people thought they knew. The only witness described four men gathered by the restaurant in the early hours. He remembered one in particular because of the scar on his forehead, he said, and because of his size. He was a giant of a man. But since the witness was a wino using the doorway opposite for comfort not many people gave much credit to his description.

Twelve days after the meeting in The Tower the war was over. The local community had threatened to withdraw their payments to the masters in Hong Kong because they were too distant to guarantee their safety from such a merciless enemy. The masters had no alternative but to sue for peace and they agreed to a set of higher percentage payments to the various gangs. In turn, they also stated a peculiar allegiance to the Smiths. There was no such thing as status quo.

Tom Smith entered into an agreement with the Chinese which remained good to this day. The small gangs had few options, since their forces were totally depleted, and since Tom had given them richer pickings from the Chinese trade they elected him their unofficial leader. There had been a vacancy. It had been filled.

Chapter 18

A chair scraped the floor as Tom Smith's youngest son drew it towards Ted's hospital bed. He sat on the hard green plastic and leant forward.

'The filth's outside with questions harder than *Mastermind*, know what I mean? There's two nurses and a doctor holdin' 'em on leashes but they'll be here in a minute. You all right?'

'Am I all right? I was blown out of my fuckin' office, swallowed half the Thames, got myself a dislocated shoulder, and you ask if I'm all right! I tell you, Brov, that was as close as I'm ever going to come. I started hearing *Songs of Praise* back there, and it ain't Sunday.'

'It could have been worse, Brov. You were lucky.'

'I wasn't lucky. I was stupid. I put it on the line trying to keep the family out of it.'

'You're part of the family,' Tommy said. 'Weerasirie told me what happened. The girl hasn't turned up yet.'

Ted concealed his surprise that the captain had told Tommy about the girl.

'There was a bastard tide. She'll turn up sooner or later but they'll have a job proving anything.' Ted paused and rubbed his shoulder before asking, 'So what's the final score?'

'Nineteen bodies. Twelve Scousers, seven women. They would have stood more chance if they hadn't been totally legless. Some of them started swimming up river! Jimmy's dead. Vic's dead. That one's a bit dodgy on account of a knife sticking out of his chest. I don't think the filth are going to wear a drownin' on that one. Liverpool is totally wiped out. There's still four missing.'

'Who was it? Do we know yet?'

'Everyone is saying Mad Mick but that doesn't make much sense. Why should he want to take out the Scousers? That sort of stunt is guaranteed to have them line up with us. As it happens they've been wiped out but Mick couldn't have guessed that. If anything they were going to side with Mick.'

Ted agreed. 'It doesn't make much sense. But who else?'

'I'll see Pop first thing. Maybe he'll have some ideas. He'll go loopy about The Barge.'

'No point in telling him about the girl,' Ted said seriously.

'I suppose not,' Tommy said. The veil was in and out of his eyes. 'The girl's mother's dead. Fok has been on the blower already, wanting to bill us. I'd like to know what it's all about.'

'You can ask your brother.'

'I will, Ted. I'll ask you both.'

'Fuck off Tommy! I've swallowed enough crap for one night. I don't need any of it from you.'

'I'm off then, before the filth arrives. They've got Weerasirie and the others but they'll sit tight. The captain was telling them it was the IRA thinking we had a police convention on board.'

Ted grinned. 'Is Peach with them?'

'Yeah, he's heading it up at the moment but the top brass will get involved in this one. The anti-terrorist mob as well. There's no way he'll keep it under wraps. It sounded like the Argies were having a go with Exocets again!'

'Well, it's about time Peach earned his keep. He can keep some of the heat off us for a while at least.'

Tommy stood up to go.

'One other thing, Tommy,' Ted said. 'Find out what happened to Peter Hough. He didn't show. Something about Denise going missing but it rang all sorts of bells. And for Chrissake watch your back. If it's not Mad Mick then there's another mad bastard knocking about who knows his way around explosives – and The Barge! Get a message to Theca for me. Tell her . . . Tell her they're keeping me in overnight. Don't bother coming because I'll be with the filth anyway. I'll see her in the morning.'

'OK Brov,' Tommy said. 'By the way, whatever the girl's about, you did good.'

Ted grunted.

Another grey day dawned; the sky was weeping for the dead. It had rained heavily during the night. A thin sheet of water covered the roads and pavements, the gutters dripped. It was after nine when

Tommy arrived at the hospital and it cost him to get in to see his father and then only for a short time and in the starkly lit bathroom, not in the ward. His father looked tired and fragile, slumped in a wheelchair, the disconnected end to the drip-tube still plastered to his arm but the nose tube had been removed. Below his dressing-gown, blue pyjamas and slippers were bridged by his white bony ankles. His pyjama collar was ruffled over his dressing-gown. A white film of beard matted his chin.

'Gor-blimey, boy, what's been happening out there?'

'Pop, it's good to see you,' Tommy began.

Tom nodded and affection touched his eyes. He smiled. 'Calm down, my son. Come and give your old man the full SP. I'm hearin' some diabolical things.'

Tommy perched on the wall radiator and, with the exception of the girl, he told his father all that he knew. Tom took it all in. His eyes narrowed in disbelief. At the end of it he remained silent, thoughtful, nodding to himself. A tiny muscle on his jaw throbbed. Eventually he said, 'That's what I heard. It's a diabolical liberty, that's what it is.' He nodded some more. 'I'd like to call Dave back but that's out of the question. The boy's got things to do. Anyway, my son, you can handle it. You're big enough now. Deep end, know what I mean? Let Ted handle the law and the financial angle. This is going to cost us a pretty penny. I want you to get over and see Mike Mountford. Get him to put the feelers out. I want to know who's done this to us. I want to know if it's Mick. I'm going to drop a fucking atom bomb on somebody. Maybe Glasgow, maybe not.'

Tommy could not remember seeing his father so pent up. His eyes burned. Part of it was directed at his own inability to lead from the front.

'See Mountford,' he repeated. 'He'll have some ideas. He'll know who's turned my boat into another *Belgrano*.' He sank back in the wheelchair. 'Barry Theroux is going to have to take Jimmy's place for the time being. You can trust him. Get him to see Jimmy's family. Make sure they're all right. They won't be, of course, but get him to do what he can. If you've got the time, then look into Peter Hough's business. Don't do anything yourself. Just check it out, quietly. I want Dave to deal with that one personally, when he gets back.' Tom sighed. 'There might be nothing to it but let's make certain. If Hough's got anything to do with this mess I'll hang him up by his fuckin' foreskin. One last thing, boy. This is going to upset your mother. Look after her. Play things down. No need to worry her more than necessary.'

Tommy hugged his father before leaving. It was more than a gesture of affection, more even than a need for comfort and reassurance. It was the cold embrace of a warrior about to go to war.

'Go on then,' Tom told his youngest son. 'You've got things to do.'

The earth at the back of Mike Mountford's garage was sterile and black. It crossed Tommy's mind as he made his way between a line of second-hand cars that, in a thousand years time, when the garage had gone and assuming that oil was still just about the most important thing to the Western world, some prospector was going to drill a hole here and think he had hit the jackpot.

The garage was dark and dirty; every surface was littered with spare parts and tools and grease. A bench was piled high with invoices and MOTs, tea makings and dirty cups and full ashtrays. A Jaguar stood over the well. To the right of that, in mint condition, a Stag stood with its bonnet up. Light flickered beneath it. A spanner dropped on the concrete floor and a woman cussed. Tommy walked across to the legs he could see protruding from beneath the car. Black leather shoes with thick soles stuck over the end of a duckboard. He touched one of them with his own foot. The overall clad legs stiffened, then, 'Is that you, Mike?'

'I'm looking for Mike,' Tommy said.

The duckboard eased out. Flat on her back on the board, holding the spanner across her chest, she looked up at him. A smudge of grease blacked her forehead and cheek. She looked about seventeen, without a hint of make-up, short brown hair cropped, her body enveloped in the massive boiler-suit. She had left the light beneath the car and in the gloom the shadows caught her features. Her dark brown eyes were deep set above prominent cheekbones.

'Who wants him?' The question was cold.

She saw a man in his early twenties; short curly black hair, steely blue eyes, brown leather jacket, loose white shirt, jeans and expensive shoes. Too stylish for a copper, and the shoes were too expensive, so he was probably a villain. He stood against the garage door with the light behind him and her squint was to increase the detail. He thought the frown, the narrowed eyes, was a look of disapproval.

'My name's Tommy Smith. Mike's a friend.'

'He never mentioned you,' she said. She struggled up from the board and began to wipe her hands on a rag. She was taller than he had first thought, around five seven or eight.

'Does he tell you about all his friends?'

She glanced up at him and again he noticed the coolness, the calculation in her eyes. When she spoke he noticed her lips and his gaze was drawn toward them. They were wide and full and the little V on the top was prominent and covered with a film of fair hair.

'Yes,' she said. 'He tells me about all his friends.' The eyes glinted now; the suspicion had been replaced by humour. Perhaps she had noticed his nervousness and he had become less of a threat.

'He must have forgotten to mention me.'

'I don't think so. The Tommy Smith he talks about is older. He's in hospital. It's not you.' She held the heavy spanner by her side, not letting it go even while she wiped her hands. She moved across to the bench and plugged in a chrome electric kettle.

'That's my old man,' Tommy said.

She glanced across at him and smiled. 'So you're Tommy junior?'

Tommy decided that she was too confident to be seventeen.

'There's a law about employing minors. Does Mike know about it? How old are you anyway?'

Her lips pursed. 'That's none of your business, junior.'

He laughed out loud. 'You're right. Do you think you could tell me where Mike is? I've been to the house but there's no answer.'

'Do you want a cuppa?'

'I want a word with Mike,' he insisted.

'He's not here.'

'You're not the easiest person to talk to, you know that? Any idea where he is?'

She shook her head, smiling now.

'What time is he due back?'

She sighed.

'Pass on that as well. It's not your day, is it? He never came home last night. I haven't seen him since he packed up here yesterday lunchtime. Some guy called for him. It's no big deal. He's done it before. Crawled home two or three days later with his tail between his legs and a hangover between his ears. He's like that. Does things on impulse. Probably met up with a friend and gone on a bender. It's happened before, more than once.'

With these few short words and in these few short moments Tommy was aware of his gut fluttering. He needed to get out.

'Who called for him?'

'What is this? He didn't tell me. A face is a face, right? A big untidy guy. Not up to much.'

'What's that mean?'

'He was driving a Lada. Now, cars I do know.'

'Dark-blue?'

'So what? Nine out of ten of them are.' She put down the spanner. The threat had ceased to exist. 'What's going on?' For the first time there was a little concern in her voice. 'Pop's all right, isn't he?'

'You're family. That figures.' Tommy smiled. 'I'm sure Mike's OK.'

'Why are you looking for him?'

'It isn't about an MOT.'

'He can't help you then.'

'Someone's been playin' battleships with our boat. We were hoping Mike could help us.'

Her eyes widened fractionally. 'That was your boat on the news?'

'Yeah, *was* is right.'

'Pop can't help you then. This is a garage not a boatyard.'

Tommy grunted. 'It needs more than a dry dock. A scrapyard maybe.'

'What happened?' She stirred sugar into the strong tea and pushed a mug toward him.

'Somebody put a bomb on board.'

'I heard that much on the news. I meant who was it? Why should the IRA have a go at your boat?'

'Who said it was the Micks?'

She shrugged. 'They're the only ones throwing bombs around.'

He shook his head. 'No, sweet'eart, I doubt if it was them. They've got no argument with us.'

'Don't call me sweetheart, junior. My name's Jill. You still haven't said what Pop has got to do with it.'

'He's got nothing to do with it. He knows a lot of people, that's all. He might have come across a whisper.'

'Junior, you're pretty low in the IQ stakes.'

'What's that supposed to mean?'

'Well, if Pop picked up a whisper about something like that he would have been on to your dad straightaway. That's what friends are like or didn't you know?'

'I didn't mean before it happened. If something was going down with explosives your old man could probably point a finger. He knows more about that scene than anyone in the Smoke.'

She studied him for a moment. A frown touched her brow. 'That might have been the case once but not now. Why do you suppose he spends half his day knee-deep in engine oil?'

'Just because he's retired doesn't make him less of an expert. And he's all we've got.'

'You haven't got much then. In any case why should he help you? He's finished with all that.'

'That's what friends are for, or didn't you know?'

Tommy did not tell her that when Mike Mountford was first released from Parkhurst it was his father who set him up in the garage business.

'What are you doing now?' she asked. 'I mean, I haven't got a clue where he is.'

'I'll try again later.'

'Well, you could buy me lunch while you waited. A girl's got to eat.'

Tommy smiled. He knew he should have got out before.

'I'll be back in ten minutes,' she said. 'There's a shower in the back. It's the one thing I insisted on when he asked me to help him run this place.'

'I'll wait in the car.'

She regarded the Rover through the open double doors.

'Not bad,' she said. 'I'll drive.'

She changed into faded denim jeans, a white sweater and white sneakers. She had added a touch of lipstick and her short hair was still damp. They said nothing in the car as she drove expertly across to Westminster Bridge. He showed her where to park in The Trading Company's private spaces and she said, 'You'll be clamped or towed,' and was surprised at his response. A smile, almost a resigned sigh as if to say you don't understand and the gentle comment, 'I don't think so.' But she understood, or at least she thought she did, and the thought sent a mild shiver down her back.

There was something about Tommy that she found curious; perhaps his confidence or his lack of self-consciousness. If it was possible, he seemed to be too natural.

He turned to her. 'What I'd like to do, if you've got the time, is to take the boat trip. It will take us 'round to the Dogs and I can get a look at what's left of The Barge. How about it? We'll be back in an hour and then we can eat at Arpino's. That's the best little Italian in town. Do you like spaghetti?'

'I'll settle for that.'

'That's good. We can get a drink on the boat. You are old enough to drink?'

She smiled.

'I told you before, junior, that's none of your business. You didn't set this up just to find out how old I am, did you?'

'Would I do that? Just didn't want trouble with the law. They're hot on under-age drinking.'

'You're safe,' she said. 'As long as you've got some ID on you.'

Playing to the tourists as they lined the quay a semicircle of Sally Anns looked quaintly ridiculous. Across from them a jellied eel and pie and mash stall had set up. A group of Japanese and American tourists weighed down with cameras and foot-long lenses paid for their *War Cry*s and turned up their noses at the overpriced pie.

Tommy barely had time to order drinks before the pleasure steamer set off. They sat in the prow along with the tourists. Jill studied her dark rum and martini mix in the plastic beaker.

'They didn't give me a cherry,' she said.

'They're right out of cherries. I'll get you one another time.'

She glanced up and smiled at the shielded invitation. 'OK,' she said.

He tasted the plastic. 'Not very sophisticated, is it? Not compared with the rest of the world.'

'It's not very anything nowadays,' she said gloomily.

Amplifiers crackled and a taped Cockney voice said: 'The stone on the bridge is self-cleansing'.

The tourists swung their heads from left to right.

'That small yellow building is the former residence of Christopher himself and from there he could look over the river and see the brickies at work. We're approaching the site of the Old Globe where my old mate Bill Shakespeare used to sell ice-creams. What's to say about the world famous Billingsgate except that the local councillors did something that 'Itler's bombers never managed? Here's Traitor's Gate, the ravens, the Bloody Tower, the torture chambers. Gor-blimey! You're seein' it all today!'

The steamer passed under the final bridge and chugged on around the slow bend. The Barge lay on her side, pulled as close to the wall as possible. In the low tide she was only half-submerged. Dozens of people crawled over her. Small boats including two gleaming police launches were tied to her hull. Up above, between a series of cranes that had just been drawn up, the area had been completely cordoned off and the long portacabin mobile incident rooms were already in place. Out of the grey the flashing lights from the vehicles sparkled like blue and gold gems.

Tommy's look turned dark. She saw the worry in his eyes as the extent of the catastrophe suddenly hit him. The news reports on the television showed nothing of the scale; somehow it had been miniaturized. The tourists babbled excitedly and pointed toward the wreckage and clicked off dozens of snapshots.

'As great rivers go it's a poor bastard river,' Tommy said quietly. 'It's got no rapids or waterfalls. Only its history makes it great.'

Unaware that she had done so, Jill had placed her hand on top of his. He turned to look at her and for the first time she saw fear and uncertainty.

Very quietly she said to him, 'You are human then, after all.'

Arpino's Pizzeria stood on the corner opposite Westminster Bridge. It was a small, bustling glass-fronted parlour that held a dozen white and red tables. It had a continental cleanness and diligence about it. The expert service from the pukka Italian waiters matched the food. Frank Arpino and his brother Marc ran it and owned fifty per cent of the place. The Smiths owned the rest. The family were regular customers and had the utmost respect and confidence in the Arpinos. The business partnership had developed into friendship. The Arpinos knew the family intimately and made a great fuss of the grandchildren. If there was ever a problem it came when the bill was settled. The Arpinos wouldn't hear of it but Tom had made it clear that the bills were to be paid. The Arpinos gave in to this and would present the bill but only when Tom made one of his infrequent visits. He would bring the grandchildren during their school holidays and on the Saturday of the boat race and he would make a great fuss of counting out the exact money. No tip.

Jill was mildly surprised by the attention and guessed that it was special before it became totally obvious. The Arpinos wanted to know about his father and about the boat, showing genuine concern. She waited until they were served before she said, 'All right, junior, I'm impressed.'

He toyed with his long glass of lager before meeting her gaze.

'That wasn't the intention.'

'Oh no?' She held his gaze for a moment longer than necessary. 'You're not what I expected at all,' she said.

'What was that?'

'Something else. Something dangerous. Something to stay a mile away from.'

'You read too much. You haven't got to believe everything in the papers.'

'I don't. But I hear people talk about the Smiths. I bet they used to speak about the Krays and the Richardsons in the same way. Quiet. Whispers. Glancing behind them before they spoke the name.'

'You can't blame us for what other people say or think.'

'Where there's smoke and all that. People aren't frightened without cause.'

'Who's frightened? We help out loads of people. They come to us. I'll tell you something, girl. For every hundred favours we dish out we get, maybe, one in return. I'd say that had more to do with giving than taking.'

'You're into protection. Everybody knows that.'

Tommy grinned. 'Protection? If that's true nobody told me. If everybody knows, like you say, why aren't the filth interested? When you get a name you have to be cleaner than clean. That makes sense. Listen, if there was anything dodgy about our affairs the Old Bill would be all over us.'

'You don't have a very high regard for the police?'

He grunted contemptuously. 'Not a lot. I agree that somebody's got to do it, but by definition the job's going to attract some pretty dodgy cases. No one else would want it.'

'I hadn't thought of it like that before.'

'Think about it now. Is it natural to want to control other people, watch them, hunt them down, play the power game?'

'I suppose not.'

'Still, if it wasn't for the police force, the loose screw hospitals would be full to overflowing! Don't get me wrong, though. Not all kozzers are bent bastards. I know a couple who actually know their dads.'

She grinned. A little cat's grin.

'But since the characters have retired or died, Fabian, Capstick, Nipper, the geezers who played by the rules, the force is filled with little grey men and they play as dirty as the villains.'

Her grin settled into a smile.

'Anyway, what do you know about protection?'

'I know it's a dirty word. You're going to tell me differently?'

For a moment he paused to watch a thread of spaghetti disappear between her lips. 'I'll tell you that the owners of the clubs and shops and restaurants got together and actually approached people like the twins and my father. They wanted a guarantee of safety from the small gangs and from the villains that hid behind the filth's uniform. And remember, there were fringe benefits as well. Some of these merchants were always in trouble; they'd be losing their licences every other week.'

'Go on,' she said.

'Well, think about it. If you pay someone who's influential it means that you're free from bother from other villains, from hooligans, from people trying to rip you off. The local filth won't bother you. Or at least, if you are going to get raided you know about it in advance, so you have time to unload any dodgy stock. That sort of guarantee has got to be worth something. Hasn't it?'

She shrugged.

'If the filth did their jobs properly and made the streets safe then you wouldn't have to employ anybody else, would you? Anyway, it's not our bag. We aren't into protection or dodgy goods or anything else. Obviously we help our friends out if they ask, but we don't tout for business. Never have done. You've been listening to the wrong people.'

She was not convinced but her expression indicated that she was not too concerned either. He should have guessed as much. The garage business was as wise as they came. You learned to drive before you could walk, and you learned to con before you could drive. Half of London's villains had something to do with the second-hand motor trade or scrap metal, which invariably meant the same thing.

'So, tell me how it started?'

His blue eyes narrowed fractionally. 'You really want to know?' Hidden in the question was a dare.

'I asked you, didn't I?' She held his gaze.

'The Smoke was about little gangs until a guy named Rafferty came into it. He wanted a cut off everything in sight and he had the muscle to back him up. Before the war my father got to know a guy named Bryant who ran the docks in Folkestone and Dover. He was down there visitin' the Hursts. They were my mum's cousins. Anyway, Bryant was into protection, labour, that sort of thing. When Rafferty began to get nasty, Pop contacted Bryant. He was doing bird at the time but that made no difference. He controlled the channel ports from inside. Bryant sent some muscle to help Pop tidy up Rafferty but only on the understanding that Pop took over this end and paid a divvy. For a while things went well. Then the percentages went up and up. Eventually people were having to pay more than they had been paying to Rafferty. By then Bryant was out and running things from Folkestone. With the help of the Hursts, Pop moved in on Bryant's people.'

'What happened?'

'The story goes that in one night they rounded the lot up, Bryant included, forced them on board a trawler in the Folkestone Harbour, then took them out to a sand-bank and made them get off.'

Jill frowned; her fork remained suspended below her lips.

'What happened then?'

'The sea came in.'

'He left them there?' Her voice was deep, incredulous.

'That's the story.'

She shook her head in disbelief.

'All that happened before I was born.'

'What then?'

'Most of the cash went into property. He put together some major deals out of war damage and turned more and more to his clubs.'

'That it?'

'That's it.'

She was silent for a moment, thoughtful. Eventually she looked up again and said seriously, 'They used to say, in these parts, that the Richardsons hurt people for business and the Krays because they liked it.'

'You're forgetting the Foremans. They hurt people for money!'

She nodded. 'I heard that too. But what do they say about your family?'

'You're going to tell me?'

'They say the Smiths hurt people out of revenge.'

He shrugged. 'Yeah, I've heard that too, but it's crap.'

'Dad knew Reggie before they went down. They met up again inside.'

'What about you?' Tommy asked. 'What happened to your mum? I know Mike isn't with her.'

'She left him when he was inside. I don't blame her for that. He got unlucky but he knew what he was doing and he knew the risks. He put his family at risk and that included me. Anyway, Mum left. She's got a flat in Stepney. She never did meet anyone else. It wasn't like that. They still see each other from time to time and maybe they'll go out to a show or have a meal. But that's all.'

'What made you stay with the old man?'

'I didn't. Not at first. But he couldn't look after himself. He was a mess. And it suited me. In some ways I've always been closer to him.'

'What about brothers and sisters?'

'One of each. My brother's still at school – lives with Mum. My sister married a fireman from up north. Hitchin.' She paused before glancing up. 'Tell me about your family.'

'I thought you knew it all. My old man's dying of cancer. He's got a few days, maybe weeks. Everyone is devastated. It came right out of the blue. He was having trouble with his leg again. We thought it was gout. This has knocked us all for six.'

'What about the other trouble? The Barge?'

'The family owns a few clubs.' Tommy spoke slowly, searching for a reasonable path between the truth and the lie. 'Here and in the Midlands. There's a guy up north who wants to take over clubland and he's trying to do it the old fashioned way. Muscle. He's trying to put us out of business. People don't go to places if they think there's going to be trouble.'

'What are you doing about it?'

'At the moment we're trying to talk to the guy. Hopefully we'll come to some kind of agreement.'

'These conversations are punctuated with bombs, are they?'

'Eh?'

'The Barge? I take it this northern guy had something to do with it? Nineteen people are lying at the bottom of the river and you're sitting here telling me that you're talking. That it's all to do with an old-fashioned take-over. For God's sake, what happens when war breaks out?'

Tommy raised his hands in mock surrender. 'I can't say with any certainty that Mick, that's the jock we're talkin' about, had anything to do with the bomb. For one thing it's not his style. We often let The Barge out to MPs. Local councillors hire it from time to time. The filth use it for their special parties. Last night we held a party to entertain some businessmen from Liverpool. If they were mistaken for any of these others – the councillors, the filth, the politicians – then the whole thing is wide open. It could have been the Micks, like you said before, or the Arabs. Who knows? It might not have had the slightest thing to do with us.'

'But you think it has?'

'Yes, maybe. These terrorist groups generally know what they're into and they've got their act together. The Irish wouldn't go out of their way to upset us. We do business and they've got too much to lose. The Arabs are staying low profile at the moment. No, I think it's personal, but I'm not sure it's Mick.'

'Who then?'

'There's a few of the old gangs still knocking about that might be on a vengeance trip or something. Some of the Costa mob might have paid somebody. Then there's the blackheads from Brixton and the Irish in Tottenham – not the IRA. There's also the South London remnants. They've started to deal in dope again. There's the Yardies, but they're small-time even if they do have big ideas. Take their shooters away and they'd be back punchin' tickets on the underground! But any of these geezers might have decided to move into the bright lights. Who knows? That's why I wanted to talk to your old man. He might have picked up a whisper that now makes sense.'

'Right then,' she said suddenly. 'Let's get back and find out whether he's turned up.'

There was still no sign of Mike Mountford. Tommy told Jill, 'Don't worry. I'll put out the word to find him.'

'Thanks for lunch,' she said. 'I hope things aren't as bad as they seem for your Pop.'

'I'll bell you later.'

'Don't forget the cherries.'

'No,' he grinned. 'I never will.'

Chapter 19

On his way over to The Tower Tommy Smith felt a heady combination of grief and excitement. There remained the heavy weight of sadness which pressed down on his chest and seemed to block his throat but there was a flutter there also and he felt guilty that his thoughts steered towards Jill Mountford instead of dwelling on his father's predicament. But she was there, forcing her way in; the things she said, the little grin, the rueful smile and her eyes on him, sparkling, savouring. And while all this happened his heart was racing faster, other thoughts were pushed aside. Even his father. And now he felt guilty.

Ted was in the office talking to Barry Theroux. Tommy closed the door and without the usual preliminaries he asked, 'Has Pete Hough turned up yet?'

'He came in this morning,' Barry said. He was a short, sallow man. Managing The Tower didn't leave him much time to see the daylight. From the moment he had arrived on the scene there had never been any question regarding his loyalty to the family. Only Jimmy Jones' seniority in the business had held him back from becoming Dave's right-hand man. 'I had a go at him. He knows he let us down.'

'Denise turned up yet?'

'No, she hasn't. He's got one of the neighbours taking care of the nipper. Is there a problem?'

'Yeah,' Tommy said. 'But I don't want it mentioned outside of this room. Pop wants Dave to deal with it personally. I didn't ask why.'

Ted knew why without asking. Dave's affair with Denise before she married Pete Hough was common knowledge.

'What happened?' Ted asked.

'He paid a call to Mike Mountford yesterday. The fireman hasn't surfaced since then. I've got a bad feeling about this. I don't know why Denise has done a bunk. When I talked to her a couple of days ago everything seemed fine. I know she wouldn't leave the kid without good reason. We'll keep a discreet eye on Pete, know what I mean?' He glanced at Ted. 'How did you get on, Brov?'

'It's too early for much but Peach gave me the first reports. It looks pretty sophisticated. The lab sheets won't be available until the end of the week, perhaps the weekend, but the prelims suggest very upmarket. The equivalent of a thousand pounds, remote controlled, three separate units. If one of them failed the other two were enough to sink her. Buttoned from the bank, even a passing car. There's been similar stuff used in Ireland and the Middle East. Most of it comes out of Czechoslovakia. The only thing he's certain of is that whoever's behind it is very well connected. We're not talking small time.'

Tommy nodded thoughtfully. His expression grew grave. Barry Theroux had already heard it a few moments earlier. Hearing it a second time did not make it lighter.

'They've found the other bodies,' Ted continued. 'The girl turned up by the Old Albert. The filth don't know what they're into yet so they're only askin' around the edges. They're certainly not convinced that the girl is a separate issue but with the water being so cold they'll never pin-point exact time of death. Even so, there's two things that worry Peach about her. The first is to do with this genetic business. If they somehow tie Vic in with her and decide to run these tests they'll have proof that she was on board and more to the point, that she was being fucked on board. Let's hope he didn't have time to unload before the bomb went off. Then there's the dope. If they find that half the bodies were doped with the same stuff used on the girl then there's going to be some very awkward questions. That's without Vic's gut feeding the fish between here and Tilbury. Fok has confirmed that his shit was loose. He better be right. If it was still in cellophane then we're in deep water and that isn't a pun. It's way over Peach's head. The top brass are watching his every move. They see it as a golden opportunity to nail us. Now's the time to pull in every favour that we're owed.'

'What about the labs? Have we got anyone in there?'

'No, unfortunately. But they are being cagey as hell anyway. Peach can't even find out who's dealing with it. He's working on it.'

'He better. We pay him enough.' Tommy sighed.

'Well somebody better come up with something,' Barry said. 'I'm getting pissed off with all this. Lookin' over your shoulder, frightened of the shadows. It's not natural. It's enough to make your piles play up!'

Tommy's smile was humourless. 'I know what you mean. We're in a corner, trapped. Sooner or later we've got to go on the offensive, win or lose.' He shook his head. 'We can't just stand back and take all this or we're never going to recover.'

The others looked on, surprised. He was beginning to sound like Dave.

Tommy and Ted turned up at the hospital to find the girls already there.

''Ello, darlin's,' Tom said. His eyes sparkled as the women fussed around him. 'Gawd, I should come in here more often!' Theca squeezed his speckled hand. 'I've been thinking about the grandchildren,' he said, addressing Sally but telling them all. 'I don't want 'em here. I don't want 'em seeing me like this, upsettin' themselves. Make them understand.'

'Of course,' Sally said.

'Now, listen, all of you, there's somethin' I want to say. The children are the future and must be taken care of. Their schoolin' and all that is down to you. Times have changed. It's necessary today for them to have an education. They've never wanted for nothin' and that worries me a bit. I don't want them growin' up thinkin' they don't have to achieve nothin'. Know what I mean? When you struggle for somethin' and you get it, then it's somethin' to be proud of. Now, I don't talk to you about the business but this is different. There might be trouble and because of it we've got to keep a special watch on the kids. Understand, my Star?' He patted his daughter's hand before continuing. 'When they go to school or to play then someone's got to watch over them. I know you don't like it but it's important and necessary. The same goes for you girls. Dave is takin' care of it but he must have your support.'

When Sally, Theca and Pat went out for coffee the boys gave him the news. When he was satisfied that they had covered everything he said, 'Dave will be back in a couple of days. By then things will have cooled down.'

Tommy held on to his mother's hand as the five of them made

their way toward the exit along the wide noisy corridor, barely noticing the faces in the crowd, other people carrying flowers and brown paper bags filled with apples and grapes, strained features, the dealings with illness and life and death.

'OK Mum?' Tommy asked reassuringly.

'I'm all right, Tommy,' Sally said.

'You're a lady.'

'And you're a gentleman, my son.'

At lunch, the day before, Theca had told Ted that she didn't know what she was going to do, that if he agreed, she would not make a decision about their future until after her father's – she did not say death but that is what she meant. She used the words, 'Until the results come through and we know what's happening'. But she meant death.

'Are you going to carry on seeing . . .?' he had asked.

'I'll talk to him, that's all. I'll tell him what I've told you.'

Ted was already resigned to the situation. He would have agreed to anything. His only concern was that the children be kept out of it for the time being.

Since then The Barge had been sunk and the Star had found herself totally confused about her own feelings. She had spent the night worrying about Ted's injuries. Tommy had explained what had happened and, without giving her details of the youngster and the reason Ted went back, he told her that Ted was hurt trying to rescue some others. On the way out of the hospital he caught her glance and recognized an appreciation. It was something he had not seen for a long time. They sat in the car for a while.

'Dad needed the loo,' she said to him. 'I helped him back. His dressing-gown wasn't tied properly and I saw this . . . tube, sticking out of his penis. He saw that I'd noticed and I felt so embarrassed for him. I feel so protective.' The tears welled up. 'I love him so much. He was such a . . . big man!' The last words were uttered in a whisper.

Ted held her hand. He could not say anything. There was nothing to say.

Chapter 20

Coddy Hughes laid on an impressive show of armed strength. From the moment the visitors cleared the main gate and were out of sight of the road his men were very evident. So were the weapons they brandished. It worked two ways, for Coddy had guaranteed the safety of the men attending the private meeting. There would be no trouble, negotiation was not even called for, simply a statement of position. Wars were costly. They resulted in police clampdowns and interruptions to business. Even the parties not directly involved were concerned. And local wars had a nasty habit of spreading.

On the gravel drive before the house the shining cars parked in a semicircle. The drivers and the minders stayed with them. They watched Coddy's men and saw the dogs straining on their leashes. It was some time before they relaxed.

As each car drew to a halt Coddy and Dave were outside to meet their guests. Valenti was the first of the Wops to get out of their car and he turned immediately to help the old man, O'Connell, supporting him by the arm. O'Connell's spine was curved, his thick black overcoat reached down to his ankles. His small cloudy eyes fastened on Coddy. He reached out to shake Coddy's outstretched hand. Standing beside O'Connell, Valenti glared at Dave. His eyes were on fire. This meeting between the two of them had been a long time coming.

'Welcome to Lincolnshire,' Coddy said.

O'Connell's gaze moved towards Dave then back again to Coddy.

'I'm glad to be here. It's very pretty country. Very green.' The old man shifted across to Dave and offered his quivering hand. Dave noticed the long discoloured fingernails, curled over like talons. They dug into his palm as they shook hands.

'David Smith,' O'Connell rasped. His breathing was heavy, drawn between every word. 'I've heard about you,' he said and glanced at Valenti at his side.

Valenti's expression remained rigid. He shook Coddy's hand quickly then walked past Dave to lead O'Connell to the house. Coddy exchanged the briefest of smiles with Dave as he recognized the snub and then followed after them. Dave turned to see O'Connell's driver.

'It's been a long time, kid,' Herman Tartt said.

Dave hid his surprise and nodded. He glanced down at the stick Tartt leaned heavily on.

'You haven't changed that much,' Dave said.

Tartt frowned. 'Whaddaya mean?' His pale blue eyes were still as dead as ever.

'You've still got shit on your nose!' He nodded toward Valenti's back. 'Whose is it? His, or O'Connell's?'

'Regular comedian, ain't you? Lemme tell you somethin', wise-guy, all this don't mean a damn. You screwed up once, a long time ago maybe, but your reprieve was only temporary.'

'Does O'Connell know you're mouthin' off like this? Or Clough? Or Valenti, come to that?'

'You gonna tell 'em?'

'No. Wouldn't want you to be sent home before the fireworks began. Wouldn't want to have to come all that way to find you again.'

'As I recall, it was you lying in a heap of steamin' pig shit.'

'Yeah, but it was you that needed puttin' back together. Typical fuckin' Yanks. The only people you're likely to damage is your own side!'

Tartt scowled. 'There'll be another time.'

'Naw,' Dave said and smiled. 'That's something you've run out of.'

He left the man glaring after him and made his way to the wide steps of Coddy's manor.

It was ironical that the chief protagonist was missing and had sent a deputy in his place. Mick's mother was celebrating her ninetieth birthday and that was a good enough reason. It was a snub, of course and, compounding it, his apology was not received until earlier that day and too late to delay the meeting.

Mick's mouthpiece Don McLachlan was the last to arrive. He was a calm, refined man of fifty, more suited to an executive office than to a meeting of the country's underworld. Immaculately dressed in a dark suit and tie, the short, neat figure acknowledged the cautious greetings from those he knew and that meant the majority of men in the room. His voice was mild and devious, it filled the small moments of greeting with a warmth that was not there. His ruddy northern complexion beneath severely short white hair lent an edge to his wide no-nonsense features. He took his place at the polished mahogany table and carefully placed his slim black briefcase before him. He looked up at the twelve faces about him. With the obvious exception of the men from Liverpool almost all the major centres were represented. The Coons from Stoke on Trent were missing but their allegiance to Coddy meant that he would represent them. There was no head to the table. It was round for that reason.

Twelve of the fourteen men at the table had carved up various parts of the country into defined territories. The boundaries were not guarded but in every other sense they were as clear and as respected as borders on a world map. Interests sometimes overlapped, some of these leaders co-existed in the same area, some business was conducted on a nationwide scale, but in all cases agreements had been reached. But just as there was conflict between nations, sometimes to do with territorial rights and border disputes, sometimes to do with business and greed, so it was with these manors. There was aggression, appeasement, wars, winners and losers. It was the nature of things.

Coddy Hughes was the host. His area covered most of Lincolnshire and a large part of the East Midlands including the ripe town of Nottingham and the riper city of Derby. In the old days he controlled the potteries, Birmingham and Manchester, but when his health began to deteriorate he handed over those areas to Lewis Rayatt and his gang known as the Coons. But things had not gone well. The Coons didn't have Coddy's ability to control, nor did they have the respect that he had earned, and the major cities that they had taken over had become lawless with smaller gangs out of control. Cheetham and Moss Side, the coconut jungles, Rusholme, the turban ghetto, were examples. Territorial battles had made Manchester especially one of the most volatile places in Britain.

With Tom Smith and Mad Mick McGovern absent, Coddy Hughes was the most respected man at the table. And respected for reasons other than power. He was trusted by the others. Coddy Hughes was essentially a businessman and his interests lay almost solely in the building industry. The Midlands, in their heyday, had made him a fortune. He was also an old fashioned man totally opposed to the drug scene, to porn and to prostitution. The inexorable traffic in hard drugs was, apart from his health, the other factor in his handing over the slum cities. He remained a force to be reckoned with and no one would take him on lightly. His army was small by other standards but it was his friendship – his family ties – with the Smiths and, to a lesser extent, his pact with the Coons that gave him the edge.

Richard Hurst had died in a car accident on the Dover Road and his brother Ian was serving a twenty-year stretch for manslaughter and conspiracy to commit murder. Roger Hurst, Ian's thirty year old son, had taken over on the Kent Coast. There were problems down there but they were for the future. The old Hurst gang had broken up completely and there were now so many independents operating it was going to take someone much stronger than Roger to pull it together. Before long someone would emerge or move in; the lucrative pickings from the channel ports demanded it. Roger Hurst's hold, perhaps even his life, was on a tenuous thread and if the Smiths lost this war he would be gone in an instant.

Lewis Hicks from Carlisle and Ray Turner from Blackpool were in each other's pockets. They might have been one. In their territory they were into everything and controlled with a vicious, unforgiving style. They were the undisputed slot-machine kings. They were into protection, drugs, prostitution and pornography. Their area was a walled city and they believed in isolationism; they seemed not to have the slightest interest in anyone else. They were an unknown quantity and just how strong they were no one knew. While their strength was questionable, Stafford Carr's, the man from Hull, was most definitely weak. He was a tall, queasy-looking man, fastidious and easily upset, never comfortable, always fussing with his lighter or cigarettes, always flicking non-existent dust from his clothes. It was common knowledge that he suffered from some kind of persecution complex and for that reason the others viewed him with more than a little suspicion. This exacerbated his condition. The decline in Hull in the industrial sense had reduced Carr's influence even further. He was now considered second or even third rate, of little consequence.

He had recently lost his most valuable contract, the importation of heroin from Holland, and now he was effectively finished.

Tony Valenti sat next to him. Then O'Connell. Next to him was McLachlan, and then John Bracey from South London.

In the old days Bracey ran one of the scrap metal companies owned by the Richardsons. He now ran his own gang operating drug smuggling out of Gatwick. Customs men, baggage handlers and airport officials were paid by him so that baggage arrived from the airport unchecked. Bracey also had financial interests in restaurants, hotels and pubs and it was heavily rumoured that he was setting up a film company. He had grown up with the likes of Billy Hill who ruled the gambling dens in the fifties and the razor king Freddie Andrews. He served two and a half years at the Scrubs for his involvement in the Royal Victoria Docks robbery and now, when most men thought of retiring, he was expanding. He was financed from the Costa mob, the South London remnants, and a good deal of his profit went back in that direction. He was an old man, his gang was not an army, and, given the present situation, he posed no real threat. He could cut off supplies, he come come up with financial help, but that was all.

John Arnold from Southampton had taken hold of Jaffa Smith's old business, tied it together with the vacuum left by Chris Holloway and Tommy Hayes and become the leading distributor of porn. The video business and the requirement for moving pictures on every street corner had boosted his turnover. Because his stock was bulky he had a large force of men but they were unreliable. The filth industry was notorious for employing objectionable characters and, although most of the men in the room dealt with Arnold, it was strictly business. It would never be friendship.

The other faces in the room belonged to Terry Ives from Leeds, Peter Bonja from Ipswich and Adrian Styles from Bristol. Styles' interests covered the whole of South Wales. Similar in strength, they were not big enough to threaten anyone alone, but if they joined forces with one of the larger gangs then they had to be considered.

There was some restless shuffling and clearing of throats; watchful, expectant glances went from McLachlan to Dave and back again.

'I apologize for keeping you gentlemen waiting,' McLachlan said through Coddy Hughes.

Barely moving his head Coddy angled it slightly on the pink neck brace and looked sideways at Dave who sat beside him. He faced the front again and tapped the silver head of his cane against the mahogany.

'We all know why we're here,' he said slowly. 'So let's not beat around the bush. I want some blunt speaking today so we all know where we sit. One thing is for sure: this uncertainty is shit!'

There was general agreement; it took the form of grunts and nods of approval.

'Everyone is going to have their say,' he continued. 'But first I want to hear from Don and from Dave.'

McLachlan began immediately. 'Dave, do you mind if I start?' he asked in his mannered tone.

Dave nodded and gave a tiny gesture with his open hand.

'Mick gave me this personal message this morning and I want to give it to you before this meeting gets underway.'

All eyes turned toward him and most showed a little surprise.

'Mick's sorry he can't be here to say this himself. We all heard about The Barge and he wants you to know that it was nothing to do with him. He wants to express his sympathy for all the innocent people hurt, especially the women, both from your place and from Liverpool. Hitting innocent people has never been our style and we know it's never been yours. Mick wants you to know that unless it's been in bed he's never personally hurt a woman in his life.' There was a murmur of laughter before he continued. 'It's a code. And we hope that you'll believe us. Also, to the point as Coddy requested, we know that your father, Tommy Smith, a man we all respect, is fighting for his life, and losing. This terrible illness is the only thing that was ever going to knock over a man like him. Not the rest of us, not the filth. It had to be something like this. Out of respect for your old man, as Mick puts it, and out of respect for the innocent victims of The Barge, Mick gives you his word that he'll start nothing until after the funeral. That is, if it has to start at all. He hopes, sincerely, that it won't have to!'

After a long pause Dave spoke quietly. 'He started it already by using my kid brother for target practice.'

The eyes swivelled back to Don McLachlan.

'We heard about that. This much I can tell you, Dave, and I think your old man will bear me out. If Mick tells you he won't start anything, then you can believe him.'

Dave fixed his gaze. 'Let me get this straight, Don. Are you telling me that turning Mill Hill into a turkey shoot had nothin' to do with Mick?'

McLachlan said genuinely, 'If Mick says that he won't start anything until after the funeral you can take it that he hasn't started anything yet. What else can I tell you? In any case, from what I hear, Mill Hill was fucked up. We don't make mistakes like that.'

Dave's thoughts raced. This admission had surprised him as it had everyone else around the table. Coddy's expression hardened. Others wondered what was going on. Everyone had taken it for granted that Mick had used shotguns on Tommy. Why had they waited until now to deny it? Why had they risked the possible reprisals? Unless . . .

Slowly Dave turned to face the man opposite him. Small dark eyes stared out of the expressionless sallow features of Tony Valenti. The surgery on his big nose had never been totally successful and the flattened scar tissue on the left-hand side gave an uneven balance to his sharp face. A small, thin man in his early sixties, he looked a good deal older. He held a cigarette close to his mouth so that he looked through a continuous flow of smoke. His skin seemed coloured by the nicotine. His thin bony fingers – they looked almost deformed – were covered in gold and a thick gold bracelet hung loosely from his wrist. His unblinking eyes never moved from Dave. The malevolence was unmistakable. It was there for everyone opposite to see. Valenti made no attempt to hide it. Dave pushed thoughts of Sharon and a moment's ludicrous jealousy from his mind.

Dave said, 'Thank Mick for his sympathies. I'll pass them on. I believe what you're saying to me, Don. Now I'm going to say something to all of you.'

He held Valenti's gaze just long enough for the American to get his point. Sitting beside Valenti, O'Connell seemed unaware of what was happening. He scratched the side of his nose with a blackened talon.

Dave said: 'Somebody in this room is responsible for sendin' The Barge into orbit. Somebody's responsible for sendin' one of Vic's bollocks to Southend and the other to fuckin' Huddersfield. Now, somebody here hasn't got the bottle to speak out. They're letting Mick take the blame. It might be the case that Mick knows all about this and knows who is behind it and is happy to let him carry on, or it might be that he has no idea and is pretty pissed off that someone is using his name. I don't know. What I do know is that if anybody around this table knows who's causing this grief then I'll remember this silence. And sooner or later fuckin' doomsday is comin'. That's something you can all guarantee!'

Apart from O'Connell and Valenti, both of whom stared straight ahead, there were some uncomfortable nervous glances bouncing off other faces. Never mind the words, the peace was a long way off. The atmosphere was palpable. Coddy could see very well what was going on and needed some relief. He turned to the Americans.

'What's your position, Mr O'Connell?'

The old man's eyes slid slowly across to Coddy. 'You better call me Augustus,' he said. He spoke breathlessly, in almost a whisper. Around the table the men leaned closer to listen. 'Shit, we're all friends here, ain't we? First-name terms, eh?'

Valenti blinked. He flicked a quick glance at his boss.

O'Connell cleared his throat and said: 'Our position? We have no position. This is a local problem. Since Nam we've learned not to get involved in local problems. Isn't that so, Tony?'

Valenti's smile was forced. It came out sickly. Stafford Carr chuckled and a few others joined in.

The old man continued. 'We'd prefer to deal with one face but that's always been the case. We have no preference as to whose that is.' He shook his head. 'You got major problems. I can see that. But from where I sit it seems to me you gotta resolve it amongst yourselves then come back to me.' He waved a throwaway gesture. 'The problem ain't here in your area at all. You always made it clear that you ain't dealin'. Shit! I know that. We all know that. If someone takes an option on your territory with regard to that one item and can come to an arrangement with you I can't see a problem.'

O'Connell had laid it on the table. Coddy's refusal to allow organized dealing had led to the present situation. Without his agreement, in principle anyway, then war was a certainty. Mick would move south and Dave north and somewhere in Coddy's manor they would meet. The Yanks would deal with the people left standing. But it would be Coddy's fault.

Surprisingly, O'Connell spoke again and pulled Coddy off the hook. 'The problem is the Smiths' deal with the Chinks.'

Only Dave recognized Coddy's relief.

'We wanna deal with one face, but we wanna deal nationwide. Understand? That means the Chinks are history!'

The attention turned back to Dave. His response was measured.

'Any dialogue with us will have to take the Chinese into consideration.'

That was it. They waited for more but the pause became a full stop.

O'Connell waved at the air again, this time in resignation. Beside him Valenti's lips curled downward into an ugly smile.

'I don't know why we're wastin' our time here.' Valenti said to O'Connell. 'These people don't wanna negotiate!' He turned to the others around the table. His voice became louder and hostile. 'There's your problem!' He pointed toward Dave. 'These people aren't reasonable. They got no taste for the cake themselves and because of it they don't want any of you tastin' it either. You wanna solve this problem then you gotta sort these people out! What the fuck are you waitin' for? What the fuck's Mick waitin' for? You can tell him from me that Christmas is a fuckin' long way off!'

O'Connell reached out a clawed hand and patted Valenti's arm.

Valenti's outburst left a long silence, broken eventually by Ian Hurst's son Roger. His freckled face and red hair gave him the image of his father. 'Whatever happens the south coast will line up with Dave.'

McLachlan smiled. 'I don't think you had to say that, Roger. If it comes to it then you, the Smiths and Coddy here will be isolated. I'm hoping that we can reach an agreement but you must know that the situation has been discussed with everyone here and the rest are against you. Some, like Lewis and Ray, want to sit it out, stay neutral, but they'll want it over as soon as possible if it starts interrupting their business and, at the end of the day, they'll be against you as well. The rest of the gentlemen here, with the exception of . . .' He paused and smiled. '. . . Augustus and Tony, who have made their position quite clear, will line up with Mick. This is not a threat. It is a statement. If you want confirmation then you can ask them now. Dave doesn't need it; nor does Coddy. They already understand the situation. We don't want a war – like Coddy said before, it's bad for business, but if it comes then you're going to be hit from six different sides. Roger, your people in Kent have been riding on the backs of the Smiths ever since your dad went down. You couldn't get an army together if you tried. The fact is, you'd be more of a disadvantage to the Smiths because they'd have to look after you and spread their forces accordingly.'

Roger Hurst was young. He had spoken out of turn and now he wished he had not. His freckles seemed to fade as his face coloured.

Dave scratched his forehead. 'Talk to me, Don. That's what you're doing, isn't it?'

McLachlan smiled. 'Maybe it is, Dave.'

Valenti grinned contemptuously. Dave met the American's gaze again and felt the hatred pouring toward him. He watched as Valenti pushed O'Connell's hand aside and half rose out of his seat. For a moment Dave thought that Valenti was going to make a dive over the table.

'I can't believe what I'm hearin' here. You people are lettin' this guy walk all over you.' Valenti's warped finger rose and began to wag at Dave. The gold rings glinted. 'Lemme tell you somethin' you mother fuckin' son of a bitch.' He was shaking, out of control. 'Without your old man you're nothin'! Hear me? Nothin'. We shouldn't even be talkin' to shit like you. Who the fuck d'ya think you are? What the fuck d'ya think this is, eh? A walk around Buckingham Palace, taking tea? Eatin' cucumber sandwiches?' He turned to McLachlan. 'You fuckin' limeys are all the same. You tell Mick from me . . .' His wagging finger nearly poked out his own eye. '. . . You tell him to take care of this fucker, or I will!'

O'Connell reached out again and caught hold of Valenti's arm. It seemed impossible that the old man had the strength in him to force Valenti back in his seat, but he did it. He leant across and whispered into Tony Valenti's ear.

For a few moments Valenti remained motionless, then he pushed back his chair and stood up. He glared once more at Dave then turned abruptly and walked from the room. The double doors closed behind him.

Dave took a deep breath and settled back in his chair.

O'Connell cleared his throat. 'You'll forgive Tony that little outburst,' he said. 'He's been under a lotta pressure lately. Personalities should never come into business. Isn't that right?'

Around the table sighs of relief replaced the shock.

Coddy tapped his cane. 'Does anyone else want a say? Anyone disagree with anything said? Now's a good time to speak up.'

He was hoping that some of the others were not as keen to back Mick as McLachlan had indicated but their silence gave him an answer.

Lewis Hicks from the north west, surprisingly neutral since he was on Mick's doorstep, said, 'I've got no axe to grind with any of you. I don't like to see old friends falling out. We've had peace for sixteen years. Things have been good. There's been no aggro. Some of you I've known all my life. I don't want to see you getting hurt. If it comes to war there won't be any winners. We'll all lose. I'd like a to make a suggestion. Mick has said that he won't start anything until after Tommy's illness . . . Shit! Sorry, Dave, but I gotta say this . . . 'till after the funeral. Now that might be sooner or later. Who knows? Only God knows, eh? But I propose that before anything is started by anyone here, we meet again. Same venue if Coddy agrees on account of it's central to all of us. We meet again in a last-ditch attempt to try and solve all this.' He waved the air. 'We can all go back and cool down and maybe rethink our positions, eh?' He turned directly to Dave. 'I've known your father since the war, Dave. He was never one for gettin' himself in a corner. Maybe he can deal with the Chinese. I'm sure we'd all be willing to come up with the ante.'

Dave flicked him a stray smile. Hicks was as neutral as hell, he decided. He had been primed. That was the longest speech he had made in his life. When his daughter got married two years previously his dinner speech had not been that long.

'I'll give my old man your regards,' Dave said.

'Anybody else?' Coddy asked hopefully.

Don McLachlan spoke again. 'What happened to The Barge was a disgrace. No one should be able to get that close.' There was a veiled criticism of the Smiths here. 'Liverpool has been wiped out. What we're going to get very quickly and without doubt is anarchy. Twenty per cent of our goods come through the Reds and there is no way we're going to let a bunch of amateurs take over. We've had no time to think this through but as we see it at the moment there are two alternatives. In order to safeguard our interests we're going to move some forces in. Quickly. Today. They are there to maintain law and order. As soon as the Scousers sort themselves out and are able to function again we'll pull back. If this doesn't sit well at the table we are willing to be a part of a multinational force.'

Stafford Carr, the tall chain-smoking representative from Hull waved his cigarette and said, 'Another alternative is to redirect your imports to us.'

McLachlan exchanged knowing glances with Dave before he said,

'Staff, with respect, you haven't even got your own authorities under control. You're losing more goods than are getting through. It's common knowledge that you lost the Dutch contract.'

O'Connell coughed loudly.

Carr grimaced and sucked on his cigarette.

Coddy asked, 'What's your feeling, Dave?'

'I've got no objection to Mick's people policing Merseyside on a temporary basis. I think it's a good idea.' He turned to McLachlan. 'With Vic dead I think you'll have some major problems. Since you'll be looking after all our interests we'll help out with the overheads.'

McLachlan looked pleased. He allowed himself the faintest smile of satisfaction. Dave was happy for other reasons. The more he could tie up Mick's men the less of a threat they became. He knew very well that once Mick obtained a foothold it was going to be difficult to shift him, but that was a future problem. His main concern was surviving the present. He had to tread the narrow path between appeasement and practicability.

It was some time later after the last of the guests had left that Dave sat in the leather armchair resting his elbows on his knees, leaning forward toward Coddy.

'Things are becoming clearer.'

Curiosity narrowed Coddy's eyes. He was keen to hear what Dave thought. Tom's eldest son had made his mark during the meeting and impressed a lot of people there with his new-found maturity. He swallowed some brandy. The flames that flicked from the logs in the massive fireplace reflected in the crystal.

'Work out the why,' Coddy said. 'More often than not it will get you the who. Tell me what's on your mind?'

Dave's voice was edged with anger as he said, 'After all this time Valenti hasn't forgotten. This has got sod all to do with Mick. He's just a tool. Willing, perhaps, but a tool nevertheless. This is a vendetta, Coddy. A fucking personal vendetta between Valenti and me. And it's happened now because for the first time, the Wop is in a position of power. He's moved up in the ranks and now he's big enough to override business. He's taken over from Clough as O'Connell's number two. Why else would he have been here? This has got nothing to do with dope and distribution. It's personal. And he's backing Mick. He's never forgotten!'

Coddy finished his drink and carefully placed his glass on the side tray.

'Every morning when he shaves he's going to see that mess in the middle of his face.' Coddy said. 'Would you forget? Every time that he looks at his wife's arse he's going to remember that you crawled all over it. Would you forget? When he looks out of his window at the grey skies he's going to think of the Florida sun and he's going to blame you for making him lose face. Do you think these things go away? Of course he hates you. He's probably dreamt of nothing else but getting you for the last ten years. The son of a bitch has just been waiting for his chance!'

'So what do I do? Sit back and wait for them to take me apart?'

Coddy cut in quickly: 'You do what your father told you. Nothing. You trust that he has got it all in hand.'

'For him to have it in hand means that he knew about it all along.'

Coddy nodded solemnly. 'That goes without saying.' He tapped the side of his nose. 'Remember the scratch on the shoulder, Dave. Go home and take care of the family.'

Dave swallowed a large measure and felt the warm glow spread out in his chest. Eventually he nodded. The old guys were still in charge.

Chapter 21

The dawn wept across Coddy Hughes' manor; its tears glistened on the early summer grass and whitened the cobweb hammocks that hung heavily on the hedgerows. The trees threw their swelling fingers into the heavy grey.

Dave found his mother-in-law, Mavis, in the massive kitchen. She looked grave. Early mornings had never been the best time of her day. He kissed her cheek while she poured some tea.

'Mavis,' he muttered.

'David,' she began and paused.

'What is it?'

'Be careful, boy,' she said. She knew the signs. Looking at her son-in-law brought back memories of her husband and the number of times he had come home with problems that had kept him awake. And then much later she would read or hear about a happening in the twilight world of gangs and villains – the underworld. Of course she put two and two together. She had never questioned him; that would never do. But she knew of his involvement. And now her son-in-law had that same look: concern, fear. A distant fear.

'Nothing for you to worry over, Mavis.'

She had heard that, too, more times than she could remember.

'I'm worried about Coddy,' she said suddenly. 'The doctors are worried about his breathing, the strain on his heart.'

'Maybe you could talk to the doctor. He's due in today.'

'Maybe I will,' she said, brightening at the prospect. 'Yes, if I get the chance.'

'I'll phone you.'

Mavis nodded reflectively; her expression held a vague look of hopelessness.

Dave's car rocketed through the early mist, swinging about the country bends and along the raised narrow roads, south, a black streak on a pool of grey.

During the drive home from his father-in-law's manor, Dave felt gutted; the realization that the present troubles were down to him weighed heavily. A vendetta! A hatred had got in the way of business. A leg-over that as far as Valenti was concerned happened ten years ago had festered all this time and had now erupted and would lead, in all likelihood, to a major war.

Dave tried, unsuccessfully, to force indifference into his mind, but his thoughts kept wandering back to the meeting, to Coddy Hughes who had guessed all along, to his father who knew also, and to his wife. Coddy's home had been filled with photographs of the girl he had married, her smile only half concealing her crooked front tooth, her bright eyes beneath the spectacles, the adoration in her look when they were pictured together at the wedding, the little things about her that he had forgotten. This throbbing mix of emotion was so intense that it blocked out the road ahead. She had never been a fearless person; her greatest daring had been during their first encounter, and he thought of her as fragile, a gentle, dignified and private woman. The ideas and images, the memories, came at him from all directions. The children were everything to Pat; she had turned them into a passion, their upbringing into an art form. When their eldest daughter had gone off at the weekend he had found her in the dark, in tears, suddenly a stranger in her own house. Her house. When he came home in the late evenings she would be waiting for him in the quiet while the children slept. There was a warmth there, an orderliness, everything was in its place, secure. It mattered. Her hand had become tender and gentle. He remembered their first meeting, the unlikely animal passion, his first explosion inside her, the bond . . . And even though time had taken away that razor edge he still craved her. In the end it all came down to that, the physical thing, the thing both symbolic and necessary, and as he thundered through the capital, her legs shifted against him, the touch of her thighs felt cool and charged, the snatch of dark hair parted and the heat consumed him. He was filled with that mixture of desire and guilt.

He drove straight home. The schools were shut for the late-May holiday and the children were playing in the far reaches of the garden. From the car he watched them for a while but they seemed unaware of his presence. He considered his children and the notion that he had seen too little of them. He could blame the business, the hours, but he knew that was just an excuse. His children were growing up without his involvement. Somehow he hoped that they realized that he was a part of Patricia and that when their mother hugged them, or listened, or spent time with them, then his spirit was there also. But he knew the nonsense of it. Their ties would always be to her; he would remain alienated, an observer, not a part of it. Dave tried to show an interest; he listened intently while Patricia gave him the news, updated him on their schooling and clubs, described the moments of their short lives that he had missed, but it was all second-hand and she had dealt with it. His business was war and violence and the safety of the family. The two were not compatible.

No one saw him as he went into the house. He guessed that Pat was in the pool, or the sauna. He made a quick call to Tommy at The Tower and to his mother at home. She was going to lunch with Ted and Theca and their children. He showered then cleaned his teeth to get rid of the journey, then wrapped in a towel he lay back on the bed.

When Pat walked in he remained silent and she didn't see him. His guess had been correct. Her green bikini bottom was wet. He watched her from the bed. His gaze was not critical so much as reflective. Her breasts had flattened slightly, her belly rounded; gravity and time were tugging southward. Her rigorous exercise and the heat of the sauna had kept her tight and fat had been steamed away, but it was there nevertheless, age creeping up, and her belly was notched with the triumph of her five babies. In the dim window light her tan was even darker. Unaware that he was watching she leant across the dresser seat to use a moisturizer and her briefs stretched across her behind, taking away the slack. Hair-line tributaries, one or two faintly varicose, reached up the back of her legs toward the elastic. In all the time he had known her, over ten years now, she had worn her briefs to bed. Even after they had made love she would put them on again. Without them she felt vulnerable and couldn't sleep.

'Sweetheart!' She saw him in the mirror and turned to face him. 'How did it go? How's Daddy?'

'Hush,' he said.

She recalled their first encounter. It had become a game between them.

'That's my line,' she said thickly. 'Tell me how he is.' She looked at him knowingly. Without her spectacles she had that faraway look of short-sightedness.

'He's fine,' Dave said.

She nodded. 'Well?'

'Well, take your knickers off and come over here.'

Moments later she was beside him, guiding his fingers to that exact, familiar place, quite satisfied to lie there indefinitely under the warm wrap of pleasure. But at the same time she knew that their lovemaking was affectionate now, dutiful rather than instinctive, and she missed the passion. She no longer lay there, afterwards, feeling that a double decker had driven right through her. It wasn't just age that had slowed it up, it was more than that. In the beginning she had been covered in love bites without realizing that he had bitten her, he had turned her inside out, his desire all embracing. She missed the intensity, the simple lust. Love had got in its way, perhaps, that shadowy idea of availability.

She went to him willingly as she always did, and wrapped her legs around his waist. She wondered at his gentleness.

In the calm aftermath, as she lay on his arm and before she got up to put on her briefs, she said, 'I never ask you about the business. The last few years have been quiet in any case. But something's happened. I know it has. You're looking worried and earlier Tom warned us all to take special care. Tell me what to expect.'

Dave's breath was flat, controlled. He broke a rule.

'Some people are trying to muscle in on your father. Because of our relationship they're having a go at us.'

She turned to face him and watched his expression grow stony.

'Don't worry. I've got people looking after the family, the kids, everyone.'

She curled up against him feeling the security of his strong arm as it wrapped around her.

The bedroom door was rapped and startled them. Jackie, their second eldest, called out, 'Telephone!'

Dave switched it through to the bedside table. Even as he lifted the receiver his gut was knotting and there was an incredible certainty in his mind that it was the hospital.

'You had better gather the family and come in,' they said. 'He has had such a bad night. His condition has deteriorated,' they said gently.

★ ★ ★

In lieu of Karen, still on her honeymoon, Dave and Pat left Jackie in charge of the young ones. Dave called Tommy at The Tower and then drove carefully across to his mother's house.

Sally, Theca and Ted had just arrived back from lunch. Sally still wore her raincoat. When she saw Dave and then Pat at the back door, perhaps it was his expression that he tried to soften, or more likely it was Pat's that looked grave, but Sally's hand flew instinctively to her lips.

'What's happened?'

'It's OK, Mum,' he said quickly. 'It's just that he's had a bad night and they want us to go in.'

He knew that the explanation was inadequate. It was always going to be. Sally turned into the dining-room, away from them, weeping into her hands, a tiny figure, at once inconsolable.

They heard her silent words: 'Oh no! Oh no!'

Dave followed her in and put his arm around her.

'We don't know, Mum. Let's get over there and find out.'

She wiped her eyes and tried for some composure before going back to face them.

Dave asked Theca, 'What about the kids?'

'They're with Nan. It's OK.'

He nodded. 'Right. Let's not waste any time.'

They trooped out to their cars. Dave had already laid on an escort. The sun shone. Tufts of cloud scudded across the bright sky. The lawns were fresh. The flowers along the borders were exploding with colour. Things at once seemed different.

In the car Sally said, 'He looked so well last night, didn't he Star?'

Theca nodded, wise enough to know that it should have been a sign.

'He looked much better than the afternoon. He had a glow to him and he was relaxed. Joking even.'

By now they knew the hospital corridor well, the flower stall and the newsagents and the bank, but in their haste they barely saw it. The footfalls echoed louder. The ward sister was waiting for them. Her experienced eyes had a curious hardness about them; filled with sympathy and touched with failure, her gaze was nevertheless steady and searching. She looked from Sally to Theca and then to Dave: twin pools of compassion that stated the dark conclusion. She had seen it before so many times.

'He's had such a bad night,' she said. Her voice was breathless yet gentle. 'We thought it best you come in. We've had to give him an injection to ease him a little, and it's made him a bit . . . Well, don't take any notice of what he says. It'll wear off in a little while. There's a bit of a smell in the room because we're having to drain off but don't worry about that.' She offered a little reassuring smile and went on, 'He's comfortable. That's all that matters, isn't it? We've moved him into a single room so you can all go in. There's a private waiting-room through here and you can use that.' She paused, getting eye contact with each in turn. 'Don't worry about visiting times. In a little while I'll get someone to make you some tea.'

The sight of him upset the others but Sally didn't seem to notice. The difference that a few hours had made was incredible. His head seemed to have increased in size, or his body diminished. His face, swollen, seemed flushed and yet grey. His eyes, great bulging angry circles kept slipping, pulling back, intense and yet uncontrollable. It looked like madness. His words hit them hard, drug-induced delirium, a seething mass of ideas spitting from his sore lips.

''Ello darlin's. Come in. Nothin's fair. Fuckin' not, you know. For a start some people are born ugly, and that ain't fuckin' fair, is it? Ted, it ain't, is it? Dave, boy, how are you? What happened? Coddy? 'Ello, darlin', my little Star. How's the kids? Love 'em. Pat, he treatin' you all right? You're lookin' peaky, girl. Beef stew, that's what you need. Cunts! Fuckin' cunts they all are! 'Ello, darlin', you hold my hand like you used to.'

Sally fussed around. If she had noticed the change she had instantly dismissed it. She sat by him, unloading her bag, holding his hand, leaning over to kiss his cheek. She was safe.

The others were visibly shaken. Theca sat on the other side of the bed but was hesitant. She gripped his hand willing him back to sense. Dave placed a chair for Pat on Theca's side of the bed and she sat there braced, in a way frightened.

Tommy was horrified. He leant against the wall to steady himself. Beads of sweat traced his forehead. Ted edged back to the door – keeping his gaze on Tom, not wanting to see the drainage bag; the few moments had been enough. A terrible stink hung in the air. He made his way back to the private waiting-room and lit a cigarette. A short while later Dave and Tommy joined him. Tommy lit a cigarette. The smoke stayed low and clung to him. For a moment it seemed that his clothes were on fire.

'I didn't expect that,' Tommy said quietly. 'I don't think I can handle it.' His hand trembled as he lifted the cigarette again. His eyes narrowed as he glanced at his brother.

Dave felt strangely philosophical. 'I hope he goes quickly,' he said. 'It's about dignity now.' He glanced at Tommy. 'You all right, Brov?'

'Yeah,' Tommy said and expelled a jet of smoke. 'Naw, I'm not. I want to break something. I want to kill something.'

A while later Pat joined them. She hugged Dave before sitting down. 'He's tired,' she told them. 'He keeps dropping off for a few seconds.'

'Is he still delirious?' Dave asked.

'Not so bad. Sally's concerned that they've taken him off the drip. She says his lips are sore because he's not getting any liquid. She's using a flannel to dampen them. The nurses want to go in to straighten him up and change the . . . bag.'

As Sally and Theca arrived to make way for the nurses, the tiny Chinese nurse carried in a tray of tea.

'Here you are,' she said. 'Have your tea. We won't be long. We'll just make him more comfortable then you can go back in.'

The afternoon dragged on. The nerves, taut earlier, became jaded; the adrenalin had wasted and left the feeling of nausea; eyes and throats became sore. The heat in the hospital increased the discomfort. The walls of the tiny waiting room seemed to move in.

Sally and Theca sat by his bed, holding his hands, sobbing quietly, willing him to glance their way. By mid afternoon his fitful sleeps fell to unconsciousness, and the last thing he said to the girls was: 'I feel so drowsy. It's the drugs. I think I'll have a little sleep.' Earlier, when that horrible delirium had worn off, he had said other things: 'You're all here, that's good,' and to Theca, 'My Star of the Veldt, you've turned out so beautiful,' and to Sally, 'I love you, girl, I always did.'

Now he was unconscious. His breathing was laboured. It rattled and rasped. They watched his still face. They held his hands. Moments of silence when his breathing stopped had them momentarily alert, gripping his hands until his breathing started and they relaxed again.

In the waiting room Tommy said to Dave and Ted: 'The Sister asked if we wanted a priest or something. I don't know what you think, Brov, but I reckon there's enough religion in that room already.'

In the ward the periods of his breathing became shorter and those silent moments became longer and the rattle, when another gasp was taken, was louder.

Dave came out and told Tommy and Ted, 'It won't be long.' He glanced at his watch as if to make his point.

Pat appeared a moment later to say, 'The Star's breaking down in there. I think she's upsetting Sally.'

Ted moved to the door.

'I'll get her out for a while. She needs a break anyway. She's been in there for hours.'

'C'mon sweetheart,' Ted said to Theca and pulled her gently from the bedside. 'This is doing you no good and it's upsetting your mother.'

For a moment the Star hesitated, pulled her arm from his grip, but then she stood up and allowed him to escort her from the room. Her eyes were swollen. She wiped them on a tissue.

'Let's take a walk,' he said. 'Come on, you need some air.'

She nodded and followed him weakly from the ward. He led her to the lift and down the main corridor. He put his arm around her.

'I'm not handling this very well,' she said. 'I thought Mum could lean on me but it's me that's gone to pieces.'

'Perhaps that's not a bad thing. Looking after you is keeping her occupied.'

They walked through the entrance and hit the damp evening air.

'I don't think I'm ever going to get over this,' she said seriously.

They remained outside for five minutes. He smoked a cigarette and Theca regained her composure. Eventually, when she began to shiver, they made their way back.

They saw Pat and then Dave behind her. Pat's expression was enough.

'No!' Theca cried.

Dave tried to catch her as she rushed by.

'Just this minute, Sis. Only a moment ago!'

It was no use. Through clenched teeth she turned back to them, to Ted.

'I wanted to be there. You! You!'

She hit him, again and again. Ted was too stunned to react. He stood immobile gazing across at the helpless, almost fearful looks from Dave and Pat.

'I needed to be there,' she whispered. 'I'll never forgive you!'

The blows weakened and she dropped her arms. She turned and hurried into the private room.

Dave moved across to Ted and touched his shoulder.

'Don't worry, mate,' he said. 'She'll be all right.' But Dave was not at all sure. At that moment he wondered whether Theca and Ted would ever be right again. The three of them followed Theca.

Moments earlier, after Ted had taken Theca from the room, Dave, Pat and Tommy had returned to make certain that the Star's distress had not upset Sally. She was composed, sitting there beside the bed, waiting, clutching Tom's hand in hers. There seemed little change in Tom. Slowly, slowly his breath was expelled, a harsh whistle, and then a pause, a still silent pause, a heart stopping moment, until once again with a quiet rattle, slowly, so slowly, his breath was drawn in.

There was nothing holy about death: it was a little thing. There was no atmosphere of sanctity: it was a silent thing. There was nothing immortal, no sign of the freeing of the spirit: it was an unimpressive thing. There was not the slightest hint of an ongoing process, hardly even an end; breathing did not cease, more, the next breath did not begin. This death was an easy thing; the thread of life was broken but so thin it was that the difference was subtle. But the silence, when the next breath did not come and people around held their breaths to listen, was absolute. Silently they watched as Sally leant closer, confirming, and then threw her arms around his neck and sank her head on to his still chest and then the silence was broken by her shriek. It was a lament, a mournful note, the saddest sound that they had ever heard.

It was over. They stood shattered, motionless, fixed expressions gazing at Sally rocking on her husband's chest, dropping heavy tears on to his blue pyjama top.

Dave suddenly moved. He had to find Theca.

And now they were all there.

Eventually the stillness was moved. Dave glanced across at Theca to see how she was coping. Her gaze was fixed on her father's face. The wetness beneath her eyes and on her cheeks glistened in the stark light. Her features slowly softened, as if the end had been for her a terrible relief. He glanced at his wife to find her coping in a different way. Like Ted, a relative-in-law only, there was a deep sadness of course, but there was not a snuffing out of one's own cells, there was no amputation of a part of life itself. The hurt that they felt most of all was for the others. Pat glanced back at Dave sensing his eyes upon her, and her eyes under her spectacles were filled with sympathy. He looked at Tommy. His younger brother was still, leaning backwards against the walled partition. A single tear trickled over his cheek.

It was over.

It was approaching eleven when they left the hospital. Sally carried her shopping bag. It contained those important things that she had insisted on collecting together: Tom's shaving gear, watch and slippers and a half-used bottle of orange squash. She walked erect and independent.

Barry Theroux ran out of the cafeteria entrance as they passed.

'It's all over,' Dave told him.

'I heard. Listen, there's a bunch of reporters out there. The hospital's sent someone out to make a statement. You don't need it.'

Dave agreed.

'Come this way. We can get out here.' He led the way and Dave ushered the others toward the side entrance. Barry hung back and whispered to Ted. 'Peach has been trying to get you.'

'I'll bell him,' Ted said.

Dave overheard. 'What's all that, Brov?'

'Detective Inspector Peach. He's been trying to get in touch.'

It was nothing, Ted discovered later. There was no further news of the investigation. Peach simply wanted to be the first to extend his sympathies. He was filth, albeit bent filth, so his sympathies were meaningless and Ted did not bother to pass them on.

They went out to the waiting cars. The night was darker. The stars glinted cruelly, polished by the events of the long day.

Chapter 22

The family motored from the hospital to Sally's house. A few reporters had gathered by the door and were pressing for statements. Half-a-dozen minders held them back. Once inside Sally had a long list of relatives and friends to call and she was on the telephone for the best part of an hour while the others sat quietly to marshal their thoughts.

Eventually, in the small hours, they wound it up and went their separate ways. Theca would return later to spend the night with her mother but first she had to collect the children. She and Ted drove a few hundred yards to Nan's house. In the car they spoke of breaking the news gently but once inside she rushed to find her children and blurted: 'Your granddad's dead and we're never going to see him again!' Her arms wrapped around them while Ted stood watching helplessly.

As they motored home he said: 'He waited until you were out of the room before he decided to call it a day. He was ready to die but he clung on until you left.'

Theca turned to him and said honestly: 'That's the only thought that is stopping me from hating you. I keep telling myself that that is so and maybe one day I will believe it.'

'What are you going to do, sweetheart? Have you decided yet?'

'I don't want to leave,' she said quickly, ready with her answer. 'I want to be with my family.'

After a late breakfast she left Sally and went across to The Tower. She found Dave in his office.

'Hello, Sis. How's Mum?'

Theca shrugged.

'I must get over there,' he said.

'That's not why I came, Dave. I've decided to stay with Ted.'

She saw the relief in his eyes.

'I'm pleased, Sis. Really. I hope you can work it out. Does he know?'

'I told him last night.'

Dave nodded. 'What about . . .?'

'I'll tell him later.'

'That's not going to be easy.'

'Nothing ever is.'

'These things happen,' Dave said reflectively. 'It's for the best.'

'We'll see.'

It was just on twelve when she met Margaret for lunch.

'I saw it on the news,' Margaret said. 'I haven't stopped crying. I tried to call.'

'I was at Mum's.'

'Yes, Jean told me. I didn't want to ring there.'

'I've decided to stay with Ted.'

'But you don't love him.'

'That's not important. Not anymore. I love my family and he's a part of that.'

'Well, I think you're making a mistake. I think it's all a dreadful waste. Why on earth did you tell him in the first place?'

'I don't know. That's the silly part. I've hurt him for no reason and yet we had reached the stage when something had to happen.'

'How can you think of living the rest of your life with someone you don't love? I know, you want to be some kind of martyr. You need to hurt and feel pain. I'm right. But, Theca, what happens when the pain of your father subsides? Oh, I know that at the moment you think it never will. But it will. What happens then? When you've got to get on with your own life again? When suddenly you find that what you had before, and that was never good enough, is all that you'll have again. What happens then? I don't think you can give Lewis up that easily. People like us can't do without passion and love and passion!'

Theca smiled weakly. She knew why Margaret was her best friend. The past and the future barely seemed to matter to her. She lived for the moment. Her exuberance excited the air about her and other people breathed it in. It was only a few days earlier that she had been doing her level best to talk her out of leaving Ted in the first place. Or at least of telling him.

'I know. I know,' Theca said. 'But the family has suffered enough. I seem to have left a trail of bodies all over the place.'

'Well, I think you should wait a while. I told you before that now is not a good time to make decisions. Why don't you wait a week or two? Get the funeral out of the way. You must give yourself time. You're talking about the rest of your life. Put things on hold. Why rush into it?'

'I have to. I can't explain it but there's a voice screaming at me to put things right. I can't ignore it. I have to tell Lewis that it's over and then I have to pick up the pieces and get some sanity back into life.'

Margaret sighed. 'Oh dear, life is so complicated. Why couldn't you just settle for a comfortable little affair like the rest of us? Passion on Wednesday night three weeks out of four and any other time you could fit it in?'

'Because I wanted more,' Theca said sadly.

'And now you're not going to have even that.'

After lunch Theca drove down to Victoria. For the first time her route was uncomplicated and she did not bother checking in her mirror. A tail now would be for her own safety and for no other reason. The Barge weighed heavily and security had been tightened accordingly. Her father's death could well have been the signal for further attacks.

She left the Mini in the enclosed square and trod carefully across the cobblestone to the back entrance of the mews. Lewis led her into the lounge expecting the worst.

She said bluntly, 'I'm not going to live with you. I'm staying with Ted. I'm sorry.'

His nod was a meek acceptance. Ted had said the right things; her father had died at the wrong time and thrown family loyalty to the fore. Lewis was angry but he hid it well. There was nothing else to do. He had to keep open even the remote possibility that at some stage in the future, when things had settled down, Theca might change her mind. He was angry, but he was not to know that Theca's decision had saved his life.

That ethereal time between a death and a funeral is controlled more by a timetable of necessary actions than by desire. For them everything was hurried. There was little time for reflection. And yet even that little time was too long. The nights were endless, restless wakeful moments filled with guilt and regret. Those dreadful feelings in the throat and chest refused to go away. And the living outside of those necessary actions was in the past. The recollection of the past poured out at every meeting; the same memories were described over and over.

And so it went on, an ungodly time, surrounded by sympathy cards from the rich and famous, from the studios and castles, from the Costa and from Brazil, the choice of coffin and flowers and cars. One day fed into the next without the necessary pause for unbroken sleep.

The soft light threw a waxen image on to his features so that he was no longer real. They went in alone. Dave was the last to arrive. Ted and Theca were in the reception, waiting for him. All day a steady flow of people had paid their respects. Sally had been the first, along with Tommy.

'Hello, Sis,' Dave said thickly.

The Star's dark eyes betrayed her. She nodded quickly. Her lips were tight. Ted's arm was around her shoulders. His nod to Dave said it all.

Dave felt flat, curiously unemotional. The things to do had left him mentally exhausted, and in the taking care of the others, particularly Sally, his own feelings had been pushed aside, postponed. He felt cold, frozen by deliberation.

He was led into the parlour and the door closed quietly behind him.

He stood just inside, not wanting to look. The room was cold; it increased his sense of chill. At the same time it was oppressive, lacking air, as if there was something else living in there. He felt a breath and it made him shiver. He looked up and as he approached his gut tightened in quick little spasms.

His father was immaculate in his best suit and tie. His black shoes, spit-polished, reflected the room like twin mirrors. He noticed the hands and fingernails, scrubbed and also polished. He was drawn to the face, the amazing relaxation, the lack of expression, and yet it was his father, ludicrously content. So real, he expected a breath, a sign, and yet so unreal he seemed to be something out of Madame Tussaud's. Suddenly it was a peaceful place; a silent life stirred. There was utter quiet and his father simply slept, dreaming a peaceful dream.

'I had a dream too, Pop,' Dave heard his own voice, quiet, detached. 'I saw you last night, in the bedroom, and I had the most wonderful feeling that everything was all right. That you still existed, somewhere.'

But when the night was done and the pale dawn was creeping at the window he was gone. The comfort of the dream faded quickly.

He leant over the glistening wood and felt his father's cold kiss.

'Goodbye, Pop,' he said softly.

There was a faint knock at the door and Ted was there.

'You all right, Brov? You've been in here half an hour.'

Dave looked up, astonished that time had been suspended, and Ted smiled out of compassion as he saw Dave's bloodshot eyes.

'Come on, Dave. Always come back again, can't you?' he said gently. Dave sighed. He wouldn't be coming back. Ted put his arm around Dave's shoulders and led him out. The embrace was accepted and in that instant Ted knew that Dave had changed, that a streak of humanity was vying with the hatred.

And so it went on; days that never ended somehow disappeared without being lived, punctuated with grief and memory and guilt. During that week the police showed an apparent lack of interest in the Smiths. Their investigations seemed to have slowed down. No one was hauled in for questioning, not a word about the drugged bodies, nothing about the girl. As far as Peach was concerned, he told them, the top brass were waiting to see what happened. The word on the street was war. The police could afford to bide their time; at the end of it they could pin the blame on who was left.

Karen and John returned from their honeymoon. It had been pointless trying to keep the news from them for the papers, albeit received by them a day late, carried stories of Tom's death. Some of the tabloids quoted police sources and suggested that a battle for the control of the underworld was about to begin. Old villains from the past, pictured against a back-drop of sun-bleached beaches, filled the captions with their memories, mostly exaggerated, of the old days when they had rubbed shoulders with Tom.

In the office, some time during that week, a morning because in the casino training sessions were in progress and, in the club, girls from the cabaret were going through their paces, John was privy to his first management meeting.

'Could it be the Chinese?' Theroux asked. 'Perhaps they got worried that Tom was going to deal them out and let the Mafia in.'

'Pop's word was everything,' Tommy cut in. 'You should know that, Barry. The chinks, even more than most, respected his word.'

'Well, someone else from the past then? The Jamaicans?' Theroux said. 'Or those fuckin' Cypriot lunatics?'

'I've wondered about that,' Tommy said. 'Someone out there jumpin' on the bandwagon, deciding to have a go while we're down. It might even be funded by the Costa. They're into dope again.'

The puzzled look from John prompted Tommy to explain.

'Remnants of the old Krays and Richardsons – and don't forget Charlie! We never crossed any of them. Kept an eye on their interests but that was all.'

Dave chuckled and said confidently, 'You're way off mark, Brov. They are old geezers now, well out of it, livin' on reputations. They talk big but mostly about the old days. How fucking great it was and all that. They were never that big, anyway, and the only reason they make the headlines today is because the press have made them Robin Hood figures. They were villains, sure, but by today's standards they wouldn't have made the ad's column. They're down there in Marbella gettin' suntans and pissin' it up on Watneys. If they're into anything it's small time, African shit and hash oil, maybe a snort or two, but that's all.'

'You tellin' me the twins were nothin'?' John asked, not convinced.

'They covered a patch of the Smoke, right? Even the local villains today cover whole cities. Take Mick. That bastard has the whole of Scotland under control. The only thing that made the twins big was their sentences. Nowadays you could top the Queen Mum and not go down for that long! The big villains today, Christ! They're government-backed. They talk in billions. Geezers in Latin America run their countries on the proceeds of dope. In Eastern Europe, in Africa, in America. You name it. Dope, arms, currency – some of our friendly banks are run by the biggest villains going. Remember that the next time you stick your plastic in the hole in the wall. These are the big villains. These people have more power than some governments. They run the fucking governments!'

John shook his head. 'Why is this distribution deal so important?'

Dave spoke matter-of-factly. 'The Yanks have bought themselves a mountain of white dust but they could end up snorting it up their own arses. We'll deal, we always said we would, but not exclusively, not to the exclusion of the Chinese. There's something about eggs in one basket here, and that isn't for us. It's not good business. Once they have a monopoly they'll be in control. That's what they really want. Fuck that for a living. It's that simple. They want to deal with one face and they want to be the only dealer.'

'So what will happen now?'

'We've got our problems with Mick, but the Yanks are in shit street too. They've got to start moving the stuff in a big way or they'll go fuckin' bankrupt. They'll put pressure on us by backing Mick, by pretending to back Mick, but they're running out of time.'

'Are you sure they're only pretending?' Tommy cut in.

'I hope they are, Brov.'

Dave kept his thoughts regarding Valenti to himself. Only Coddy Hughes shared his fears. And since the guinea bosses didn't know that it was their own Tony Valenti causing all the grief, they probably thought it was Mick, and everything was going to plan. Clever bastards! But it wasn't Mick. Dave was almost certain of that now. And that was his one good card. It would give him time.

'Why did your old man want you to deal with Hough personally?' Theroux asked. 'We normally take care of the business.'

Although he had not asked it the question also puzzled Tommy.

'Probably because I took him on in the first place,' Dave muttered.

It was the obvious conclusion but it was the wrong one and it was going to be a few days before Dave was to understand his father's complex reasoning.

Chapter 23

His city had been castrated by the planners; not much of it was left now. Dave drove through the squalid streets lined with vulgarity, the fast food chains painted predominantly in red – somehow, tasteless, superficial junk food went down well with the current lack of architectural taste – the launderettes and bingo halls and video shops. What the hell had happened, he wondered, that it had become a city of neglect? Had he really slept through it all? Unaware?

He wondered at the thousands of little people behind those squares of reflecting glass as they went about their business unaware that a major war was being fought – unaware that in the safe streets of the city there was another world, a dangerous place, where the stake was life itself. Unaware too, that he was their leader and he had the power of life and death over every one of them. They were alive today because they did not interfere.

He cut a line through the intersection where the ugly block fortress of the Bank angled across to the columns of Mansion House. The past silently echoed from the solid grey façades as their stiff reflections slid across his windshield. The street life, no different, produced a gut reaction and he stepped angrily on the accelerator. The car leapt forward through a set of reds and belted down Queen Victoria Street and left to the river. He pulled up on the Embankment just beyond Blackfriars where he could look over the steely grey warships at Southwark and the National. The river was high; gulls wheeled and dipped over the swell, squawking soullessly into a warm southern breeze that carried the scent of the sea. The reflections of fluffy clouds raced across the surface; ghosts from the age of sail.

Dave thought of his grandfather sinking slowly under the heavy metallic water and his father who had lived through it all and he was stung with nostalgia for those times he never knew. In that moment his mask slipped; the hardness melted away and he felt the downturn of his lips as they began to quiver. In that moment he could have wept. He shrugged off the sentiment as though it was something repugnant, a mark of weakness, and his facial muscles tightened in anger at his own feelings. Back came the hooded eyes and contempt with which he held all but a fraction of mankind.

'Fuck you, son!' he said to the river and reached down to start the car again.

His father had said adamantly: 'Do nothing until after the funeral.' The words, spoken in a calm knowing way came back to him. 'Just hold the fort and keep things ticking over.' The humour in the eyes, the certainty that things would work out, that everything was under control, was just as evident now as when the words were spoken. Somehow his father had planned for the future, was – even in death – in control. But Dave was less than confident. How could his father have guessed about Valenti? Even so, for the next few days he would play a waiting game. But, once the earth had been sprinkled on the polished mahogany, then Mick and all who ran with him were going to pay for causing the Smiths additional grief at such a time. He didn't know how he was going to achieve it with the Mafia and half the other gangs lined up against him but, in his mind, there was nothing more certain.

One thing at a time, he kept telling himself as he took a right into The Strand and let the traffic carry him along Fleet Street. He turned back into Queen Vic and headed up Bishopsgate toward Spitalfields.

His father had wanted him to deal with Pete Hough personally. Was it the old man's way of telling him that he knew all about his affair with Denise? Dealing with Pete Hough and with Denise would bury another of the family's skeletons. Dave nodded grimly. Perhaps his father had enjoyed the irony.

He turned south into Commercial Street. A few moments later he turned again through a pebble-dashed archway set in a terraced row into a small courtyard surrounded by two-storey warehouses. Just inside the entrance two men leant across a car engine. They were close enough to block the way of any unwelcome face. They recognized Dave and acknowledged him with a slight nod. Dave parked next to another black Rover. Barry Theroux walked slowly towards him while the two men closed the high double gates.

'All right?' Barry said as Dave climbed out of the car.

'Yeah. I ain't all that on these early morning calls though.'

Barry yawned. 'I know what you mean.'

Dave turned to look at the crumbling buildings. 'What have we got here?'

'Used to be a milk depot,' Theroux said. ''Till the supermarkets fucked up the trade.'

Theroux turned to his own car and opened the boot. Carefully, using both hands, he lifted out an axe and held it towards Dave. The curved handle was three feet long.

Dave took it one-handed, felt the weight then ran his finger along the sharp edge.

'Nice one,' he muttered. He rested it on his shoulder.

'Where is he?'

'This way.' Barry pointed toward a steel door in a red brick building. 'Cold storage. We turned the fridge back on to keep him cool. He's stark bollock naked; probably got frost bite by now.'

'Has he said anything?'

'Not a word. Taking it very personal.'

'Let's get on with it.'

Together they walked up a slight incline toward the building. At the large sliding door they were met by another man carrying a sawn-off 12 bore. Theroux nodded and the man drew back the heavy steel door. The cold air hit them immediately. It came out in a dense cloud.

Dave turned to Theroux.

'You comin' in?'

Theroux shrugged. His sad eyes were resigned. He followed Dave into the cold bare room.

Pete Hough was at the far end. He was hugging himself and stamping his feet. His face was ashen, his body tinged with blue. Hough saw Dave and moved forward. He saw the axe and stopped abruptly. Fear widened his eyes.

'Dave, what . . .?'

'It's time, Pete. Let's not waste time.'

'What are you talkin' about?'

'If you don't know, Pete, then you can't talk me out of it, can you?' Dave swung the heavy axe from his shoulder and held it out with both hands. The head glinted in the stark strip light.

Pete Hough had seen Dave in action many times. He knew how heartless he was. In his time, especially that spent in the Scrubs, Pete Hough had mixed with the real evil bastards but Dave was in a different league. He wasn't human. There was not the slightest compassion in him.

As Dave advanced waving the axe from side to side Pete Hough stood as if mesmerized, defenceless. He barely raised his hands.

'Have a heart, Dave. I done you some good turns in the past. I think they've got Denise. I couldn't take the chance.'

'Denise was still at your gaff when you had a go at Tommy.'

'I swear that wasn't me, Dave. Tommy came to me. I even tried to get hold of you.'

'Don't fuckin' lie to me you toerag. Don't you insult my fuckin' intelligence. My phone wasn't engaged at five in the morning. You were letting Valenti know that he'd fucked up. That's why you came back to us the next day. He wanted you on the inside. Telling him all our moves!'

'Tell me what to do, Dave. Is there anything I can do?'

'Not a lot, Pete. You didn't really think that you could fuck with me, did you?'

'Come on, Dave. For old times' sake. I've been with you a lot of years.'

'That's the shame of it.'

'I know you ain't religious, but your old man was. Can't you give me another chance on his memory? Vengeance is mine, and all that?'

'All that means, my son,' Dave grinned, 'is that after I've finished with you, you've still got to worry about Him.'

Abruptness crept into Hough's voice. 'You're finished, Dave. Can't you see that? Valenti's backin' the whole country against you. What's the point in havin' me now? Next week it will all be over. You'll need some friends.'

'Why the fireman, Pete? We know you ferried him out.'

'Honest, I never knew they were going to top him. They told me they wanted him out of the way for a while. It made sense.'

'Why?'

'He was the only one who could have fingered Valenti. He knew too many people in the game. Even after all this time he's pretty well tuned in. He would have picked up a whisper. They all like to mouth off and you gotta admit The Barge was a pretty tasty job. You gotta admit that. But I swear to you that topping him was never an option.' He shook his head regretfully. 'My hands were tied. I don't know what's happened to Denise. She wouldn't have left the kid.'

'Yes she would. If she thought her life was on the line she'd do anything, same as you would. She's done a runner. You should have followed her. She knew me. She knew what I'd do when I found out!'

Dave swung the axe. Hough tried to dodge but he had left it too late. The blade hit him just above the ankle. He heard the crunch of bone and felt a terrible pain explode in his leg. He stumbled forward and tried to grab Dave's neck but his strength had gone and instead he sank to his knees. He looked back. His foot was a yard away, on its side. He could see the flesh and bone protruding from it and the blood gathering in a little steaming pool.

He looked up. Even through the pain his face was a mask of disbelief. He began to cry. Tears streamed down his face and dotted the dark concrete floor.

'You didn't need to do that,' he gasped.

Dave stood over him. 'Let's go back ten years,' he said calmly. 'About the time Valenti lost his fuckin' nose.'

Hough's sobbing stopped with a sudden intake of breath. His eyes widened as he stared up at Dave.

'It was you, wasn't it?'

Hough swallowed hard. His face twisted as another wave of pain swept up from his leg.

'Please, Dave, I'm bleedin' to death. I'll tell you everythin' but don't –.'

'Tell me about it.'

Hough broke down again.

'If there's one thing I hate, it's grovelling. How did you know where to find me, Pete?'

'I knew how long it took the car to get back.' Hough's voice quivered. His breath came in short bursts. 'It had to be the Hursts in Folkestone or Coddy up north. Once Jimmy said you were knee deep in pig shit, it had to be the farm. Coddy's manor.'

'All this fuckin' time.' Dave shook his head in disgust. 'How much did Valenti pay you?'

Hough shook his head. 'Please, Dave –.'

'Whatever it was, it wasn't enough!'

Hough screamed as he saw the axe come down again. He snatched his hand away but part of it remained on the cold dusty concrete. For an instant his fingers continued to claw at the floor. As he lifted his arm blood spurted over his face and covered his chest. Through a red mist he watched Dave's approach and heard his voice, calm and deep: 'Cheers, Pete. Try not to worry about all this too much. It isn't personal.'

Hough's scream bounced off the icy cold walls. Dave stood back and steadied himself before swinging again. The blow landed on Hough's neck. For a moment Hough's head hung at a ridiculous angle, swinging on skin and sinew until the body collapsed and it hit the floor. A pool of blood turned black in the dust.

Dave dropped the axe to his side and bent low over Hough's head. The face was turned toward him, the eyes still open, the mouth wide in a silent scream.

'Now, don't you fuckin' well do it again,' Dave said.

Barry Theroux walked across to stand at his side.

'You all right?' he asked. 'Feel better?'

Dave nodded. 'Yeah,' he said breathlessly. 'There isn't anything wrong with revenge.

Theroux grunted and switched his gaze from the body to the head. The air was filled with the sweet sickly odour of blood.

'Keep the head frozen,' Dave said. 'Once Denise has surfaced I want it dropped off in the Smoke. I want some headlines in the *Standard*.'

Theroux nodded grimly. 'We've got to tighten up, Dave,' he said stonily. 'Make sure this sort of thing can never get out of hand again.'

'It's not over yet,' Dave said.

Theroux went on as though he hadn't heard. 'The only way to do it is to make people so scared they wouldn't dare take us on. Like Leeds United in the seventies!'

A smile tugged Dave's features. He turned to Theroux. 'That severe, eh?' he said.

Dave caught Tommy at The Tower and told him that the fireman was dead. He was surprised at Tommy's sudden dejection over a man he barely knew. He explained that Hough had been working for Valenti and that it was Valenti himself who had ordered the destruction of The Barge. He told him about Sharon so that Tommy understood the nature of the personal hatred Valenti had for the Smiths and for Dave in particular.

'It's not the wiseguys we're fighting,' Dave said. 'It's Valenti himself moonlighting. The Mafia didn't sanction the hit on The Barge. Sure, they're trying to put us under pressure but that's all. It's Valenti.

He's not playing the game. It's his own personal war. And he's played it perfectly. His bosses think it's Mick causing all the grief. And what's more we can't touch the bastard and he knows it.'

'So what do we do?'

Dave sighed and shook his head.

'We wait until after the funeral. Pop was working on something, so we'll wait and see. After all, that's what you wanted and that's what he asked us to do. After that we've got a choice: we back off or we go to war!'

Quietly the family was getting ready. Safe houses had been set up, men had been armed, trusted reinforcements had been recruited, police connections had been primed so that they would clamp down on Mick's business and make his movements difficult, informers were paid for information on Mick's organization, his strengths and weaknesses, men had been shifted from Kent to strengthen Coddy Hughes. The Hurst's old empire was defenceless so there was little point in keeping even a token force there. And while this was going on so was the talking. Promises were made and deals struck with other leaders to secure their backing. Financially the situation was crippling. The consolation was that Mick would be making the same moves and running up the same costs.

Tommy had not yet come to terms with the discovery that his family was heavily involved in the procurement of minors. For the first time in his life he felt a sense of hostility and loathing towards the business. Only slightly satisfying was the certain knowledge that his father had no part in it. On his way across to see Jill Mountford he wondered what other dreadful secrets he would uncover. His outrage compounded the anger he felt at the loss of his father. He felt, almost, that he was losing control.

The sadness was there, overwhelming all else, and something even more than that, a detachment, an illusive sense of isolation, that he no longer had the chance to earn his father's respect and approval. He felt, as all children must, that he had been cheated of the right to prove himself, that he would never recognize that important mark of pride in his father's eye. His ambitions had been downgraded because of it, his possible achievements had become necessarily less important. For this selfish reason the bitterness was more acute and the anger burned that much deeper.

He went to the garage first but found it closed. He found her at the house. She had heard him drive up and met him on the path. She wore a pair of tight cords and the white sweater he had seen before. She led him into the front room.

'I heard about your dad. I'm sorry.'

'Yeah, well, it happens, I suppose. It don't make it any easier, though.'

'Mike still hasn't surfaced,' she said. She met his steady gaze. 'I've been thinking about you.'

'I've been tryin' not to think of you.'

'Were you successful?'

He shook his head.

'I've been dreamin' about cherries. Bowls full of 'em.'

She laughed.

'What?' he said.

'It doesn't matter.'

He led her to the sofa. She caught something in his expression and turned hesitant.

'What is it?'

'Jill, sit down. I've got to talk to you.'

Her brow crinkled. 'What is it?' she repeated cautiously.

'You're not going to see him again, sweet'eart.'

'How do you know? What's happened?'

'Listen to me. I know. I've heard. I do know.'

Her lips trembled. 'I don't believe you.'

Tommy gazed at her. His eyes were dark, his lips tight; there was an honesty that she could not ignore.

'What happened?' Her voice shook.

'I don't know what happened. The Yanks had him taken out. That's all I know.'

She stared at the floor. Her expression was grave and hard. Suddenly her eyes flicked up filled with accusation.

'It's to do with your father and all this trouble!'

Tommy nodded. 'I'm sorry, but I had to tell you. I found out just an hour ago. He had nothing to do with us. The Yanks thought he would finger them for The Barge job.'

'Damn your family,' she said.

'It's been damned for a long time.'

'I'm shaking like a leaf. I don't know what to do.'

'Let me help you.'

'What can you do?'

'I can do anything that you let me. Everything or nothing. I want to help you. I want to be with you. You haven't been out of my mind since I first saw you. I just wish I could do something to put this right, but I can't.'

'Hold me, Tommy. Please hold me.'

He reached forward and embraced her. Her face buried into his chest and he felt the wetness of her tears through his shirt.

'Will I ever know what happened?'

'I don't know. Maybe we'll hear something, get a whisper, but I doubt it. He's just never going to come home.'

'Oh, how can I bear this?'

There was no answer. He held her closer.

'I loved the old sod so much.'

'I know.'

'It's so unfair. Why him? He was harmless.'

He held her for what seemed like hours and listened to her intermittent sobbing, not wanting to move, finding his own solace in her touch. The light from the window began to fade, sucking the colours from the room. She had calmed, perhaps even dozed. She struggled to her feet. Catching hold of his hand she led him into the hall. He thought she was leading him to the door and was dismayed. She did blame him after all. When she led him instead to the stairs the relief surged through him and threatened his balance. She led him to the back room, her bedroom, and to her bed.

'Make love to me, Tommy,' she said firmly. 'Let's forget everything else for a little while.' She pulled off her white sweater and coyly uncovered her breasts. They were soft, hung slightly with puppy fat, and the dark nipples were the size of old half crowns.

'Fuckin' hell,' Tommy said.

'What is it?'

'You're gorgeous.'

She gave a little shiver as the chilled air touched her. She struggled out of her tight cords. There was a determined, unemotional look about her. Her skimpy pants were a dull contrast to her pale skin. A trace of dark hair curled from beneath them. Shyly she threw up her hands to shield herself from his look of helpless admiration.

It was a sad embrace. There was something innocent yet despairing in the moment, a sadness, a joy, an expression and perhaps a commitment. She held on to him and refused to let him withdraw and in that moment she whispered, 'Oh darling!' and he was filled with wonder. They cried together, not out of ecstasy but out of life itself. Later, as they lay entwined under the cover of darkness, with Venus a trembling spark on the glistening windows, she said, 'Darling, I'd like to come to the funeral,' and he stroked her cheek and said, 'I'd like you to come and be with me.'

Chapter 24

Tosca filled the air. It was being performed in Milan and the BBC were broadcasting it live. It began at 11.30 a.m., UK time. So did the funeral.

There were flowers everywhere. They spread up the rise of the cemetery, either side of the narrow concrete paving slabs, right up to the mound of freshly dug earth and the hole beside it. They circled the trunk of a young birch that threw its shadow across the hole.

Once the coffin was lowered and the earth was scattered to end the obsequies and the old soldiers had made their salutes, it was over. There was something so final, so absolute, that it left nothing of the past. It was the cold beginning of something else. They left that rise straight-backed and determined.

Tosca played on, quietly now, out of the back veranda doors and the open windows of the detached houses backing on to the cemetery. On the way down the hill, with his arm around his mother's shoulders, Dave said to her, 'You're a lady, d'you know that?'

She tried a quick smile. 'And you're a gentleman, David,' she said, then added, 'I'm all right, really. I'm all right now.'

He was a tall man, this old man, pock-marked, hawk-like. His movements were stiffened with age but there was a dangerous power there also. It was not an easy thing he had to do but he relished the prospect. It began with a girl, an ex-stripper, an ex-whore, and she was the key which would make all things possible.

'The family needs your help,' he told her and she had understood. She had known that sooner or later the business would call. It had been, almost, her destiny. She had left a note for her husband telling him that the Smiths had a job for her and she placed her child in the care of a neighbour. Before he left the house, of course, the pock-marked man took the note and slipped it into his great coat pocket next to the .38 Smith & Wesson which he always carried.

There were things to do, specific paths to follow. They filled his mind. They were written in blue on a noboboard in his headquarters on Mount Pleasant. Only three other men were privy to this information and they were his men.

They needed lay-outs of Runnymede and they needed to log the movements of the wiseguys living there.

They needed to establish a safe house within walking distance of the river. They needed to install hardware, some of it hot from Glasgow, and that was not going to be easy. Most weapons that had been used ended up at the bottom of the Clyde.

They needed a caretaker to look after the safe house and the soldiers who would live there and then to clean up afterwards. Cleaning services that guaranteed the removal of every dab and flake of dust needed booking well in advance.

They needed supplies for the army – food, booze, trusted girls, videos, comics. They could be there for up to a month.

They needed four fast cars.

They needed a make-up artist and a soldier who resembled Vinny Grey, one of Mad Mick's key men.

All that and that was just the London end.

In Glasgow they needed to install Denise.

They needed a safe house there to keep Vinny Grey.

They needed to log his movements.

He began the meeting with his three senior men.

'We've worked together before so you know what we're into. You were all with me in Chinatown. We've got one more job to do and then that's it. Retirement. We're getting too old for all this shit anyway. But this is the big one. It's bigger even that Chinatown. Anyone we use has got to be one hundred per cent. Even the slightest question mark and we don't use him.'

So it began.

Vinny Grey was known as the Snake. It had to do with a strange tattoo of a cobra on his left forearm. Where Don McLachlan looked after Mick's financial interests, Grey was the undisputed leader of his forces. He was Mick's muscle and had been with him ever since

Mick had first made his mark on the Scottish scene. Over the years he had proved his leadership qualities and ran his army with rigid control but he had one weakness that few people knew of. He was partial to the pretty darkly tanned face.

Denise had been learning her trade for a number of years and she was the perfect bait to use on Vinny Grey. At fourteen she had arrived penniless on Charing Cross Station to be snapped up by the first ponce in the queue. She had looked older than her age and he had introduced her to the sex-show circuit. She took off her clothes in various clubs and pubs, making her way through the London Streets to six or seven different venues on a single night. The pimp used a heavy hand to control her; he hit her in places that didn't bruise and stuck heroin into her veins. He held her down while his friends took away her dignity. Stripping led to live sex acts on darkened stages with men she didn't know. Three at a time, two from the audience, became her speciality. When Dave Smith found her she had been close to death. Her pimp hadn't been paying for the dope he was feeding her and Dave worked him over to within an inch of his life. Rehabilitated, she began to work for the Smiths and became one of the highest-regarded toms in London. It stayed that way until Dave himself took an interest in her. When he eventually lost interest she was pregnant and for whatever reason, decided to have the baby. Peter Hough replaced Dave and she married him and let him believe that the baby was his. Now she had a chance to repay the Smiths for saving her life and she threw herself into it with little regard for her own security.

Once installed in one of the clubs frequented by Grey, Denise used her old routine. Subtly, but leaving in his mind no doubts whatsoever, she made herself available. For him there was no escape. Denise was special. She toyed with him. It became a game. It took her moments to be noticed and less than an hour to get him drooling. She flashed her eyes wickedly and she used her body, baiting him with glimpses, sitting on his expanding lap and gently shifting her weight. He never stood a chance. And she kept him that way for a week, until she was given the word, and so eventually, the day before the funeral, she gave in. But on her terms. She made love to him in a motel bedroom. Because of the secrecy that she demanded, he arrived alone. He had finished once and had started again, forcing an anal entry, when two men burst into the room and dragged him down and covered his mouth with a rag full of chloroform. No one he knew saw him again for forty-eight hours. By then it was all over. It was too late. And no one that mattered believed him.

It was surprising how safe the Americans felt in Britain. Their confidence was built around the fear of reprisal and the fact that they were mere onlookers, albeit instigators, of the present situation. Where, in the States, the families employed an army of bodyguards, those that headed the British end made do with two or three. This complacency and their involvement in the local problems was to lead them to extinction.

The three leaders went to Tom Smith's funeral and remained in a small group at the bottom end of the cemetery. Their presence was not unnoticed but neither did it cause concern. It was the Smiths' loss of control that had the Americans putting distance between themselves and the family gathered around the family plot. That they were there at all was respect enough and if the Smiths were to regain their position then relationships could easily resume. The old man, O'Connell, dressed in black, held at the elbow by his driver, the tall blond-haired Herman Tartt, bowed his head and clutched his personal bible with thin, bony fingers. His weak eyes could barely make out the crowd on the hill but he could hear the mournful notes of *Tosca* filtering from the windows. The younger men, Valenti and Clough, dressed in similar black suits and overcoats, stood beside him, ready to move quickly to their vehicle as soon as the service was finished, before the crowd came back down the hill. They had made an appearance. That was enough.

Their drive back to Runnymede was interrupted by heavy lunchtime traffic and it took them half an hour to reach the detached group of houses on the bank. There was no sign of the kids playing in the gardens and that was surprising. Tartt let the three men out of the car before driving to the garage and using his remote control on the door. He parked inside, switched off the ignition and opened the car door. His last thoughts as he noticed the garage door closing was that he had touched the remote control button on his handset. In the dim light a lick of flame flared and, from an explosion, slugs tore into Tartt's face and blew the back of his head into the passenger seat.

The last act of the opera blared from the open doors of the patio. A canopy of willows produced a dappled pattern on the shimmering water; the boats moored at the water's edge breathed sluggishly. The gardens that ran down to the footpath were dressed in early summer colours; golden jasmine on the arches reflected in the still ornamental pools where carp moved languidly between the lilies. A whisper of breeze stirred the lilac and the camellia leaves. Under a brilliant red rhododendron lay a dead child, a boy of about eight, and from a gaping knife wound in his neck blood trickled into the pond and coloured the water pink and the carp began to dart quickly producing occasional flashes of light on the surface.

On the perfectly rolled lawn, on a tartan blanket, a baby girl babbled happily and played with colourful toys while a couple of red admirals fluttered around her; a couple of flies buzzed around the corpse and made preparatory landings on the open neck. The pond water thrashed with activity.

The scene was mirrored by the huge French windows of the dining room where crimson skids on the glass had begun to dribble. In there, O'Connell had taken two bullets in the chest. A third had smashed through his teeth and lodged somewhere in the back of his head. He had slid down the thick toughened glass of the French windows next to his wife who had died moments earlier. Clough saw the bodies of his children before a single bullet caught him in the forehead. Tony Valenti had no children and had no idea that his wife Sharon was upstairs. Twin barrels from a sawn-off took away his face. Out of three families, twelve people, only two remained alive. The baby girl on the lawn still played with her toys and in Valenti's front bedroom, his wife Sharon, on her hands and knees, groped about for the telephone. While they waited to complete the final executions some of the men had dragged her upstairs. She was held down by two men while a third, a man with a strange snake tattoo on his forearm, had raised her skirt and ripped off her pants and had bored into her anus until she had screamed. He had done it that way because that was Grey's preference. And when he had finished and the others had left him to get rid of her, he fired a shot harmlessly into the bed, and whispered in her ear in a strong Glaswegian accent that her beautiful arse had saved her life.

The final tragic notes rang out loudly. The silence that followed the applause and the shuffling of the audience was absolute, uncomfortable, a mark of the drama that had gone before. Into the early summer gardens, away from the baby, the birds flew back to chatter and flit and a warm breeze whispered through the shooting foliage and where there was none, suddenly there was life.

He was a tall man, this old man, and he had a vague memory of Dover cliffs; through a red haze the cliffs had turned pink; Tom was holding him in his arms; the boat was rocking; he was so cold, shivering. There were numerous caves in the cliffs; most of them filled up at high tide. He wore his old army jacket and before him he placed his old revolver. It was dark in the cave. Through the entrance he could see the solid grey green swell and the gulls swooping and crying plaintively at the rising tide. He swallowed his pills and his scotch and felt quite easy about it all. He laughed out loud. Who'd have thought it would end this way? As the faces of the dead moved about the dark shadows of his cave he laughed at life. The little Chinese girl was there somewhere, screaming at him. He chuckled. He would never forget the look on her face as she understood his intention, as he picked her up, still on him, and carried her over to the vat. He would have liked to have killed Denise too, but Tom Smith had been adamant that she was to be returned home safely. It had crossed Fox's mind that she would remain a weak link, that out of everyone involved she was the one who could tie the Smiths in with Glasgow and possibly even Runnymede. Still, he knew that the old man would have his reasons. Tom Smith always had his reasons. Nevertheless, he would have enjoyed killing her. She was the right age; the right shape. Wrong fucking colour, of course, but he could have closed his eyes. He supposed that she would have been like the rest – and there had been plenty of others. It was not a sexual thing now – he was far too old for that – but he would have liked to have seen her dangling with her limbs jerking like a puppet, the fear in her face, her body naked, those smooth fucking contours, beaten and ripped and destroyed. Yes, he would have liked that, marking her soft skin with his gnarled hands. The idea glazed his eyes and tugged his cracked lips into a faint soulless smile. His eyelids were suddenly heavy, his vision slipping. Christ! These pills didn't hang around. The screaming faded; the ghosts faded; he was left alone. It was best this way. It was the only way. When there was nothing else to live for then it was quite easy to die. Sergeant Adam Fox, Scratch to his few friends, fell asleep and the sea came in.

★ ★ ★

They pulled Denise out and dropped her off on the Mill Hill Broadway.

She entered the house the back way, as was her custom, struggling with her case along the alley and across the small square of back garden to her door. She set the case down in the hall and closed the back door. Before taking off her jacket she filled the kettle and plugged it in next to the cooker. She slipped out of her jacket and carried it toward the hall cupboard.

A slight noise behind her had her turning and for a moment her heart stopped. Even as she turned Dave's arm snaked around her neck and she was jerked back into his shoulder. She gasped and let out an involuntary cry. Her hands gripped his arm to loosen the constricting hold. He dragged her into the living room.

'Why are you doing this?' The calm sound of her own voice surprised her; its tone was accusing.

'Where have you been, Denise?' Dave's familiar voice whispered into her ear. She felt his hot breath.

'North. Where d'you think?'

'Tell Mick all about us, did you?'

'I've been helping you, for Chrissakes!'

'Yeah, like Pete helped us?'

'What's that suppose to mean?"

'You know what it means, Denise. But it doesn't matter anymore, does it? It's all over.'

'Where's Pete? Where's the kid?'

'Pete's dead and I've got the kid.'

She was silent for a moment before she said quietly, 'You're his bleedin' father.'

'As soon as I saw him I thought I might be. He's got my good looks. You should have told me about him, girl.'

She let go of his arm and ripped open her blouse. Buttons flew to the carpet.

'Your bastard kid was fed on these, Dave. Paki-nigger colour, ain't they?'

'I've seen them before.'

'Even a cruel bastard like you can't kill the mother of his own kid!'

Her thoughts raced. Tell him about the set-up, about Fox. Make him believe! She mouthed the words but they emerged as strangled noises as she began to choke. His weight forced her down. She kicked out. Her flared black skirt rose. She heard his voice.

'Goodbye, Denise.'

She saw the glinting blade snap from his hand. She stopped struggling and he eased the pressure on her neck.

'Relax sweetheart,' she heard. 'Don't worry. I'll take good care of the kid.'

Out of dark eyes she watched the blade sweep around toward her naked side. Her hot breath expelled in a long gentle sigh.

From the kitchen the boiling kettle began to scream.

'Oh, Dave.'

It burned, red hot. She watched her own blood seep down the handle over his hand. He released the grip on her neck.

'Hold me,' she said. 'I feel so cold.' She took his hand and held it tightly. 'Oh God, it hurts so much.'

He felt her stiffen, her legs twist away and then relax so that her body became heavy. Her hand fell away from his. Slowly he moved his hand down the front of her knickers, over the smooth skin of her belly. Moments earlier her bladder had relaxed. She was wet. The heat was still there. He smiled faintly at the novelty.

The room was gloomy and heavy, the lack of air almost intoxicating. He caught sight of himself in the wall mirror. What he saw surprised him. Blood was everywhere. It had smeared across his cheek and run down to his chin. It stained his white shirt. But it was his eyes that shocked him, fiery and shot through, reptilian. In that moment he was overwhelmed by a combination of pain and exquisite pleasure, of utter violation and destruction. He used her pants to wipe the blood from his cheek. When he looked in the mirror again he saw his own rage. His eyes were hooded, deadly, filled with hatred, but there was something else there also, something beneath the ice-cold fury. It was the brutal acceptance of his own evilness. Beyond his reflection, over his shoulder, he could see the girl. She looked quite beautiful. Her eyes were open, her features as soft as he had ever seen them. The knife was still embedded in her side. The pool of blood had spread out on the carpet. Her skirt was around her waist, her legs apart, just as he had left her.

Chapter 25

'It's all over. It's a matter of picking up the pieces. You're big enough to do that by yourself.' Coddy's voice was marked both by relief and fatigue.

Dave knew that his father-in-law was a late riser and would have left his bed in order to take Dave's call in the study. It was six-thirty. The early sun tumbled through the sparkling garden and flooded Dave's front windows. He heard the chink of bottles and saw the milkman walking back down his drive. A minder watched the milkman from a black Rover parked beneath the oak then got back to his *Mirror*.

'Your old man knew what he was doing. You should never have doubted it, Dave.'

Dave nodded into the phone.

'Monopolies dictate supplies and prices. Never forget that. There was no way Tom would allow such a thing. You think your old man was a Tory, for Chrissake?' Coddy chuckled. 'That's a thought.' His voice levelled off again. 'He knew that by throwing you and Valenti together at the meeting, the Wop would lose control, be seen pressing Mick into a corner. The idea that anyone could lean on him, never mind a bunch of Yanks, would send Mick into orbit. That's what everybody thinks anyway.'

Dave said: 'Will you come down for the service? They're having one here before flying the bodies home.'

'Of course. I wouldn't want to miss that. There might be another one further north before long.'

'I know what you mean. Every flight from New York brings in more of their armed forces, and they're all asking the way to Hadrian's Wall.'

'Mick's going to need a good hiding-place. Maybe that old thatched cottage on my estate, what do you think?'

Dave chuckled.

'I'll bring Mavis,' Coddy went on. 'She can spend some time with Pat. Now it's safe again maybe they can do some shopping.'

'Yeah,' Dave said flatly. The thought that it was all over was somehow depressing. His feelings seemed to travel down the line.

'You know, Dave, some people like to think that they rule. The politicians, the councillors, the civil servants, even some members of the bench and the armed forces, and definitely some of the police. But they're false pretenders, every one of them. They're alive today because they don't interfere. Understand?' Coddy paused and then said quietly: 'You're holding a heavy responsibility now, boy. You go and make your father proud of you.' That was it. The conversation ended and Dave hung up.

He made his way to the bathroom, stripped off his towelling robe and stood under the shower. The steaming water cleared his head.

Coddy had been right. The burden was now his. In the beginning the murder of two villains had given a man respect; and there was a time also when a single act of violence in a dingy Chinese restaurant in the middle of Soho had elevated a man and his family to a position of power in the capital; now another act of violence had raised that family to a similar position, but nationwide.

Dave was still under the hot shower when Pat called into the bathroom.

'Peter Hough's been on the television. Breakfast news. His body's been found.'

'Oh? Any other details?'

'It's horrible. His head was found on a wall by Traitor's Gate.'

'That is horrible. I wondered where he'd got to.'

When he walked into the bedroom moments later Pat said, 'He worked for you, didn't he? Peter Hough?'

'Yeah.' Dave shook his head. 'But he wasn't all that. Know what I mean? Unreliable sort.'

His mother was staying with them for a few days, until the press lost interest and left her alone.

Over breakfast she glanced at the child who sat at the end of the long oak table. His new school satchel lay next to his cereal dish.

'You can't keep the child,' Sally said to Dave.

Patricia watched them from the kitchen. She looked at the boy and saw again the remarkable likeness and knew that her mother-in-law was wrong. They would keep him. There was no doubt about that. Curiously the thought was not upsetting.

'The authorities will have something to say about it,' Sally continued. 'You can't just bring someone's child home. It's not that easy, David.'

Dave smiled at his mother's apparent innocence. 'Mother, we can do anything we want to do,' he said.

Sally gave him a fearful look. He grinned at her.

'You're a lady,' he said.

She did not respond.

The will was read sometime later and in it Tom Smith had written: 'To each of my grandchildren . . . including David Hough'.

The sun was a watery ghost above the wet tiles; the paving slabs of the footpath had darkened with the rain. The rain had stopped but the air was close and held the smell of rain. Across the glistening road a milkman was finishing his round, his float filled with empties, glass on glass, rattling; a hawk-faced man with protruding cheekbones and chin and dark button eyes sunk into sleepless holes.

The youngster hesitated to watch the milkman stack another empty crate and pulled back on Dave's hand until he slowed his pace. Dave glanced across at the milkman and muttered, 'Some people are pretty and some are ugly but by Christ some are pretty ugly!' He looked down at the boy and grinned. 'You don't understand a thing I'm saying, do you?'

The youngster looked up, at once attentive but frowning in an exaggerated fashion as youngsters do. He shook his head and gave Dave a broad grin and flashed his small pointed milk teeth.

'Listen to me carefully,' Dave said to him. 'This is important.' They walked on. Holding hands seemed natural. Father and son. The boy did not look up. He barely heard his father's voice; his thoughts were still with the milkman. 'This is a fine country, my son,' Dave said. 'Don't let anyone tell you any different. Here, you can do anything you want. You can have anything you want. All you got to do is know what you want; the rest is easy. You name me another place in the world that's as fair as that?'

The boy did not look up but Dave heard the tiny whisper. 'I'm goin' t' be a milkman.'

Dave chuckled. 'Why not, my son? That sounds like a good job to me!'

Hand-in-hand they walked on toward the nursery school and crossed the road at the zebra crossing just beyond where, in the beginning, the empire had begun in the darkened smoke-filled rooms of the Eagle; father and son moving through the streets of the capital, cherishing the moment and considering their opportunities in this country fair and fine.

ALLISON & BUSBY CRIME

Simon Beckett
　Fine Lines

Denise Danks
　Frame Grabber

John Dunning
　Booked to Die

Chester Himes
　All Shot Up
　The Big Gold Dream
　Cotton Comes to Harlem
　The Heat's On
　A Rage in Harlem

Russell James
　Slaughter Music

H. R. F. Keating
　A Remarkable
　　Case of Burglary

Ted Lewis
　GBH
　Get Carter
　Jack Carter's Law
　Jack Carter and the Mafia Pigeon

Ross Macdonald
　The Barbarous Coast
　The Blue Hammer
　The Far Side of the Dollar
　Find a Victim
　The Galton Case
　The Goodbye Look
　The Ivory Grin
　Meet Me at the Morgue
　The Moving Target
　The Way Some People Die
　The Wycherley Woman
　The Zebra-Striped Hearse
　The Underground Man

The Lew Archer Omnibus
　Volume 1: The Chill,
　　The Drowning Pool,
　　The Goodbye Look
　Volume 2: The Moving Target
　　The Barbarous Coast
　　The Far Side of the Dollar

Margaret Millar
　Ask for Me Tomorrow
　Banshee
　Mermaid
　The Murder of Miranda
　Rose's Last Summer

Richard Stark
　Deadly Edge
　The Green Eagle Score
　The Handle
　Point Blank
　The Rare Coin Score
　Slayground
　The Sour Lemon Score

Donald Thomas
　Dancing in the Dark

Marilyn Wallace (ed.)
　Sisters in Crime

Donald Westlake
　Sacred Monster
　The Mercenaries